PRINCE OF OMERTÁ

By

Giovanni Gambino

Club Lighthouse Publishing E-Book

ISBN: 978-1-927337-08-0

Cover Art: T.L. Davison

Certificate of Registration

A Club Lighthouse Crime Drama Edition
Published in Canada

PROLOGUE

AFTER MAKING HIS WAY through Manhattan's bumper-to-bumper traffic, Joey DeSante stepped out of his new, flashy red and white Cadillac which was double parked in front of the '21' Club at 21 West 52nd Street. He handed the keys to the parking attendant, warning him, "Be careful. I just got it. Don't want any scratches. Keep it under fifty when you park it."

"Yes sir, Mr. DeSante," the attendant answered, laughing slightly. "Don't worry about a thing. I'll watch it." As if to defy DeSante, he sped off with tires screeching. DeSante grimaced.

"Hey, you son-of-a-bitch," DeSante shouted. It was too late. The attendant was out of hearing distance in a few seconds.

Inside, DeSante, a *capo bastone* – an underboss – for Dominic "No Pain" Esposito, the boss of one of six *Mafia* families in Manhattan, went straight to the bar. He ordered Scotch on the rocks, Chivas Regal no less, and finished the drink quickly to help steel himself for the meeting he was to have with Johnny Valenti, an enforcer for the same family. Valenti was more than an enforcer, who generally concentrated on breaking bones. Valenti's speciality was murder. He was the family's hit man. While Valenti would be reluctant to brag, he was very good at his chosen profession; indeed, among the best in the business, a business which, given its inherent dangers, had a high mortality rate.

DeSante was nervous. This would be a very sensitive, delicate meeting. He could not risk Valenti picking up any wrong signals, disturbing signals. DeSante did not underestimate Valenti. The truth was he respected him. He knew Valenti had lots of street smarts. Valenti would not have survived in his profession unless he had keen instincts. To be successful, DeSante would have to be at his best. Given the potential consequences, failure was not an option.

He ordered another drink. As he waited, DeSante was greeted from all sides by waiters, bartenders, porters. That was one of the reasons he frequented the Club. He liked being recognized, particularly in a place as famous as the '21' Club. DeSante took pride in the attention accorded to him in such a prestigious environment. It boosted his ego, and he needed the reinforcement.

The '21' Club was one of New York's most prominent restaurants, catering to presidents, business and political leaders, Hollywood celebrities and sports stars. Tourists flocked to '21' not so much for the food. They came, hoping to see, and have dinner with, someone famous.

Customers could impress their friends by stating they had dined with the likes of Ernest Hemingway, Marilyn Monroe, JFK, Gerald Ford, Humphrey Bogart, Al Jolson et al.

As he revelled in the special treatment from the club's employees, DeSante, not quite a world celebrity, scanned the crowd waiting for guests to acknowledge his presence. None did. DeSante did not notice that no one noticed. He may have been in denial. He bathed in the recognition from the Club's help, proud that he had some identity in this historic New York landmark which, to its credit, had its own history with the underworld.

During Prohibition, the Club operated as a speakeasy, storing thousands of cases of illegal hooch in a room hidden behind a specially designed impenetrable door adjacent to the kitchen. The door was about a foot thick and weighed some two and a half tons. It was opened by inserting an eighteen inch meat skewer through a very small crack in the cement wall. The design was ingenious. Anyone who had been partying at the Club and had one or two too many would not have been able to open the door. Even sober federal authorities, who were confident the Club was violating Prohibition's ban on the sale of liquor, failed to find the evidence.

In addition, an architect designed a system permitting the club to destroy illegal liquor should it be alerted to a police raid – and it had the good fortune to have exceptional friends in the police department. When notified that the cops were on their way, the club would set off an alarm, alerting customers to finish their drinks. Bartenders then would press another button and the shelves on the walls would flip upside down and the wine and liquor bottles would slide down into the city's sewer system.

After Prohibition, when the consumption of liquor was again legalized, the restaurant remodelled the former liquor closet and operated it as a dining room. It seated about twenty, and guests were charged several hundred dollars a plate to experience some of the bootlegging ambiance of yesteryear. Expensive wines, now legal, lined the walls.

DeSante called Valenti just after Valenti had completed a contract, inviting – luring was a more accurate word – him for some drinks and dinner at the '21' Club to celebrate the successful mission. Rather than give Valenti a plaque that he would not be able to show off or mount on a wall, DeSante would reward Valenti for his fine work with dinner at this very special place. "Fine work" was defined as having a dead body with no police showing up, at least for a few days, to question suspects or "people of interest." Valenti had achieved both objectives. He deserved a night out.

Valenti accepted the invitation, never reflecting on the fact that DeSante was not one to spend money on others. He watched his pennies very closely. He was generous when his own desires were involved – the Caddy, Chivas Regal, etc. – but frugal, very cheap, when having to open his wallet for friends. It was incongruous for him to underwrite a celebration, particularly since Valenti was just doing his job, carrying out an assignment. No reasons for special recognition. Valenti was expected to be successful. Indeed, this particular hit could have been classified as "routine." It had hardly challenged Valenti's special talents.

Valenti did not reflect on the inconsistency. He was grateful for the invitation and looked forward to visiting the '21' Club, which was not one of his haunts. He had heard about the Club and was curious why it attracted so much attention. As far as its fame was concerned, it did not mean much to him one way or another.

He was more at home in a neighbourhood bar. Unlike DeSante, he did not need recognition to satisfy his ego. Indeed, hit men liked to remain inconspicuous. The fewer people who knew them, the better.

No question about it though, he should have been more sensitive and curious about DeSante's motivation. Nothing should be taken at face value in the mobster underworld. That is rule Number One, never to be overlooked. Valenti did not know it, but he had violated the rule and screwed up.

During the last few months, DeSante had become disenchanted with Valenti. He could not really explain it but just the mention of his name made him angry. He did not like the fact that Valenti was successful, that he was praised by the top of the echelon, and that it was obvious Valenti had a prosperous career ahead of him. DeSante suffered from a severe case of professional jealousy. Not that DeSante was suited for Valenti's line of work. Not many were. That, though, did not matter. In short, Valenti just pissed him off.

Then, one day, he overheard his name mentioned while Valenti was talking to Numero Uno – "No Pain." That's when he could no longer get Valenti out of his mind. Hey, who could blame him? He did not know in what context his name was used. When your name is mentioned to the best hit man in the Big Apple, who wouldn't worry? So DeSante decided to do something about it. He could no longer live with his suppressed fear and festering hatred of Valenti.

When Valenti arrived, he joined DeSante at the bar. The two exchanged bear hugs before Valenti ordered a beer. Valenti glanced around almost like he was looking for a coin-operated pool table. He did not understand what all the fuss was about. No barmaids with big tits, short skirts and long legs like at Joe's Tavern in Brooklyn. No tight asses he could pinch. Overall, Valenti thought, the place was too stuffy. Stuffy, schmuffy. What the hell, it was a new experience. He could say he had been to the '21' Club.

"No problems, right?" asked DeSante in starting the conversation.

"Went smooth as silk. Ain't gonna find him for at least couple of days."

"Good."

"Deserves more than a beer."

"Hey, you ordered."

The two indulged in small talk and, once again, had Valenti been more alert, he might have detected some tension in DeSante's voice. DeSante was forcing himself to be congenial and it was noticeable except to Valenti. Perhaps Valenti was still in the decompression mode from his most recent assignment. Maybe the adrenalin high had not tapered off. Job pressures can make one careless.

"Got myself a new Caddy," DeSante said. "Leather seats, the works."

"You always had style. I like my Ford."

"Johnny, this is a real car. Man, it is unbelievable. Never had such a smooth ride. Broads go crazy in it."

"I don't give a shit what I drive as long as it gets me where I'm goin'."

The conversation was stilted. DeSante was ill at ease. He was aware of his nervousness, and he did not like it. It was risky. He clumsily steered the small talk into a particular direction – that they settle for drinks and cancel dinner.

"Mind if we go after a couple?" DeSante asked. "Really don't have time for dinner."

"No sweat with me," Valenti said. "Too highfalutin for me anyway. Almost didn't come when you said I had to wear a coat and tie. Damn thing's chokin' me. Glad to get out of here. Next time, treats on me at Joe's."

Then he told Valenti, bending the truth a little bit, that Esposito wanted to discuss the hit, and after their drinks they needed to see Esposito at his home on Staten Island. "Let's go," Valenti said. "Don't need this fancy food. Give me a burger, some fries."

"Wanna drive the Caddy, and I'll follow with your Ford?" An unusual offer since the car was new and DeSante was very protective of it. Still, Valenti failed to read anything into DeSante's unconventional generosity. He should have.

After protesting that he did not want to risk an accident, Valenti accepted graciously and, admittedly, with excitement. Valenti left the bar, walked to the front door and then suddenly returned to leave a tip. He saw DeSante by the public telephone. He waved, but either DeSante did not see Valenti or he was ignoring him. The latter was more probable. Valenti did not react to DeSante's apparent slight.

Outside, the parking attendant handed Valenti the keys to the Caddy, alerting him, "The trunk is not tight. Seems something stuck in a crack."

Valenti checked quickly, too quickly. Not only was his inspection sloppy, he also failed to notice a small red spot near the trunk's keyhole. It was blood.

Valenti drove off, enjoying the Caddy, its feel, and how it responded with a burst of speed to the slightest pressure on the gas pedal. He could get used to this. DeSante was right. This was some classy car. Totally engrossed in driving the Caddy, he turned on the radio just as he heard a siren, and saw the all too familiar red flashers in the rear view mirror.

Valenti steered the Caddy to the curb to permit the scout car to pass. Instead, New York's finest pulled up right behind him, in a position to give the cops a good view of Valenti. Within seconds, another scout car stopped behind Valenti. This was not a routine traffic stop.

"What the hell?" Valenti said to himself.

Valenti was puzzled. He had not been speeding nor did he believe that he had violated any traffic laws. It could not have been about the hit. It was too soon, and, more importantly, he was confident he had left no clues. He was a pro. Whatever it was, he still believed it was a minor problem, that is, until one of the cops told him through the scout car's roof-mounted speaker system to stay in the car.

"Just do what I tell you to do. Roll down your window and open the door from the outside."

When Valenti, hesitated, the cop repeated his instructions, adding, "I don't want to have to tell you again. Do it and do it now."

Perplexed and angry, Valenti, becoming understandably concerned, did as he was told. Slowly he rolled down his car window and awkwardly he reached out and opened the door.

"Get out, put your hands behind your back, clasp them together, and walk backward toward our car."

Shit, these guys meant business. This was obviously serious stuff. The cops sure weren't interested in giving him a traffic ticket. When Valenti, walking backwards uneasily, reached the area of the trunk, he heard, "Stop right there."

Four officers got out of the two scout cars. They had unsnapped the covers of their holsters and had their hands on the handles of their weapons. They did not take their eyes off Valenti.

When Valenti ventured to ask, "What did I ….," one officer cut him off. "Keep your mouth shut. That's all."

Using good judgement, Valenti did not argue. One ordered him to place his hands on the car's roof. He patted him down.

"Don't even move a muscle," the officer warned. Through the car's open window, the cop reached in and removed the keys from the ignition.

While three cops watched Valenti, the one with the keys unlocked the truck. Valenti heard the officer say, "Well, well, what do we have here?"

"Hey, Joe, bring our friend over here."

One of the cops grabbed Valenti by the elbow and shoved him toward the trunk. "Move your ass."

"Can you explain this cargo in your trunk?" asked the officer who had opened the trunk.

Valenti didn't say a word. He just stared, glowered might be more accurate.

What "we had here" and what Valenti was unable to explain was the body of a two hundred eighty pound man who had been killed by a shot that blew off half his head.

As the officers handcuffed Valenti, the pieces fell into place. DeSante inviting him to dinner. DeSante getting him to drive the Caddy. DeSante on the phone in the '21' Club. DeSante pretending not to see him when he came back to leave a tip. The son-of-a-bitch was calling the cops. Valenti finally put it together. It was just a little too late.

DeSante had set him up.

CHAPTER 1

JOHNNY VALENTI GOT OFF his cot and started packing his things.

His "things" didn't amount to much. A few packs of cigarettes, shaving stuff, some hardcore sex magazines, a couple of sweatsuits and a portable radio. That was about it.

He dropped all his belongings into a laundry bag that had the prison's name on it. He didn't like that, but he planned to toss the bag as soon as he unpacked at the hotel room that would serve as his home for a while.

His cellmate, Bubba, watched as Valenti prepared to leave after eighteen years.

"Watcha gonna do on the outside?" Bubba asked. "Got a job?"

"Don't know, Bubba," Valenti replied. "I'm gonna be okay. Always have been. I ain't worried. And when you get out, look me up. If I can, I'll hook you up."

Bubba was pleased. Valenti meant it or he wouldn't have offered. Valenti was a man of his word, even when it cost him.

"You been a good cellie," Bubba replied. "Not many in here I would trust but you, Johnny, are different."

Yeah, trust, not having it, cost him eighteen long ones. He would get even, that's for sure. It had been eighteen years but he had not forgotten who betrayed him. There was work to be done. True, he was to blame for not picking up the signals at the '21' Club. He should have been more alert. He rationalized there was no reason for him to have been suspicious. No reason to suspect that DeSante was worried about Valenti moving up the organizational ladder, moving up too fast in DeSante's opinion. He had seen no hint of animosity, jealousy.

Valenti would make up for whatever mistakes he had made. He was, above all, a man of principle. No question, he killed people to make a living. Everyone's got to make a buck. But there are rules to abide by. Like not talking to the cops. Not selling out colleagues. It's easy to have principle when nothing is at stake. However, men of honour, like Valenti, don't break rules even when facing a long prison sentence. And Valenti was proud that he hadn't crumbled under pressure from the cops. He did his time, never squealed, never complained.

When the guards unlocked his cell, he shook hands with Bubba and gave him a hug. They held on to the hug for a few seconds while patting each other on their backs.

"See you down the road," Valenti said. The guards asked him to move along -- one last order -- and escorted him down the hallway past the other cells.

Farewells rang out from prisoners looking through their bars from every quarter of the cell block. Valenti had engendered respect, respect as defined in a lawless world. To earn it you (a) never ratted, no matter what the consequences, and (b) you needed to be able to hold your own, without whimpering about what a tough life it was. Valenti easily met both standards.

Almost all at once came shouts of, "Good luck, Johnny," and "You're one lucky son-of-a-bitch."

He was warned, "Stay away from my old lady." Another inmate was more forthcoming, stating, "Go see mine. Maybe you'll be luckier than I was." That brought a roar of laughter from Valenti's former prison colleagues.

He enjoyed the good-natured ribbing and laughed when he heard, "Come visit some time." *Absolutely, I will*, he thought. *Can't wait to come back here.*

Understandably, he was immensely enjoying his last walk through the Adirondack Correctional Facility (known as Ray Brook Prison) in the hamlet Ray Brook located in the town of North Elba between the villages of Saranac Lake and Lake Placid in Upstate New York.

As the gates closed behind him, Valenti took a deep breath. Man, this was heaven. He couldn't believe he was a free man.

Freedom. He had a hard time accepting he was out. He looked back. The gates were locked but he was on the outside looking in. He waved to familiar faces in the yard. His former colleagues watched with envy as he strolled outside the gates to a life as a free man.

He did a couple of knee bends. He stretched his arms into the air. He picked up a stone and threw in across the ground like someone trying to skip a rock along the water's surface. Then he screamed, "Oooooooeeeewww!"

God, for the first time in eighteen years, he did not have to ask for permission to do anything. He could do the knee bends, throw the stone, and no one would tell him, "No." Weird, indeed.

This would take some time getting used to. Walking with your head up, and eating, sleeping, even taking a piss whenever he wanted. No guards looking over your shoulder. He would revel in every second of his adjustment to freedom. Damn right.

As he looked around, he spotted Luigi with his Mercedes in the prison's parking lot. Luigi was standing outside of the car, leaning against the right front fender, with his arms folded. He was smiling from ear to ear.

Luigi "The Fixer" Giancamilli was Valenti's friend – best friend – since early childhood. They were inseparable, bonded like brothers. They played on the same ball teams, visited their first whorehouse together, exchanged phone numbers of the "best" girls in the neighbourhood and, most important, had no secrets from each other. Compared to Giancamilli and Valenti, Batman and Robin were strangers to each other.

As they entered a life of crime, Giancamilli, and his street boss, recognized he had a weakness, a serious weakness. He could not kill, or even break a couple of legs. While he could do it in a pinch, if he had too, he just did not get any job satisfaction from it. At first, the wise guys made fun of him but later, when big stakes were involved, they used him in a different way, taking advantage of his special diplomatic skills.

He was good at negotiations and was astute at settling disputes between competing factions. That was how he acquired his nickname, "The Fixer." Giancamilli was always asked to settle things before Valenti was called in if his services were needed. They made a perfect team. Good mobster, bad mobster, a strange inversion of the good cop-bad cop strategic team.

Needless to say, Giancamilli had a big advantage as a negotiator. Those on the other side of the table understood the potential consequences of not reaching an agreement. They knew Giancamilli had muscle power waiting in the wings. But Giancamilli was man enough not to play the violence card. He let it speak for itself.

Valenti headed toward the Mercedes. Giancamilli never had a penny to his name but still always managed to drive the best cars, wear the most expensive clothes and jewellery. Valenti's pal always went first class.

When he reached the car, the two men embraced, kissing each other on the cheeks. Giancamilli gave his friend a bear hug and picked him up off the ground.

"Good to see you, Johnny," said Giancamilli.

"Same here, Luigi," answered Valenti. "Yeah, same here."

Giancamilli was uneasy, he did not know what so say. How do you welcome someone, someone who just spent eighteen years in prison?

Trying to make his friend feel at ease, he offered, "You look good."

"You too, Luigi."

As Valenti looked over his friend's shoulders, he saw the two broads in the back seat of the car.

"Get in the back and keep them company," said Giancamilli.

This was an order, the first one on the outside, one that Valenti was pleased to follow. *Some welcome,* Valenti thought. He got in and sat between the two bimbos. He barely was settled when the women went to work on him. They did not even take time to greet him or ask for his name. One undid his belt buckle while the other unzipped him. They pursued the assignment from Giancamilli with commendable dedication and enthusiasm, and while they were somewhat businesslike and seemed to lack sincerity, Valenti was not looking for true love in the back seat of a car only minutes after being released from the can after eighteen years.

"My homecoming present to you, Johnny," said Giancamilli, looking into the rear view mirror.

"How'd you know what I wanted? You must have looked at my wish list. Beats tickets to a ballgame."

As they sped along the highway, Valenti leaned back and let the two bimbos carry out their assignment. When the broads finished, he asked Giancamilli to stop the car. He got out and joined his friend in the front seat.

"Thanks," said Valenti. "One would have been enough to do the job. I gotta admit, two were better. Hope you got a discount hiring two."

They both laughed and engaged in small talk about the Yankees, broads, mutual friends, and more broads.

For a few minutes, Giancamilli noticed that his friend was quiet and introspective. He gave him a few minutes to "catch his breath."

"Tough in there, eh?"

"Dozen and a half is a long time."

Valenti thought back and the eighteen years flashed through his mind. He remembered how, in the very first week, he had to establish himself, his turf. He let the word go out that killing was his profession – for professionals. If they fucked with him, figuratively or literally, they would pay a price. That got him some respect, some space.

He was a name dropper. If he encountered trouble, he recited his resume, listing the crime bosses he worked for, names that would evoke fear. He was successful. Overall, he had little trouble. One inmate made a mistake, deciding to test Valenti. The result was he spent months of his ten-year sentence recuperating from countless injuries. And, he was warned, that when released, he better disappear. That seemed to do the trick for Valenti. Not surprisingly, he never had trouble again.

He thought about the time – eighteen years, an eternity. He was in prison during the administrations of five different presidents, during the time the nation developed its space program, landed on the moon and accomplished other exploits in space. While doing time, his Yankees won four World Series, in 1960 and 1961, his first two years in prison, and in 1977 and 1978, his last two. Was the timing some kind of omen? Valenti was hardly aware of this "coincidence," but even if he had been, he would not be prepared to return to prison just so the Yankees might win another World Series. Even the Yankees would understand that.

Controlling his sexual desires was another matter. He had lost out on more broads than he wanted to count. To assuage his raging hormones, he engaged in self-satisfaction. He hated himself for resorting to what he considered perversity, but it gave him some relief. He had not engaged in that activity – he never had to given his success with women – since he was fourteen. In prison, reluctantly, he traded relief for self-loathing.

Almost as bad as the sexual frustrations was the boredom. It almost drove him insane. The repetitive daily routine. The same faces day in and day out. The schedule always identical. At times, he did not want to leave his cot, knowing the day's activities he would face.

He thought that as the time for his release approached, he would be upbeat, happier with each passing minute. The opposite happened. With about three months to go, he became depressed, continually looking at his watch. It moved so slowly.

He counted the minutes, the number of meals he had left in prison along with the nights left to sleep in his cage. The clang of the metal door on his cell in the latter stages of his imprisonment almost drove him up the walls. The sound gave him hot flashes. God, the wait was interminable.

Giancamilli understood that Valenti needed time to adjust. He stole quick glances at his friend who, to his surprise, looked pretty good. Overall, he had not changed much. He had worked hard to maintain muscle tone and his weight, exercising in the prison's gym. He had kept in shape. There was not an ounce of fat on his body. Controlling his food intake was not much of a problem given the quality of prison food. So, overall, he was fit.

He was still extremely handsome with pitch black, curly hair except for a tinge of grey on the temples. The grey gave him a look of maturity he had not had eighteen years earlier. He had a dimple in his chin and a two-inch scar on his right cheek, earned in a street fight when he was ten. He had a dark complexion and black eyes, and when he laughed, women reacted like they did to Italian stars in the movies. Valenti, the "babe magnet," would surely take up where he'd left off in the sex department.

For the next fifty miles or so, they hardly said a word until Giancamilli interrupted Valenti's trip down memory lane. "It'll take some time."

He added, "They know on the street what you did. Everyone knows you didn't talk."

"No big deal," said Valenti. "For me, it was the only thing to do. I don't rat. Never ratted."

"I know that. They also know. I think you will be able to call in some chits when you need them."

"I didn't do it for the chits. It's the right thing to do. I don't know no other way."

"Yeah, everyone knows that too and that's why you probably can collect them because you didn't expect them."

Valenti did not respond.

"Luigi, what did DeSante tell Esposito and the others?" Valenti asked. "That always bothered me. Didn't they ask?"

"Said you borrowed the Caddy and did some freelancing. That you took care of some prick who screwed you. They apparently bought it. Don't know much more. Maybe they didn't want to know the whole story. Who knows?"

Yeah, who knows? They should have known, Valenti thought. He never broke the rules. He abided by the chain of command. He followed his organization's protocols. Freelancing? They had to be kidding. He had enough on his hands with assigned hits.

Despite all his anger, doubts and feelings of having been abandoned and double-crossed, he was never even tempted to sell anyone out. He thought back to when the feds offered him a deal.

"Look, talk just a little," the feds insisted during hours of questioning and cajoling. "We know that DeSante was involved. That you worked for Esposito. We took DeSante in, and we don't buy that crap that DeSante loaned you the car. His story is bullshit, but someone's gonna take the rap. We don't give a shit who does, and that someone is you unless you talk."

"What don't you understand about *omertá?*" Valenti asked. "I ain't gonna change my mind, and I don't give a shit what you offer me."

Omertá, the code of silence, was as sacred to Valenti as the Torah to Jews, the Koran to Muslims and the New Testament to Christians. Maybe even more sacred. Some might have considered Valenti an *omertá* fanatic, an *omertá* fundamentalist.

For Valenti, *omertá* was the First Commandment not only because he was committed uncompromisingly to keeping one's mouth shut, but because he violated most of the original ten anyway. With some exceptions. He honoured his mother and father and did not worship idols. As to the others about not committing murder, stealing, or coveting the neighbour's wife, those were another matter.

Had Valenti drafted ten commandments, he would have had allegiance to *omertá* at the top of his list. He would have taken the Ninth Commandment from the original tablets, the one about not bearing false witness against thy neighbour, and moved it to the number one spot, and he would have written it a little differently. Something along the lines, "Thou shall not squeal on him, especially to the cops."

The problem was Moses delivered the commandments some five thousand years before he was born. As they say, timing is everything.

No matter how strongly the feds argued with him, he would not violate the code even if he could avoid jail time. They wouldn't give up. Their offers would have reduced his possible sentence from fifty years to twenty years even to five years. Valenti held firm.

"If you get fifty, Valenti, you'll get out at seventy four," the feds argued. "You'll be an old man, that is if you don't die in prison."

Valenti held strong. He was a stand up guy and he stood up. As far as he was concerned, only dolphins flip. He would not compromise on *omertá*. Ultimately, he would have his revenge without violating a – *the* – sacred principle.

"I don't rat," he told them. "It was a rat, a stoolie, a turncoat, who put me away so you think I'm gonna turn into one?"

The feds kept pushing. They argued, they'd settle for just a few key names, with each name being worth, let's say, two, three years or so.

Valenti didn't budge. One of his standard replies was, "Once I'm in the can, I don't got to worry about being run over by a car. I don't need to pay rent or taxes. The government feeds me and takes care of me. When I get out, I'll be in better shape than ever since I can't drink, screw around with broads, stay out late. I'll feel younger than ever. So I'll take whatever you give me."

Ultimately, he was sentenced to twenty years, and after serving fifteen, his lawyers went to work and managed to get him out after what Valenti called a dozen and a half. While he detested his legal mouthpieces, all of them, he had to admit they did a good job in getting his sentence reduced, and winning him parole.

His lawyers produced letters from well-known people in the community, community leaders, who testified that Valenti had made a mistake. He had acknowledged his mistake (the entire incident was just a simple mistake), deeply regretted it and that, underneath it all, he was a man of good character. It never occurred to parole board members that these leaders might be ex-officio employees of Valenti's former bosses. Maybe it did. Perhaps the board members had been approached to join the payroll of Valenti's employers.

Further, Valenti swore that after eighteen years of living among the most violent and amoral people in the U.S., indeed on earth, he had been rehabilitated. That was not an easy thing to do given the environment. He told them, it's not the company you keep, it's what's in your heart.

He never went with the "I am innocent" route. It never worked even though, ironically, he did not kill the man in the trunk. Yeah, sure, he'd killed some others but that's not what he was tried for. The "I'm a victim" defence had been tried endlessly and only seemed to piss off parole board members. They had heard it countless times. They did not even respond to "I'm innocent" protestations. Instead, it increased the board members' scepticism.

Does he have a job? Will he be able to get one? Those questions were more difficult for Valenti because he was fairly confident that if he answered his former bosses were waiting for him he would not get the board's vote. So his answers were vague, something along the lines, "I will dig ditches if I have to."

He also added a sentence recommended by cellmates who maintained it was absolutely essential for him to tell the board, "I believe I have paid my debt to society." He did not know what that meant. Debt to society? He didn't do anything to society. Society had nothing to do with it. He had no gripes against society. Society didn't squeal on him, set him up, sell him out. DeSante also didn't owe a debt to society. He owed one to Valenti. And he was going to pay it. No doubt about that. Regardless, he accepted the advice. What was there to lose, and he sort of liked the sound of the phrase.

At the end of the interview, a board member asked him, "Will you ever do this again?" Displaying the utmost diplomacy, the board used the word "this" and not "murder." How do you ask a man, "Will you ever murder again?"

Valenti, not hesitating said, absolutely not. He had learned his lessons, and learned them well. "This" – murder – was the furthest thing from his mind. He looked forward to a law-abiding life. He did not say that he wanted a "house with a white picket fence" nor did he wipe away a tear or so. That might have appeared a little insincere, that might have been overdoing it.

Recognizing the stakes involved, he worked to impress

those who had his future in their hands. A little humility never hurt anyone. Indeed, at times, it can do a lot of good. He was prepared to grovel a little bit, even more than a little bit. He did not mind kissing ass if it got him out.

He was successful. The parole board was moved by his apparent sincerity, and approved Valenti's early release. Its decision took two years, or ten percent, off his twenty year sentence. Nothing to sneeze at.

It was time for Valenti, at forty two, to get back on his feet, but first and most important, he would seek justice, his brand of justice, by doing "this" again.

He had lied to the parole board.

CHAPTER 2

VALENTI LOOKED AROUND HIS hotel room while contemplating his future. Giancamilli had given him a few hundred bucks, and arranged for the room on Manhattan's Upper East Side. It wasn't the Waldorf Astoria but it would do until he got on his feet.

The hotel was run by an ex-con for ex-cons. Having experienced the problem of finding appropriate housing when he was released from prison, the owner adopted his version of a fair housing policy and operated the place for residents who were short of cash. He rented on credit with an interest rate that made Shylock's demand for a pound of flesh seem moderate. He defended his rates, telling his tenants he had a high-risk clientele. He knew, first hand, whereof he spoke.

While Valenti tried to keep a low profile in the building, he occasionally ran into his neighbour, Israel (Izzy) Baker. Baker, who had Americanized his name from Barkowicz, had done a little time, three years, for supervising blacks who ran numbers in Harlem. He was tough too, once commanding a customer to swallow number slips when undercover cops entered a grocery store he was working. The black guy, not wanting the slips rammed down his throat, did as he was told.

Baker walked with a limp, a limp he earned while convincing three customers to pay their debts. When they balked, he took on all three. They paid, although he was left with a bum leg which was his badge of honour and courage, and a warning to others not to mess with him.

Baker, a compulsive talker, irritated Valenti because he always was making referrals as if he earned a commission for doing so. In fact, he did.

"Johnny, you need help collecting?" Baker would ask.

"I can get you Shtarka. That means strong, real strong, in Jewish, and this guy is a bull." Baker was referring to Steve "The Shtarka" Gray (changed from the Polish Szczepan Grabowski) whose speciality was knees. He wasn't bad with arms and elbows either.

"He's good, Johnny. Break 'em in a minute. Don't charge much either," Baker assured his neighbour.

"Thanks, Izzy. I don't need Sharka, Smarka or whoever. I'm better on my own."

"His name is Shtarka, Johnny. Only three to five percent of what the deadbeat owes," Baker retorted. "Good deal. And if he gets caught, he don't talk. Guaranteed. He believes in *sha shtill* which is like *omertá* in Jewish."

When Valenti seemed unmoved, Baker implored Valenti to listen to a story which spoke to the Shtarka's effectiveness. Emphasizing that the Shtarka's pedigree went back to the Purple Gang, a mob organization made up primarily of Jews operating out of Detroit in the 1920s, Baker pleaded his case.

"The Shtarka is assigned to collect from an Orthodox Jew and goes after him on a Saturday," Baker explained. "Johnny, on Saturdays, an Orthodox Jew only prays in a synagogue. He can't go in a car, touch money, work, or do anything.

"Shtarka finds him in the synagogue. The Jew refuses to leave. Shtarka and his men drag him out when the Jew wraps himself around a post yelling, *'Yir kent mir derhargenen affen ort. Ober Shabbas for yich nit.'"*

Baker stops and looks at Valenti who just shrugs, raising his eyebrows to indicate he has no idea what Baker is talking about.

"Johnny, that's Yiddish and it means, 'You can kill me on the spot, but on Saturday, I don't drive.'"

Valenti chuckled, asking, "So, what happened?"

"Shtarka laughs so hard he has tears in his eyes. Then, he gets a bat from his car, walks back, breaks both arms holding the post and leaves. He let the Jew observe his Sabbath."

"My kind of guy," Valenti said, remaining steadfast that he did not need any help from Shtarka or anyone else.

While Baker annoyed Valenti with all his talk, overall, Valenti liked him primarily because he was Jewish and the Jews had their own mobsters. Some of them were real famous, and anyone with mobsters in his heritage couldn't be all bad.

Sitting in his room, Valenti was grateful to Giancamilli for finding the place. He was also indebted to his friend for the piece. Good pal, Luigi, the best. One of the few who could be trusted, and Valenti valued trust more than anything else.

Valenti was ready. During the two months since he got out, all he did was plan his next move. He pursued his goal as thoroughly as an academician writing a PhD. Nothing would be left to chance. The violation of *omertá* would be avenged. The thought had consumed him for eighteen years.

Over and over again during his years in jail, he had replayed the night at the '21' Club in his head. If only he had been more alert to the clues at the bar, no matter how subtle. He remembered other hints in DeSante's behaviour that should have tipped him off. DeSante often had let slip that he was a little upset, more than a little, at Valenti's accelerated career path. At the time, DeSante's complaints had left no mark on him. In his cell, replaying events and conversations, he saw the picture more clearly. There had been signs, danger signs. If only...

He had made a mistake, a big mistake in judging – misjudging – character. Ain't ever gonna happen again. Engaging in self-pity, he knew, served no purpose. It was time to get his revenge, to settle the score. With Luigi's help, he would make up for eighteen years.

Giancamilli sympathized with his friend's determination to get even. Indeed, he thought that Valenti had to strike first. There was no other choice. If DeSante found out that Valenti had been released, Valenti would become the target. Giancamilli totally endorsed his friend's obsession. He did not even define it as an obsession. It was something Valenti simply had to do, not only to get some justice, which was important and deserved, but to survive.

A few months before Valenti's release, Giancamilli had discovered where the rat, DeSante, lived and gave the address to his friend. Night after night Valenti watched trying to find the answer that would get him into his target's apartment building. After about three weeks, he found it. The doorman would leave his post for forty five minutes or so at about 12:30 a.m. on Tuesday and Friday nights. He was as regular as clockwork.

Valenti noticed the doorman did not walk away from the building. He went inside, apparently to an apartment. Valenti assumed it was for a broad, single, divorced or just cheating. The guy was risking his job but, Valenti thought, he had a good deal. Getting paid while getting laid.

To double check the schedule, he watched for another – an extra – three weeks. The doorman's urge in his crotch was always on schedule, like Mussolini's trains. Three more weeks of Tuesday and Friday nights away from his post.

It was time to act. After his six-week stakeout, on a Tuesday night, feeling confident, Valenti was sitting on his bed in his hotel room, inspecting his piece, a 7.62 mm Nagant M1895, which unlike most other revolvers, could be fitted with a silencer. The Nagant had been used for assassinations by the Russians during World War I and later by the Viet Cong in the Vietnam War. If it was good enough for the Russians and the Viet Cong, Valenti assumed it would do the job for him.

The gun wasn't easy to come by, but Giancamilli was an effective underworld researcher. Someone always seems to know someone who could help and Giancamilli tapped into them. He had started his search before Valenti was freed and, along with the two broads, gave the revolver to him as a present.

Giancamilli could have obtained a silencer from Carmen "The Mechanic" Evola. The Mechanic was a master at making silencers to order in a shop behind his restaurant in Brooklyn. This time, for this very important job, Giancamilli did not want any trail at all. He wanted as much distance between the silencer, himself and Valenti. Thus, he went deep underground for the Nagant.

This was in keeping with Valenti's strategy. He was not ready to have word out on the street that he was back. After his victim's body was found, people would talk. So Giancamilli was extra careful not to give the gossipers any reason to suspect his friend.

Not that Evola couldn't be trusted. In keeping with his unofficial, self-taught trade, Evola abided by the motto, silence is golden and much safer than the alternative. He liked breathing.

Making sure the cylinder was empty, he looked down

the barrel and pulled the trigger a half dozen times.

Click, click, click. It sounded good. It was good to have a piece in his hand again. Cool. Smooth. A little old-fashioned in how it looked. Style didn't matter to Valenti. He wanted effectiveness and, most important, as much suppression of the revolver's explosion as possible since the job would be carried out in an apartment building.

He was glad that he was about to close the books on this case. God, it had gnawed at his insides. It gnawed so bad it almost hurt. Many a night, he tossed and turned thinking about DeSante, the bastard. It would soon be over.

During the eighteen years, and in the two months he was out, he made a promise to himself. One more hit. Just one more. That's it. He had enough. He would do something else. While he wasn't sure what, he had few doubts he would land on his feet. He would deal with his career plans at some other time. First things first. He had to complete the job and then he would consider future employment opportunities.

He tucked the gun into his belt in the small of his back. It was a little cold which gave Valenti a feeling of comfort. The cold steel brought back memories. Been a long time.

It was 11:30 p.m. He left his hotel and headed for the subway station. No cabs that might be traced. An extra, perhaps unnecessary, precaution. Why take chances? He took the No. 6 train downtown to 42nd Street where he got off.

He walked three blocks to a brownstone. In the shadows, he waited. The street was relatively empty of pedestrians. He worked to stay out of sight. Ten minutes.

Twenty minutes. He was calm and patient. It had been eighteen years, so another few minutes didn't matter. He needed patience. He remembered an old Sicilian proverb: *Give me enough time and I will put a hole in you, the worm said to the walnut.* Yes, he needed to be patient. The worm was wise, and the analogy was appropriate. With enough time, and in this case, it was really only minutes, he would put a hole in the walnut that had cost him years of his life and given him so much grief. No reason to worry or panic. He had done his homework, studied the schedule.

It must have been at least a half hour, maybe more, before the doorman left for his liaison, a few minutes later than usual, according to Valenti's notes. Valenti sprang into action. He put on gloves and rushed into the building. Using the intercom in the foyer, he buzzed the apartment of Joey DeSante.

He pushed the buzzer several times a few seconds apart. Valenti fidgeted nervously. He wanted to be finished with the job in ten minutes, fifteen max, hoping to be gone before the doorman was scheduled to return.

"Come on, come on …"

Suddenly, he heard, "What the hell do you want? It's one a.m., you shit."

"Mr. DeSante, the gas company is here saying they need to check apartments for leaks. Someone reported smelling fumes. I'm alerting everyone. They'll be up to your place soon."

"Yeah, I ain't going anywhere." For a fleeting second, DeSante was bothered by the doorman's voice. Something "wasn't right." He couldn't put his finger on the problem. He was still drowsy from just having been awakened, which led to his mistake, a fatal one, of not thinking a little more about the call. Ironically, he was making a mistake similar to the one Valenti had made, and one which would cost him dearly.

Valenti jimmied the lock of the front door, bounded noiselessly up the steps, and was in front of Apartment 3B in a couple of minutes. He checked the hallway and it was clear. He knocked lightly on DeSante's door, making as little noise as possible. After a few seconds, he knocked again.

"Hold your fuckin' horses."

Valenti heard shuffling, movement. The chain was removed and the lock turned. The door was opened only about an inch when Valenti pushed himself inside and immediately closed it behind him. When their eyes met, it was like a Montague looking at a Capulet.

"Long time no see, Joey."

Joey DeSante was stunned. His heart skipped a couple of beats. Sweat broke out on his forehead instantly. Suddenly, it hit him. The voice on the intercom. It wasn't the doorman's. Why hadn't he stopped to think? Shit.

"Johnny, I didn't know…"

"Didn't know I was out? Is that what you were going to say?"

"No, I …." DeSante was having trouble collecting his thoughts. Considering the circumstances, that was understandable. He was, all in all, speechless, like a spouse who was caught cheating. DeSante's situation was a little more serious.

Valenti reached behind his back and pulled out the Nagant. He screwed on the silencer to the end of the barrel.

DeSante's blood drained from his face. His face twitched and he trembled as he watched Valenti closely. He looked at the revolver with the silencer that was pointed at him without so much as even a slight quiver.

"Johnny ...."

"Shut up."

"I wanna explain."

"Shut your stinkin' mouth. I'll explain. You sold me out. I don't know why. Don't even know who the guy was in the trunk. Thought about it a lot in the can. I don't give a shit why. You were a *capo bastone*, and I played by the rules and never said nothin'. Those are our rules. Don't squeal on bosses even if you're innocent. Now, my time has come. Unlike you, I ain't using the cops. If you had any balls, been a man, you would have come after me yourself. Instead, you went to the cops."

Valenti saw a dark, wet spot appear in the crotch of the pants that DeSante had hurriedly put on when awakened. Slowly, the spot grew larger down one pant leg.

"I can make it up to you," DeSante pleaded.

"Too late by about eighteen years."

"Johnny ...."

"Johnny what? Sorry? You didn't mean it? Time to forget? What?"

"I'll do whatever you want."

"As I said, eighteen years too late."

DeSante might have believed that after eighteen years, Valenti had changed. That he had mellowed or softened, and that his anger might have dissipated. He could not have been more wrong. Valenti's desire to avenge

DeSante's misdeed had only hardened over the years. It hardened with every passing day. And the only punishment that Valenti thought would balance the underworld's scale of justice was murder. He never considered anything else -- beatings, money. Nothing would do it for him except to kill the man who had committed the unspeakable crime of using the cops to send him to prison. Unthinkable.

"You're a complete shit," Valenti said, spitting at him. "You screwed up my whole life. Everything fell apart because you sold me out. And for what?"

DeSante tried again. "Let me explain ... I can ..."

"I said shut up. Explanations don't matter anymore."

Then Valenti said nothing, letting DeSante suffer and contemplate his upcoming fate. Valenti watched intently and with satisfaction the fear he was witnessing, the trembling, shaking, DeSante's sweating, the paleness of the face. He could almost hear DeSante's heart beat. DeSante's eyes pleaded for a reprieve while Valenti's rejected any compassion.

Valenti would have liked to watch DeSante overwhelmed with panic for a half hour or maybe more. If only Valenti had time to just sit there with the gun pointed at DeSante and savour the moment. As much as he would have enjoyed that luxury, Valenti was cognisant of his time constraints. He was committed to his deadline of fifteen minutes. It was a trade off. He could minimize risk by keeping to his schedule or indulge himself in understandable but short-lived pleasure of seeing DeSante petrified. He decided to minimize risk.

DeSante puked. "Johnny, I'm sick."

"Don't worry. You won't be for long. Joey, you shit on *omertá* and I can't let that go. Without *omertá*, we're all nothin'. We're absolutely nothin'. You got that, nothin'."

Those were the last words DeSante heard – Valenti's philosophy on *omertá.* That's how Valenti wanted it. Valenti stated his sacred principle with as much homage and respect as parishioners in church reciting The Lord's Prayer.

Then *pfuuuuuuufft.* That was the only sound in the room – *pfuuuuuuufft* – and DeSante slumped to the floor, landing on his side. Valenti stood so close to DeSante, he could smell the urine.

With the toe of his right foot, Valenti pushed on DeSante's shoulder, rolling him over on his back. A second shot was not necessary. The first one had penetrated the heart. Good, because a Nagant required reloading one cartridge at a time. So Valenti was extra careful with the first squeeze of the trigger. He did not want to have to take time to reload. He didn't have to. His aim had been perfect.

Almost immediately, he noticed that the gnawing pain in his gut caused by DeSante double-crossing him was gone. In jail, he had worried that he would get ulcers. With just one *pfuuuuuuufft*, and, zip, no more cramps, pain, stomach-aches. Better than a Tylenol that took at least twenty minutes to cure a headache. And the pill didn't always work. This did.

He slipped on DeSante's overcoat, pulled up the collar, and put on one of DeSante's Brooklyn Dodgers baseball caps. He bent the brim low to cover his eyes.

It had been twenty years since the Dodgers, affectionately called "da bums" by their adoring fans, had moved to Los Angeles. DeSante never got over it. When the Dodgers abandoned Brooklyn in 1958, DeSante was thirty-nine. He thought it was sacrilege, like the Pope converting to another religion. It was abandonment, abandonment that left him heart-broken but he remained loyal to the Dodgers.

He had never gotten over the loss da bums suffered in the 1951 pennant playoff series with the Giants. Leading by 4-2 in the bottom of the ninth and ready to clinch the pennant, the Dodgers' pitcher, Ralph Branca, screwed up and the Giants' outfielder, Bobby Thomson, who had a history of great success against Branca, made him pay by lifting the ball over the left field wall for a three-run homer, clinching the game and the pennant.

Arguably the most famous home run in the history of baseball, it became known as the "shot heard 'round the world," and even the poet, Ralph Waldo Emerson, who coined the phrase in writing about the American Revolution, would have agreed, assuming he would have been a Dodgers fan.

What was even worse, the loss came after the Dodgers led the league by 13 ½ games in mid-August when the Giants went on the winning streak to tie for the pennant at the end of the season. The only consolation for DeSante, and it was not much: the Yankees took the Series 4-2.

Given DeSante's career in the underworld and breaking some rules himself, he thought the Giants deserved some credit because they allegedly used some devious and illegal means to win the game

Reports were that Herman Franks, a Giants coach, following orders from his manager, Leo Durocher, used a telescope from centre field at the Polo Grounds, to steal the Dodgers catcher's signs. With instructions from Franks, an electrician by Franks' side activated a buzzer in the Giants' bullpen. One buzz for a fastball and two for a curve. Sal Yvars, a reserve catcher in the bullpen, would listen for the signals. If Yvars held on to a baseball, the batter would know a faster ball was coming. If Yvars tossed the ball into the air, the batter should expect a curve ball.

According to Yvars' relay from the bullpen, Branca would throw a fastball and, Branca did not disappoint. Thomson, properly alerted, obviously had a little advantage and became part of baseball lore.

Thomson always denied that he ever looked at Yvars. He said he was too busy concentrating in the batter's box. That was a little hard to accept. He may not have looked directly at Yvars, but no one asked him if perhaps he took just a little peek.

DeSante could identify with those kinds of underhanded tricks, and much worse. If only his Dodgers had not been the victims of such skulduggery

DeSante went into depression, and friends suggested he see a shrink. DeSante ignored the advice because there was always "next year" so he passed on getting psychiatric help, saved his money, and hoped the bums would make up for choking so badly in future seasons.

This one-two punch left DeSante heart broken. So when they moved, he bought three dozen or so Dodgers baseball caps and he was never without one. It became his trademark.

Looking down at the body, Valenti whispered, "I bet if I had played for da bums you wouldn't have turned on me."

He made a quick inspection of the room, checking that he had not dropped anything or left any clues. Everything seemed in order. One final hurdle, the doorman.

While Valenti, at five foot ten and a hundred eighty

five pounds, was a couple of inches shorter and a few pounds lighter than his victim, he didn't think the doorman, if he were back at his post, would notice. Still, there was the possibility that the doorman might challenge Valenti. What if the coat and cap did not work and, for whatever reason, the doorman stopped him and asked questions?

He had thought about that in his hotel room. Not a problem. He would do what he had to do. No, he would not like it, but he would not compromise on the promise he had made to himself in jail. He would not leave any witnesses, if at all possible. He didn't want the doorman telling police about "someone" leaving the building at about one a.m. So, while hoping to avoid ruining the doorman's afterglow from his tryst, he was prepared to expend one more bullet. He reloaded and put the pistol with the silencer still on the barrel in his pocket.

He left DeSante's apartment, turning the doorknob from the inside to its locked position and closed the door. When he reached the foyer, he saw the doorman had returned, earlier than Valenti expected. Must have been a quickie, Valenti thought. To avoid speaking, Valenti gave him an informal military salute with his right hand. He slipped his left hand into the coat pocket, curling his forefinger around the revolver's trigger.

"Going for a walk?" the doorman asked. "Be careful. Some tough guys in the neighbourhood."

"Yeah, I know," Valenti answered, adding a second salute while suppressing the temptation to laugh at the warning about the neighbourhood. "Thanks." He was glad he did not have to use the piece again. The doorman would have been happy too.

He took the No. 6 train uptown back to his hotel. With his mission, eighteen years in the making, completed successfully, he was ready to start a new life.

CHAPTER 3

VALENTI SLEPT LATE INTO the morning, awakening just before noon. He felt like a new man. Life was good, never ever better. He was free. He had his revenge. For the first time in almost two decades he did not think about DeSante. The ultimate Dodgers fan was history. What more could a man ask for? He was, to quote another good Italian, Frank Sinatra, sitting on top of the world

At the same time, he also felt a little bad for the doorman. How would he explain to the cops and his bosses that some gunman got by him to take care of DeSante. The guy would probably lose his job. It just didn't seem right to Valenti. The doorman really hadn't done anything wrong except to bang some broad while on the job. That might merit couple of days suspension but not a firing.

Aiding and abetting murder by dereliction of duty, well, that was another matter. The building's owner would have a right to be a little fussy ab out that. The doorman would probably be canned. Couldn't be helped. Not much Valenti could do. Life wasn't always fair. He could testify to that. Maybe the doorman was eligible for unemployment benefits.

True, it wasn't his problem but he felt a little guilt. Whatever happened, even if the doorman managed to save his job, one thing was certain. The doorman would have to make some other arrangements with his lover. Maybe he would have to give up his lunch hour.

Valenti turned on the TV for the weather forecast. He ignored the news even when the anchor announced "a breaking news story." Suddenly, he turned to listen when he heard the name "DeSante."

"...body was discovered about two hours ago when blood from the victim seeped through the floorboards and into the apartment below. He had been shot once through the heart.

"Police said the killing was a professional job. They have no suspects.

"The doorman, Joseph Tilman, told police he had seen DeSante leave the building about the time police said the victim was shot in his apartment. Police officials maintained the body had not been moved. Police authorities are investigating the apparent discrepancy.

"DeSante was described by police as a capo bastone, *an underboss, for one of New York's Mafia families that dealt in gambling, prostitution, racketeering and other illegal activities.*

"Our reporter, Joan Wilkins, caught up with Joseph Tilman, the doorman, at his home just minutes ago. Joan ...."

"Yes, I'm here – live – with Mr. Tilman. Can you tell us how you could have seen the victim leave when police said he was found shot in his apartment?"

"All I can say is, I seen the guy go for a walk. Told him to be careful. That's all I know."

"Could the man you saw have been someone else?"

"No way. It was him. Always has that silly damn Dodgers cap on. He's sort of crazy about that. Little nutty, if you ask me."

"Did you see anyone strange enter the building?"

"No, like I told the cops, no one. I watch pretty good. Been doing this job for twenty years. I don't know nothin' else."

"Did you ever leave your post even for a few minutes?"

"Never. I never leave. I gotta go."

"That was Joseph Tilman, the doorman of the building where the body was found. Bob, back to you."

"Thank you, Joan. This really is a mystery. We'll stay on top of this story and have more details for you on the nightly news at six."

Valenti was proud that his work was described as "professional" and he had to chuckle at the doorman's account of having seen DeSante leave. Valenti owed his successful mission in part to DeSante's uncompromising allegiance to the Dodgers. Couldn't have done it without da bums.

"Hey, Valenti, you did alright last night," he said to himself. "Pretty good job even though I ain't had any jobs for some eighteen years."

Valenti's record was 5-0. He had never failed. If he were to count his very first job, for which he was assigned a partner, he was 6-0. He didn't like having help, but the bosses insisted. He was untested at the time, and they did not want to take any chances.

The reports on his performance in his debut were good, very good. He was described as meticulous, always prepared, one who avoided unnecessary risks, did not leave any telltale clues, and, most important, he was cold-blooded. He was fearless. There was no hesitancy at the moment of truth. Like a bullfighter aiming his sword at the *toro*, Valenti never flinched. He was as cool as a cucumber – always. DeSante could have been a character witness to Valenti's competence.

Valenti was allowed to solo after his first hit while

some apprentices required a partner more than once. Given the evaluation of Valenti's work by his tutor, a thug who no longer even kept count of his hits, he progressed more rapidly than others. His mentors reported he never showed any signs of conscience or remorse, not even a hint.

He turned off the television. Now what? It was time to think, to make decisions on how he was going to make a buck. In the last two months while concentrating on DeSante, he had lived like a hermit. No one knew that he was out and in town, except Giancamilli. That's the way he planned it. He didn't want his old bosses, the Espositos, to know he was back on the street. If they didn't know, he wouldn't be a suspect in the hit. Eventually, when he surfaced, they would probably put two-and-two together. He would deal with that when the time came. Valenti really didn't care. For now, he wanted to stay under the radar as much as he could. It also provided him with some "adjustment" time. No use hurrying back to work.

More important, he didn't want them to think he was available for future jobs, that he was back in the business. He wasn't. DeSante was an exception, a very special exception, a one-time deal. At some time, probably very soon, he would give his eighteen year and two month notice, hand them his resignation. That would not be easy but a guy's got to do what he's got to do. He was firm about his decision. No more whacking, no more hits. His decision was not based on any moral code. He had not concluded that murdering people was wrong; indeed, those he whacked – rats, deadbeats – had it coming. He just wanted to do something else. The world was a big place to explore, and life was short, indeed very short for those who crossed Valenti's professional path.

He felt a little like a college graduate considering

various career options. Admittedly, Valenti came to his employment crossroads from a different perspective than someone who had just graduated from a university, but the decision-making process about what to do in the future was the same. There were choices to be made, and he did not want to make a mistake.

In what served as a kitchen in his room, he picked up a plastic bag and some rope. He put the revolver along with DeSante's coat and Dodgers cap inside the bag.

He left the apartment and took a leisurely stroll toward the East River. It was a sunny day, cool and breezy. Valenti was as free as a former jailbird. It was good to be alive. Probably for the first time in his life, he looked around and appeared to take notice of the city. On the way, he continually picked up rocks, some heavy, and put them in the bag. At the river, he wrapped the bag tightly with his rope. He leaned against the guardrail, holding the package between his hands. He looked around. He was alone. He let go, watching the package make a big splash and sink.

"Hope it wasn't something important," said a woman a few feet behind him.

For a second, a shiver ran through Valenti's body. Shit, where had she come from? "Nay, nothing I needed." *I gotta be more careful,* Valenti thought.

"I'm glad."

"Thank you, ma'am, so am I."

Valenti deposited and entrusted the Nagant, as he had other pieces he used to carry out his assignments, to the waterways surrounding New York City.

CHAPTER 4

VALENTI MOVED INTO GIANCAMILLI'S apartment, telling him he would stay "just until I get on my feet." He had a roomie again, like Bubba. There was one major difference. No bars on the windows or on the front door. He was free to come and go as he pleased. Giancamilli liked the company, but both understood this was temporary housing for Valenti.

Sharing living quarters did create a tense situation because Valenti had worked for the Espositos while his life-long friend was employed by the Marceses, a competing mob family. The two crime families had a rivalry like high school or college football teams except, it was safe to say, the stakes were somewhat higher. At times, they were deadly.

The fact that the two were on different sides did not affect their friendship, but suspicion always hung over them because the heads of the two families worried that they might share "trade" secrets. It was like wondering whether Macy's would tell Gimbels. Would Valenti tell tales out of school, sharing proprietary information with Giancamilli, and would Giancamilli give Valenti inside dope?

The two families' fears were unwarranted, unnecessary. There was no reason for them to fret. Both had pledged not to discuss the businesses of their respective employers with each other. They understood respectfully that they were competitors, friendly competitors in deadly pursuits. There were consequences of breaking the allegiance to those giving them their paychecks. Admittedly, it wasn't just honour that kept them honest. Potential crippling injuries or death were effective motivators to keep them from whispering secrets in each other's ears. They did not need any additional reasons to avoid engaging in shop talk.

With Valenti free and working for no one, and with only an unwritten mob loyalty code to bind him, Giancamilli worked on his friend to join his professional family, the Marceses. He urged him to divorce his previous family.

"Hey, Johnny," he continually told his friend, "we need a guy like you. Lots of opportunities, and not just in your speciality. Why not? You're quitting the Espositos anyway. It was their *capo bastone* that sold you out."

Valenti held firm, turning him down. True, he wasn't planning on working for the Espositos. As Giancamilli said, one of them had betrayed him, and, to make matters worse, they didn't treat him right or his family. When he went to prison, it was like he had never existed. They just forgot about him. He could even buy that they no longer gave a shit about him. He understood why they shunted him aside, not knowing if they would ever use him again. Nevertheless, it wasn't right, given all he had done for them.

What gnawed at him was they abandoned his parents as well. He'd expected them to help, maybe send his parents a few bucks every week. Without him, his parents barely made it from week to week. Valenti was pissed at his bosses. He had expected more. The Espositos owed him something, and taking care of his parents would have helped them make ends meet.

If he had a soft spot in his heart, it was for Papa and Mama Valenti, who settled in Little Italy in lower Manhattan near the financial district after immigrating from Sicily in the 1920s. They followed a large immigration that started in the late 19th Century and reached a population of almost four hundred thousand by 1920. The immigrants came mostly from the south when their homeland was suffering massive unemployment.

His father, Antonio, ran a bakery with his mother, Rosita. It served almost exclusively an Italian clientèle and, overall through the years, business was not so bad. They could make it. They weren't going to be the Rockefellers, but they didn't want to be. The Rockefellers were rich – so-called filthy rich – but not Italian. The Valentis were satisfied that the bakery kept the proverbial roof over their family's head.

Valenti had fond memories of bringing friends into the bakery and his parents always giving them pastries. It cost them but they never failed even though their generosity impacted the shop's meagre profit margin.

Over the years, business spiralled downward with the neighbourhood continually changing. Little Italy became littler and littler with the Italians relocating to its fringes while the Chinese were moving in.

More problems piled up when gangsters fled the area because the feds infiltrated Little Italy to spy on them. The mobsters didn't like being watched from windows by men with binoculars from neighbouring apartments, so they just picked up, moved out, and opened shop elsewhere. In an unexpected development, the anti-mobster programs prompted law-abiding Italians to leave as well.

When he was working, Valenti would send his parents a few bucks, helping them over the hump. If they had known how that money was earned, his parents would never have accepted it.

"They don't need to know," he told Giancamilli through the years. "They'll never know."

Of course, his parents had an inkling that their son did not make a living as a bank vice president or school principal. They weren't dumb. Whatever their suspicions, they had no idea that he got paid for shooting people between the eyes or through their hearts. And they never did find out. Explaining his prison sentence, he had told them he got caught for fraud, for forging checks.

"Chicken shit," he told them, trying to ease their pain. "Don't worry, I'll see you soon."

The Valentis "accepted" their son's story. They weren't going to push despite their suspicions. Gossip in the neighbourhood about their son obviously reached them, and while they did not watch television news or read the papers, they heard about the news stories that sometimes mentioned Valenti's name. They put their faith in the word "alleged," the adjective which always appeared before the kind of work the media claimed their son and his colleagues were involved in.

If truth be told, they did not want to know the truth, whatever it was. While their son might be among the best in his field, it would be difficult for any parent to brag about having a son who was a hit man.

While in prison, he could have gotten permission to see his parents. If he had taken advantage of this privilege, he would have been in chains and with guards watching him. That hardly would have made for a warm family reunion. So he never made use of that privilege. He did not want to put his parents through that humiliation.

Valenti learned of their passing while in Ray Brook. His mother died three years after he was sent to prison, and his father had a fatal heart attack five years later. The time had come for Valenti to pay his respects to his parents before he had a more sensitive meeting with his former employers.

As he drove to Green-Wood Cemetery in Greenwood

Heights, Brooklyn, he experienced emotions that were unusual for a man who had blood at temperatures below freezing running through his veins.

He recognized the emotions primarily because he rarely, if ever, had them. They included sadness, sentimentality, regret and, some guilt. Guilt, not for what he did for a living, but guilt that his parents would have been ashamed. More than ashamed.

An only child, Valenti showed signs very early that he was someone who marched to his own drum. He was a drummer to whom rules, regulations, laws meant nothing. He did have an innate allegiance to his own set of principles and ethics that led to his unswerving commitment to *omertá*. He knew right from wrong as defined in his world and, later, in the professional underworld. He had, from the beginning, a mobster's sense of honour.

It was because of an inherent code of honour that he would not squeal on classmates or friends and acquaintances that engaged in criminal behaviour. Many times he was asked by principals and teachers to identify troublemakers, but he would never budge. He would do their time whether it involved staying after school, or serving suspensions. He never ratted regardless of the punishment he faced.

He had no mentors who taught him this code. It just came naturally and he never reflected, even when he graduated from beatings to murders, on the possible contradiction in his definition of honour. A rat deserves the ultimate punishment. Simple as that. No room for debate. Totally justified.

When informants squealed on him in his classes for causing the respective problems, he would have his revenge. In what was an elementary version of a hit, he would beat the shit out of the ratters.

Overall, he was viewed as one tough son-of-a-bitch. Unlike other teenagers as well as pre-teenage gangsters who paraded their toughness, Valenti intimidated others with his silence. Just one look from cold, threatening eyes was enough for Valenti to achieve his objectives. What he wanted, he got. He frightened everyone.

If teachers threatened to talk to his parents about absences, not doing his assignments, beating his classmates senseless, fondling girls in the halls, or smoking in the boys' restroom or on school grounds – or other school no-nos – he glared at them, saying, "You ain't gonna talk to no one. You leave them out of this."

Wisely, most listened and took his less than gentle warnings seriously. They were shaken by the starkness of the threats coming, ironically, from the high-pitched voice of a twelve year old. One teacher, after he scheduled a Valenti parent-teacher conference, saw Valenti, who at the time was in the sixth grade, sitting under a tree about thirty yards from his car. The teacher found the four tires of his car slashed, and the doors along with the windshield smashed. The young boy stared coldly and threateningly at the teacher. He did not say a word. He didn't have to. The teacher cancelled the meeting.

His teachers adopted a *laissez faire* attitude toward Valenti. They gave him a wide berth. Their instincts, very good instincts one might add, told them that would be the best policy even though they did not know they were teaching and counselling a future hit man.

He was feared in his neighbourhood, so much so that he was able to shoplift brazenly, simply taking whatever he wanted from bakeries, grocery stores, gas stations and other retail outlets. Shopkeepers would not call the police. They did benefit from their reluctance to call the cops. In return, given Valenti's commitment to fairness, if they needed him to take care of others who were screwing them, Valenti was always available. What's fair is fair. He was their insurance, and it cost them only a few of their products. Valenti had his neighbours' respect, admittedly a strange kind of respect.

When he was fifteen, he and Giancamilli, his partner in juvenile crime, did have a very close call with the cops that almost cost him his life.

He had a bad case of puppy love and told the father of his love interest that he was serious about his daughter. The father, a wealthy man who owned a trucking company, humiliated Valenti in front of others, disparaging him, and his parents.

For his revenge, Valenti and Giancamilli hijacked one of the man's trucks. Unfortunately, two cops, in a nearby patrol car, noticed. They chased the truck, and when Valenti and Giancamilli abandoned their stolen vehicle, the cops continued after them on foot.

The two thieves made a left when they should have turned right and were caught in a dead-end street. Angry, Valenti spit in the face of one of the cops. The cop pulled his gun and pointed it at the boy's head.

Giancamilli, the fixer, even at his young age, pleaded with the cop who had lost control. Inadvertently, or in his anger, the cop pulled the trigger just as Valenti happened to duck while kicking the cop in the groin. The bullet, barely missing Valenti, hit the cop's partner. The two gangsters-in-training escaped.

That incident along with his rebellion against any kind of law whether it covered jay walking, stealing, burglary or more serious anti-social behaviour only enhanced his reputation and soon the *Mafia,* like sports scouts recruiting young talent in middle and high schools, wooed him, signing him on when he was just sixteen. Just like prospective star athletes, he worked in the "minors" as the *Mafia* groomed him. He progressed rapidly into his speciality within about three years.

His bosses quickly learned, to their surprise, pleasant surprise, about his uncompromising commitment to *omertá.* He already had a long history of abiding by and being true to *omertá.* They were more than pleased that Valenti had developed a junior version of the principle as a boy, that it was not a principle they had to teach him upon joining the big leagues. It was like recruiting a baseball player to the majors who already had the talent to hit a curve ball. Not too many around.

After he made the big time, he sometimes served as a sort of guidance counsellor/mentor/tutor to the less experienced when they wanted to deal with unacceptable violations of the underworld's rule of law. He played the part of big brother, particularly since he had not had the privilege of having such help when he was learning the illegal ropes.

On one occasion, years later, Valenti was visited by his godson, Luigi "Little Lou" Marcese, the fourteen year old son of Eduardo "The Brains" Marcese, who headed the most powerful *Mafia* family in New York City, Giancamilli's parent company that Valenti would ultimately join.

Little Lou told Valenti the following story: His best friend, Ricardo Pavaro, the son of a single mother, found out, after pressuring his mother for years about the whereabouts of his father, that he was the product of a rape.

His friend was crushed. After a long investigation and covert research, he located the rapist who was now a man of the church, a minister. Ricardo wanted to even the score for his mother, and for having made him a bastard. Could and would Valenti help? Was he in that kind of work? If not, could he make a recommendation?

The boy had come to the right place. For Valenti, rape was almost as serious an offence as the violation of *omertá*. It was a condemnable crime in the criminal world. Raping defenceless women was simply unacceptable, and subject to only one punishment.

With information from Little Lou, information the boy gleaned from Ricardo, Valenti, with Giancamilli's help, tracked down the father and kidnapped him. They grabbed the minister by the elbows as he was lighting candles on the altar, and marched him out of the church without saying a word.

They called Little Lou and told him to bring Ricardo to an abandoned warehouse in a secluded part of the city that evening. When the boys arrived, they found the rapist tied to a metal post.

At first, the clergyman believed that he was the target of a robbery, or perhaps being held for a ransom. That is until he noticed his physical resemblance to Ricardo. He thought he was looking in the mirror. It was scary. He immediately understood.

When the boys faced the clergyman, Valenti handed Ricardo a revolver. Ricardo inspected it. He did not flinch or protest at the implied solution being recommended by Valenti, his elder, his mentor. He trusted Valenti, a man with extensive experience in these matters.

The rapist, aghast, pleaded. "Don't do this for God's sake. It was a long time ago. I was young, an alcoholic. I'm not the same man. I'm a man of God. I'm a minister."

Desperately, he made his final appeal, "Please, please ... I'm your father, and serve God. Please ..."

Ricardo was not placated, coldly responding, "You're gonna see God soon, and you ain't my father. You're nothin'... you're a piece of shit." Without another word, Ricardo had his revenge.

Valenti was impressed. This kid had balls. If only the *Mafia* had a human resource department, he would have sent it Ricardo's resume with a recommendation. Like Valenti in his youth, this kid had talent, and a future. *It's not easy to find good help. Need to be on the lookout constantly for employees with promise.*

As he did with Ricardo, Valenti reached out to young people and his neighbours as well. Before going to prison, he and Giancamilli opened a fruit store as a cover for their more profitable business. Like other retail operations that served as fronts, the mob referred to the fruit store as a laundromat because it cleaned dirty money. Indeed, one guy looking for Valenti spent about an hour searching for an actual laundromat. He risked asking where he might find Valenti and when he did, he never understood why he was in a fruit store.

Valenti's neighbours, who viewed him as a man of honour, a man of integrity, did not care if he made his money from businesses not exactly sanctioned by cops patrolling the streets. Of course, some cops more than sanctioned the business. They were silent – very silent – partners. The neighbours, frankly, often were envious and wanted part of the action, but without the risks.

"Valenti's Ventures," which offered opportunities to make a quick buck, tax free, brought the neighbouring shoemaker, Mario Gallio, to Valenti.

"Mario, you want to buy some fruit?" asked Valenti,

somewhat facetiously.

"Johnny, I gotta six kids, my wife is sick, and the shoe business not so good," answered Gallio. "I wanna invest some money with you."

Gallio went on to complain how the banks are "crooks, stealin' my money. The whole world is crooked. Everyone cheating me all-a the time."

"Mario, there are good and bad guys in the *Mafia* too. Things are changing. Used to be able to trust *Mafia* guys. No more. Don't know what's happening."

After bewailing the state of morals in the *Mafia*, Valenti asked, "How much you got?"

"I have-a five thousand dollars in cash," said Gallio holding up a brown paper bag he was carrying.

"How much you want for the money?"

"Johnny, I know you're a fair, good man. I'll take-a whatcha give me."

"Deal," said Valenti without another word.

Gallio was grateful. He would realize a substantial return on his investment, almost guaranteed. There was no paper trail and he would not have to pay taxes. Nor did he face any potential dangers from authorities since no records existed. The only risk was that Valenti might go out of business as a result of being arrested (which did happen) or he might be killed. Gallio made his decision on the principle that all investments have risks, some larger than others. Gallio had considered his odds and considered them pretty good.

As soon as word leaked out on Gallio's deal, Valenti was visited by other neighbours. His fruit store became a kind of local chamber of commerce headquarters offering investments for small businessmen. Valenti agreed to help most of them.

Valenti's largess pissed off Giancamilli.

"They're cowards," Giancamilli protested. "They want us to do all the dirty work for some fast money. When the cops get us, they turn their backs. They ain't gonna know us. Say they never heard of us at all."

Valenti did not waver in continuing his philanthropy for two reasons. He genuinely wanted to help and, more important, he told Giancamilli he was planting seeds for favours that might prove valuable someday. You never know. As they say, bread cast upon the waters

At the cemetery, he found the graves and stood with his head bowed. Instinctively, he looked around hoping that no one was in the cemetery to see this side of him, this weakness. Scanning the area at cemeteries was also a habit developed when attending funerals of colleagues who warranted the "secret" watchful eye of federal authorities. Out of sight, these uninvited funeral guests would record the names of mourners at the burial ceremonies. This time Valenti was alone.

"Mama, Papa, I'm sorry," he whispered. "Ain't your fault. You were good. It just happened."

After another few minutes, he told them, "See you around. I'll be back."

His belated eulogy was heartfelt, if not particularly eloquent or expansive. Given the circumstances, even those with special talents at expressing themselves would have had a difficult time. It ain't easy to explain to parents how you became a hit man, and then ask for forgiveness.

Valenti had done his best, and then he left for a meeting which would be much more pressure-packed than the cemetery visit, one in which he could not be weak, emotional or equivocal.   And he would need to be convincing.

He got into his car and drove to meet with the head, the boss, the top honcho, of the Esposito family.

CHAPTER 5

JOHNNY VALENTI AND DOMINIC "No Pain" Esposito faced each other. Esposito was behind a huge desk.

"Been long time, Johnny," Esposito said when Valenti arrived. "Glad to have you back. Yeah, sure is."

"Thanks. Glad to be here," Valenti lied.

"You look good, Johnny.   Kept in shape, huh? Nothin' around the mid-section. You're solid."

The two looked at each other like two prize fighters in the first round. Their eyes reflected respect and suspicion. They parried on a number of issues, feeling each other out. The main subject, Valenti's future, could wait until they finished with meaningless preliminaries.

It was Esposito who had recruited Valenti as a soldier – an enforcer – when Valenti was about sixteen. One night, three years later, when Valenti executed, literally, his first hit, Esposito heard about his skills, immediately called him to his office, and promoted him. He told Valenti he would be used exclusively to carry out contracts. The hours were good as was the pay. He was assured of a good future, lots of opportunities. The market was good. Never a shortage of rats, deadbeats, turncoats or others who needed whacking.

Valenti's reputation immediately soared in the gangster rumour mill, and Esposito was extremely proud that a man of such a reputation worked for him. The message to the other families was that Esposito hired only the best, and Esposito wanted the help of a man who was fearless and feared on his payroll.

"So, Johnny, you hear about DeSante?" asked Esposito. It was not so much a question as an attempt to see if Valenti would reveal any telltale signs of involvement.

"Heard on the news."

"Whatta you think?"

"I think? Dominic, I think nothing except no loss."

"Got shot with a .22. Must have been an amateur who did the job."

Immediately, Valenti recognized the trap. If he corrected Esposito, that it wasn't a .22, the game would be over. The cops used this devious trick frequently. While investigating murders or crimes in which guns were used, they would reveal to the press the calibre of the weapon they were looking for when, in fact, the gun involved was of a different calibre. They hoped the shooters, reading news stories about the crime, would conclude the cops didn't know what the hell they were doing, keep the weapon that, ultimately, would help them with their case when the suspect was caught.

"Didn't know that," said Valenti. "We got some amateurs around. No sweat off my back."

Esposito did not press the issue. Valenti would have an answer for everything he asked, so why bother. While Esposito was suspicious of his visitor's involvement in the DeSante murder, he respected Valenti as a pro. He would not push to have Valenti violate his commitment to *silenzio*, nor did he want to upset him before asking him to rejoin his organization. Esposito, not the most patient of men, decided diplomacy was in order.

"Just a loser," Esposito offered. "Shouldn't be a problem."

By "problem," Esposito meant that while DeSante had rank – indeed, he was number two in his organization –

Esposito did not plan to avenge DeSante's killing. He was giving Valenti a signal that he understood, and even agreed with the concept of revenge. He would expect Valenti to retaliate for having been sold out.

Addressing the issue indirectly, Esposito said, "Sorry, Johnny about what happened. I didn't know anything. I know you kept your mouth shut. That's big in my book."

Valenti was not impressed. He thought, *He's sorry. Big deal. It cost me eighteen.*

"I couldn't get into it at the time," added Esposito. "Had lots on my plate. I wish I could-a helped you. Really, I wanted to. Had problems with some of my guys and the feds were pressuring me. The take wasn't what it was supposed to be. You know how things are sometimes."

No, I don't, Valenti thought. *Too busy? Who you kidding?* Valenti said nothing. He sat quietly, assuming Esposito would get the message that he did not understand. He wanted Esposito to know he was pissed, more than pissed.

Esposito waited for an answer, some kind of indication that Valenti would forget, forgive. He did not get the signal he wanted. After a few seconds, Esposito decided against being too defensive. He would not try to explain his non-involvement in the railroading of Valenti. After all, this meeting for Esposito was about rehiring Valenti. As they talked, Esposito studied his employee carefully watching his eyes, his body language.

He had not built his empire by being impulsive. As head of one of six mob families in New York, he was involved in about everything that was illegal, including prostitution, money laundering, racketeering, gambling, and a variety of other enterprises. Esposito worked on a strategy of diversification, protecting against possible cyclical downturns in any one of his businesses.

Drugs were another matter. Esposito hated them because, inevitably, some of his soldiers dipped into the cookie jar. They became addicts which invariably meant that when they were arrested they were vulnerable, more likely to talk. The cops would entice them with anything and everything, even providing junkies with a fix. As far as he was concerned, drugs were an unnecessary risk.

He was tough and as fearless as Valenti when he was on a job. He got his nickname – No Pain – from a scar across his cheek that he earned in a street fight when he was in his early twenties. Mob folklore had it that when he was slashed with a knife on his face, he did not flinch, did not raise his hand and simply kept fighting as if nothing had happened.

His opponent was aghast, hesitating just long enough to lose the fight, and suffer wounds that were more serious than Esposito's facial wound. Esposito's opponent survived, barely, never to have another knife battle. Not that he wanted one.

"So, Johnny," Esposito asked with a mixture of curiosity and irritation. "Whatcha gonna do?"

"Don't know exactly," Valenti said. "I'm getting out. No more of the old stuff."

Esposito feigned surprise. He had half expected a resignation. It happened often after his men were released from prison. Many lost their stomach for the business after doing time, serious time. And eighteen years can be classified as serious time. It ain't exactly an overnight stay. Moreover, he expected Valenti to be angry with him since one of his men – his number two guy – was responsible for his years in prison. Couldn't begrudge a man a little grudge.

"Johnny, we need you."

"Yeah, well, Dom, I had enough. Gonna do somethin' else."

"Doing what?"

Valenti did not want to tell Esposito. He was ill at ease and a little embarrassed saying that he was going to try to make a living lawfully. He did not think Esposito would believe him. Valenti hesitated before answering.

"As I said, don't know. I'm goin' clean."

Esposito controlled the impulse to burst out laughing. A hit man, whose record would qualify him for the *Mafiaso*'s Hall of Fame, if one existed, going clean struck him as funny.

"You're kidding, Johnny? You gonna make it on the other side with what, three hundred dollars a week? Come on. This is Dominic Esposito you're talking to. Your boss. I know you."

Valenti was tense. He stretched his arms while sitting, trying not to show any signs of irritation in this exchange with Esposito. Esposito would pressure him as much as he could. Getting out of a job was proving more difficult than interviewing for one.

"I'm gonna give it a shot," Valenti offered. "I'll make it. Thanks for wanting me back."

Esposito gave it another try, making an open-ended offer.

"Johnny, you tell me what you want to do, and I'll make it work. I wanna make it up to you. You been loyal. Whatever you want. Well, almost whatever."

"Thanks, not interested. Lots of things have happened. I lost some of the fire in my belly, and you know my parents are gone."

Esposito immediately picked up Valenti's reference to his parents. Valenti's message was not lost on Esposito. He expected Valenti to be angry.

"Yeah, I heard, sorry about them Johnny," Esposito offered. He started to explain why he had not helped them but thought better of it. It would not do much good now. Just like his explanation about DeSante hadn't helped.

"Johnny, you come back work for me, and you can team with Tommy Boy again," said Esposito. "I know Tommy Boy wants you back with us."

Valenti smiled at hearing the name. Tomaso "Tommy Boy" Galente was, like Giancamilli, one of his boyhood friends. He was closer to Giancamilli but he trusted Galente just as much.

"Yeah, would be nice," said Valenti. "Tommy Boy is good people. No deal. Made my decision. Thanks anyway."

Esposito decided not to argue with Valenti. Obviously, Valenti was serious. It would be futile to try to change his mind. Esposito saw a very determined look in Valenti's face. He didn't like it but he would not pressure his employee, his former employee. He accepted the resignation although not exactly graciously.

On a practical level, he did not want an unhappy hit man on his payroll. Somewhat risky. Never could predict where that might lead to, what kinds of mistakes Valenti might make by not giving it his all, not having his heart in his job.

"Johnny, Johnny, Johnny. You win," he said, taking Valenti's head into his hands. He slapped Valenti's cheeks with both hands, adding, "All I got to say I better never hear you working for someone else."

Valenti ignored the implied threat. The threat was not just implied, it was real. He controlled his instinct to lash back. This was not the time or place. Maybe it would come in the future. While he could not know it as he was quitting his job, he would get his revenge. He would have his day. Someday, the stars would align for him.

He swallowed hard with the warning ringing in his ears as he left to see if he could make it on the right side of the law.

CHAPTER 6

VALENTI HAD SUCCESSFULLY COMPLETED two of the items that needed attention after his release from prison -- DeSante and Esposito. For Valenti, quitting the Esposito family was more difficult than whacking DeSante. The face-to-face with Esposito had created some tension, friction, even some risk. He could not be confident that the issue would not come up again, or that Esposito would not strike back. To Valenti, the risk was worth taking and, if Esposito were to revisit the issue violently, Valenti would, as they say, cross that bridge when ... For the time being, he checked DeSante and Esposito off his list. Done, finis. He had been productive.

Now there was one more item that needed attention before he could go on with his life: Fiora. This would not be as sensitive as the other two items. It was more a matter of achieving closure. It fell into the category of a nice thing to do, not something that was necessary. It just nagged him. He wanted to see her, find out what had happened to her, and officially indicate that each needed to go their own way, if she had not already done so. And, most important, he wanted to hear about his child.

He had been dating Fiora for about two years when he went to prison, and the week he was sentenced, she told him, she was two months pregnant. It was an "almost" exclusive relationship. Periodically, given his lifestyle, Valenti would violate his unofficial fidelity to Fiora. They weren't passionately in love. He liked her and Fiora thought Valenti was a good guy, and in her circle of friends and neighbourhood, good guys, even good guys who were hit men, were hard to come by. While they never really talked about marriage, the assumption was that eventually they would become husband and wife. DeSante had screwed up their plans badly.

Fiora had written to Valenti for the first few months. Slowly, she wrote less and less until she stopped, about three months before she delivered her baby. Valenti did not blame her. He had answered a few of her letters and he lost interest as well. Still, he could not forget about the possibility that he had a child, that he was a father.

With information from Giancamilli who had located Fiora, Valenti took a cab to a flat in Queens. He paid the driver, got out of the cab, and spent a few minutes on the street in front of the house collecting his thoughts.

He was confident, with some reservations, that this was the right thing to do. It had been eighteen years. Would she want to see him? Would she really care one way or another? Why mess up her life by showing up, and without notice?

As he pondered these questions and others, almost without thinking, he found himself on the front porch where he rang the doorbell. As he waited, he looked around the neighbourhood, hands in his pockets.

Just as he was about to ring the doorbell again, she opened the door. She was wearing jeans, a white blouse and her pitch black hair with a few strands of grey hung over her shoulders. Except for a few wrinkles at the sides of her mouth and along the corners of her eyes, she had not changed much. Very pretty, even beautiful.

They looked at each other just for a few seconds before she instinctively said, "Johnny."

She said his name matter-of-factly, simply as a sign of recognition and not with any emotion. If she was surprised, she did not show it.

She had read about the DeSante murder in the newspapers and wondered, very briefly, whether her former boyfriend might have been involved. The thought crossed her mind, even though she assumed he was still in prison and couldn't be involved. She recalled how, without explaining any details, he had told her he was innocent, at least of this murder, and had made no secret of wanting to get even for being railroaded. He did not say get even with whom. She did not know that DeSante was responsible for having her boyfriend imprisoned. Her only clue was when Valenti occasionally mentioned DeSante's name during court proceedings, he did so filled with hate.

She also considered that Valenti might have mellowed over the years. Perhaps Valenti's hatred for DeSante had abated. Who knows? Who cares? Overall, she did not give DeSante's death much thought. When the news of DeSante faded in the media, so did her thoughts about Valenti. Wasn't her problem. She had a new life. Had a husband and a daughter. She already had reached "closure" and as she looked at Valenti, she thought she could have done without this visit.

"Fiora," he said, echoing her greeting.

They stood facing each other each not sure how to start the conversation. She broke the tension, asking, "When?"

"Couple of months ago. Been a long time. You look good."

"You too."

After a few seconds of nervous glances at each other, she offered, "Want to come in?" She almost hoped he would reject the invitation. He didn't.

"Ain't gonna stay more than a few minutes. Just want to see how you're doing."

She led the way to the living room where she sat down on a recliner while motioning him to the sofa.

Valenti looked around the room before he said anything. She watched him closely not knowing exactly what to anticipate. Why was he here? Did he want to pick up where they left off? Did he believe she had waited eighteen years? Not possible. No one could expect anyone to wait eighteen years. She decided to let Valenti start the conversation.

"You doing alright?"

"Yeah," she answered. Then she added strategically, "I'm happy."

"That's good. That's real good, Fiora. Glad to hear that."

He nervously rubbed his hands. They looked at each other, and then quickly looked away.

"Johnny," she began. "I couldn't wait. I'm married. I hope you ...."

"That's good too. You done the right thing. He good to you?"

"Yes, he's a good man. Works hard. Takes care of us."

The use of the pronoun "us" did not escape him. Did she have more than his child? Several others? He hesitated to follow up on the opening.

"Glad you found a good guy. Hope he ain't involved."

"No, he's a house painter. Drives a cab sometime. We're paying the rent."

As he looked around, his eyes fell on a photograph on a corner lamp table. The photo was of Fiora, a man Valenti concluded was Fiora's husband, and a teenage girl. He stared at the girl in the photo. He tried to decide if she resembled him at all. Fiora was watching him inspect the photo.

"That her?" he asked.

"Yes."

"Got others?"

"No."

"What's her name?"

"Nicole."

"Nice. Handful, I bet."

"Not really. She's pretty good. Look, Johnny, I didn't know you were coming and I have …"

"Yeah, I was leaving anyway. Got things to do myself. Just wanted to see you, find out about ..." He stopped abruptly, asking, "Does she know?"

"No, she believes my husband is her father. I married him when she was just one. Perfectly natural. She has no reason to think otherwise. I thought it best."

One year old? She did not wait very long. Maybe dated only a few months. He wondered whether he should feel hurt. What surprised him, is that he did not feel anything at all. He felt bad that he did not feel bad.

He did not ask about her husband's opinion about Fiora's deception. Did he agree? Did he consider himself a fraud acting as the real father to a child he did not father? Doesn't seem right. Nicole should know the facts.

Valenti thought about asking Fiora about her husband's role in hiding the truth. He concluded she probably would tell him it was none of his business, and he would have to agree. Not after an eighteen year prison sentence for murder. He may have been innocent of the murder for which he did time, but he had a few other skeletons, literally, in his closet that a teenage girl might not be particularly proud of.

"You did the right thing. No need for her to know. Thanks for telling me."

Valenti got up to leave. On the porch, he moved to give her a hug. Instead, he just patted her shoulder.

"You take care, Fiora. I won't bother you again."

Without protest, she replied, "Okay."

CHAPTER 7

IT HAD BEEN A month since Valenti had visited Fiora, and he had some trouble not thinking about her. Well, not really Fiora but Nicole. He was a father, and he was not sure what role, if any, he needed to play in her life. He was confident that moving on was the thing to do. Yes, he believed that Fiora was right in not telling Nicole about him. What was the point? He put his faith in time. Time would take care of whatever guilt troubled him. And, in time, not a lot of time, he forgot, or at least put her out of his mind.

He had more immediate concerns, the primary one being how to succeed in his new role as a used car salesman. He pondered that as he stood among hundreds of used cars in the lot of *Benny's Best Deal Auto Sales.* Since deciding to give up murdering people, Valenti had applied for several jobs – short order cook, racetrack ticket seller, bartender, construction worker – and a bunch of other blue-collar jobs. Being "honest," he always marked an X in the box asking whether he, the applicant, had a criminal record. As a result, he never was hired.

He decided to lie. He answered "no" to the question whether he had a record or did not fill in the box. His deception led to his job at *Benny's.* Benny, the owner, gave Valenti a crash course in auto salesmanship, but Valenti failed miserably in successfully implementing Benny's instructions. He hadn't closed a deal after three weeks on the job. He bullshitted a lot of potential customers with the merits of the respective cars. In the end, he had no sales to show for his efforts.

Maybe Esposito was right, Valenti thought. Maybe he wasn't cut out to be a law-abiding citizen. Whatever the case, he was not ready to surrender. He swallowed hard and grimaced as he walked up to a couple on the lot. This was getting very tiresome, the false smiles, the lies, the arm draped around a customer's shoulders.   God, what a man had to do to make a living.

"Hell of a car," he exclaimed as the couple inspected a '75 Ford. "Little mileage and driven only about five, six miles a day by a retired school teacher."

He felt shitty in a shitty job. How the hell do all those guys do it? It just ain't right to try and screw these people into buying junkers. He was more at ease putting some guy out of his misery. The victim always deserved it. He was making a point, upholding a principle. And principle was important. But this? Trying to shaft some poor soul by convincing them to buy a clunker that hardly would make it out of the lot, that was something totally different. It was really abhorrent.

"The price can't be any better," he added. "Tell you what I can do. I can see in your eyes you just got married, that special loving look, so I'll cut fifty bucks off."

The potential sale became another failure. Was this the twentieth, twenty first, or twenty second lost sale? He didn't know, couldn't remember. He had lost count. This failure wasn't really

his fault.   He could not have known the couple, married twenty two years, was splitting up and the purchase of a car for the wife was part of the divorce settlement. Valenti had no skills at evaluating personal relationships.

He did not have to feel bad long about his ineptitude. Benny, being suspicious, checked Valenti's background and discovered the slight omission of being a convicted felon for the crime of murder.   He fired Valenti not reflecting on the possible consequences, potential fatal consequences, he might face.

Valenti grabbed Benny by the neck, choked him just long enough to see the face turn red, eyes bulge, and to watch Benny trying to say, "Please stop," when he let go.

"No hard feelings, Benny. It's okay."

Valenti lied to Benny. It was not okay. He was pissed, angry, frustrated as Giancamilli, in their apartment, was constantly murmuring in his ear, like a man to a woman reluctant to give in, "Come on, Johnny. The Marceses want you."

"Johnny, the Espositos disrespected you," Giancamilli said. "No one wants to be disrespected. The Marceses, they care about *famiglia*. They'll take care of you."

He was not ready to give up. After several more weeks of applications and interviews, he was hired as a cab driver. All he found was more frustration with passengers jumping out without paying, short-changing him, not tipping, women with huge dogs climbing into his cab, and young children ripping the shit out of the back seat.

The job as a car salesman started to look good. His patience to be a law-abiding citizen ran out one night when he got lost and found himself and his cab surrounded by eight not so pleasant looking hoodlums. They did not want a ride.

Most cab drivers would sit in panic with the fear of being robbed and/or beaten. That's what these guys expected. They had done this more than once.

Valenti, though, took a slightly different approach. He waved his right hand, like a driver at pedestrians indicating they can cross in front of the car, at the two standing in front of the hood. The two laughed hilariously, imitating Valenti's gesture with their hands before they went flying into the air as Valenti crushed the gas pedal to the floor.

He didn't even bother to look in the rear view mirror.

He had enough. He had given it a try. He wanted to be a "good" citizen, obey laws. It was becoming clearer by the day that he was obviously not suited for that kind of life. Maybe it was genetic. Maybe society was not ready for him even though he had told the parole board he had paid his debt to society. Maybe society had not been listening. It was time to meet with the Marceses.

"Luigi, go set it up."

Giancamilli embraced his friend. "You won't be sorry, Johnny, you'll see." Giancamilli was proud that he had won agreement from his number one draft pick.

"Johnny, it'll be good to work together again," said Giancamilli. "Like the old times."

A week later, Valenti was in the home of Eduardo "The Brains" Marcese. When he arrived at about nine a.m., Marcese was just finishing a card game that had begun the night before.

"Good to see you, Johnny," Marcese said, welcoming his prospective employee. "Have-a drink, smoke-a cigar. Be with you soon."

Marcese signalled to the players that he needed to end the game. All of them left except Carmen Rossini, a very rich man who walked with a limp and stuttered.

Rossini had been pestering Marcese for a long time to make him a member of the mob. He felt that as a mobster – officially – he would have more status, more respect than being identified as a very successful and wealthy businessman, even a businessman that cut corners, lots of corners. Most important, he wanted the fear, the awe that mobsters engendered, and the honour.

When he cheated his customers, they mumbled and

grumbled that he was a shyster and sometimes even tried to talk him into giving their money back, and some even sued him. He believed, that as a mobster, he would not have to endure back talk.

He saw how society treated mobsters like celebrities while publicly holding their noses to show their disdain. "Legitimate" celebrities almost genuflected before gangsters. Hollywood and the media played their part in making them heroes. On the streets, mobsters would be asked for their autographs. Rossini wanted into this world.

Given Rossini's handicaps, Marcese refused, making an elitist judgement like college fraternities and sororities that worried about their images. Rossini, in effect, was blackballed by just one vote – Marcese's. It was the only vote that counted. For Marcese, respectability was important, and Rossini did not meet Marcese's standards for membership. Rossini didn't just limp, he stuttered as well.

"P..p...p...l...eeeese," begged Rossini again, "mmm...mmm..a...ke meeee a mmm..a... mmm...an."

Marcese hesitated again. "You-a talka with a stutter. I no understand. It's like you talk-a Japanese."

Tired of just trying to talk his way in, Rossini tried a new tactic. He took out a checkbook and stuttered, "Hhh...o...w mmm...u...ch?"

When Marcese did not answer, Rossini wrote a check for ten thousand dollars.

"Www...i...l ttth...is do iii...t?" Rossini asked.

Marcese, looking at the check, feigned disappointment. "You forgot-a zero."

Rossini ripped up the check and wrote another one for a hundred grand and, just like that, Rossini was a mobster.

"Welcome, Carmen. With this check, I understand you better. Your talk-a not-a so bad. You gonna do good with us."

Rossini left with his chest puffed up. He could tell the world he was a part of the Marcese family. He could brag that he was a member of the powerful *Mafia* family and watch, with pride, the envy in the eyes of his listeners. Life proved good for Rossini that day.

Marcese, on the other hand, put his hand on Valenti's shoulder and said, "Money covers all-a defects." He continued, quoting another proverb, "Money makes the mute speak," adding, "It can't help Carmen with his stutter." He laughed hilariously at his witticism.

What Rossini did not understand nor would he ever find out was that he would never be considered a full member only used – exploited – on the fringes. He would be treated like the family member everyone tries to hide.

Eduardo "The Brains" Marcese had made it to the top of his family, whose speciality was international drug dealing, with his brains, ergo, his nickname. He tried to avoid violence using it only when absolutely necessary. For him, it was always a last resort.

When Marcese parked his new Jaguar, of which he was very proud, outside his office, two auto thieves, one black and one Puerto Rican, broke into it and drove it away. Marcese noticed, and had his men follow them.

The thieves' destination was an auto shop where the two, with several assistants, within minutes dismantled stolen cars like the Jaguar, and sold the parts. It was a very profitable business.

Others at the top of *Mafia* organization charts would have broken some bones, maybe even burned the garage down or whacked the offenders to warn others to be more careful whose cars they stole.

Not Marcese. Yes, he had the two thieves beaten. The beating, however, was intended to get the attention of the thieves and their bosses, that they listen to the proposal he was about to make, which was to sell the cars themselves not the parts. The beatings were not intended as a punishment. He used the violence as an attention-getter. And he was successful. Those he talked to listened.

He outlined an elaborate plan that included working with law-abiding car dealers to obtain new vehicle identification numbers. With this information they could develop a black market for their under-priced vehicles. The owners of the auto shop were impressed along with being a little – more than a little – frightened, and signed on.

Thus, with Marcese's help, a whole new enterprise was born. Marcese got a piece of the action – a big piece – and his new partners entered into the venture that, to their surprise, proved more profitable than the used auto parts business. The two thieves who stole the Jaguar leading to the new business did not receive a bonus. Considering the actions Marcese could have taken, they were happy – more than happy – to settle for a weekly paycheck.

Furthermore, Marcese, in forsaking violence when its use was unnecessary, was more patient than others and accepted that mistakes, like the ones the car thieves made, were sometimes inevitable. He never forgot how one of his men whacked the wrong whackee. Marcese could not believe it. The intended target and the victim were not even similar in physical appearance. Marcese thought about sending a condolence card to the survivors of the innocent victim, expressing, like cops do, his sorrow "for your loss." He decided to forego sending the sympathy card, even anonymously.

It was his instinct for opportunities, where others saw none, and his shrewdness that earned Marcese his nickname, "The Brains." He was also the arbitrator of disagreements among neighbours, issuing Solomon-like decisions to keep the peace.

Only a week earlier he had issued one of his renowned "legal" decisions in a case involving a local restaurateur named Gianluca who was accused of serving spoiled fish, and poisoning the beautiful pregnant wife of a local businessman.

The couple and the restaurant's owner could not settle the dispute, with the husband threatening lawsuits and violence. Ultimately, all three ended up before Marcese.

The husband testified to his side of the story. "He served us bad fish. I rush my wife to the hospital. They say she got food poisoning that caused her to lose-a the baby. I work-a hard to make my wife pregnant."

"I must ask-a a question," Marcese interrupted. "You say it was hard-a work making your wife pregnant. Is that true?"

"Yes, Mr. Marcese, that's-a so."

"I believe you." He asked Gianluca for his side of the story.

"Mr. Marcese, you eat at my place all the time. Twenty five years I no have this. That night, how could only one person get sick? It no make sense. How can that be?"

Marcese paused, thought for a few minutes and issued his opinion which was, no matter how interpreted, an order.

"Here is what I am-a gonna do. Since it was so much trouble making your wife pregnant, you gonna turn her over to Gianluca for three days and nights. He will return your wife pregnant. I hope-a you learn that there is nothing wrong with a little hard-a work. Case closed. Get your asses out-a my house."

Those kinds of stories about Marcese's "brains" spread his reputation far and wide. And Marcese revelled in the fame and respect he engendered among his Italian neighbours

"Johnny, welcome to my house," Marcese said as he embraced Valenti. "Waited long time to meet-a you."

"Thanks, good to be here."

Valenti was facing the head of one of the more powerful mob families in New York City, more powerful than Esposito. His reach was farther, his employee payroll larger, his connections better, and, most important, he was more profitable. And in America, the land of opportunity, profitability engenders respect and increases power.

Marcese, being shrewd, waited before discussing the business agenda – there was only one item on it – he had prepared for Valenti.

"You're *famiglia*, Johnny," he said. "I knew your grandfather in Cinisi. We come from the same town. He was *famiglia* and now you're *famiglia*. You been to Cinisi?"

"No, maybe someday."

"Once we do business, I send you. I'll pay. You need-a to see your hometown."

Marcese was nothing but smiles, showing how pleased he was with Valenti's decision to join him. He was trying to impress Valenti, but he was also very elated to be talking to a fellow Cinisensi. Not many around in New York.

Marcese was proud of Cinisi for two major reasons. It was the birthplace of Giovanni Meli who wrote some of his most well-known poems in the city in the mid-1770s.

Probably more to the point for Marcese was that many of the leaders he looked up to came from Cinisi. It was a training ground, preparing men like him for the future.

Marcese bragged about Cinisi's heroes. Admittedly, he had more praise for the bosses Cinisi produced than for Meli. Poets are a dime a dozen although few were born in Cinisi. Even without much education, Marcese knew you can't make much of a buck with poetry no matter how beautiful the rhymes or how moving the message.

"Hear lots-a of good things about you, Johnny. Not just from Luigi. Lots of others, too. We can use you."

Valenti was appreciative. It was always nice to hear that you have a good reputation, even if you achieved it murdering people. It was better to be respected for being a good hit man, than chastised for being lousy at the job.

"What about Esposito? He's gonna be pissed," said Valenti.

Before he had a chance to protest, Marcese picked up his phone and dialled as he winked at Valenti.

"Hey, Dominic, Marcese here."

Valenti was uneasy, nervous. He did not want to be the subject of negotiations between Esposito and Marcese. He would have liked to have discussed such a phone call with Marcese, develop some strategy, decide on the best approach, before the call was made. It was too late.

"Been good. Everything's good," Marcese said on the phone.

"Listen, I been talkin' to Johnny Valenti. He needs a

job, and we got a place for him. So, I thought, only right to call you."

While Valenti could not hear Esposito, he assumed his former employer protested vehemently. Valenti had not forgotten Esposito's not too subtle warning.

"Dominic, Dominic, I understand...you gotta understand too. I need him. Got some special problems that Johnny can fix. I've been waiting for someone like him. He wasn't working for you anyway. Let's work this out."

Valenti picked up on the implied threat – "you gotta understand, too."   Marcese was more powerful than Esposito, and Esposito would not want to anger Marcese. There was more at stake than Valenti who did not really mean much to Esposito, or for that matter Marcese. In the end, Valenti was like a professional athlete: to be used until he was useless. For the respective crime families, it was a matter of pride. Neither wanted to look weak or lose anything even if the loss was meaningless. In this case, both wanted Valenti, given his expertise, on their payroll.

"Dominic, someday I'll do you a favour," Marcese said. "You know, you scratch my ass and I'll …. what's that? Oh, yeah, scratch my back and I'll scratch yours."

Marcese listened for another thirty seconds. He said nothing. His eyes moved from side to side as he analyzed the arguments from his adversary.

"Deal. Last time I do this. You got my word, Dominic. Next time we meet, I buy you a drink and give you one of my cigars."

Marcese hung up the phone, got out of his chair, and walked over to Valenti who stood up. Valenti was tempted to ask what Esposito had said. He decided against it. It didn't matter anyway. If he had something to hide,

Marcese wouldn't tell him the truth anyway. So what was the point?

As Marcese was about to embrace Valenti, they were interrupted in their meeting by Marcese's cousin.

"Johnny, meet my cousin, Benito. Benito, this is Johnny Valenti. He gonna work for us -- me."

Benito Palazoa shook hands with Valenti and, somewhat nervously, asked Marcese if he could talk to him privately.

Without waiting to be asked, Valenti left the room. About ten minutes later, Palazoa passed by him in the hall without saying a word. Palazoa looked very angry, and did not make eye contact with Valenti.

"Come back in, Johnny," Marcese shouted.

"Benito never learn, Johnny. Always need money," said Marcese. "He asks me for a couple thousand I said no. Why?

"If I give it to him and he no pay it back, I lose the money and a cousin. If I say no, I still lose a cousin but have the money."

Marcese laughed uproariously. "Your new boss pretty smart, huh Johnny?"

Marcese told Valenti that his cousin and others would come to see him only when they were in trouble. In good times, they were nowhere to be found.

"I never see them except when they need help, Johnny. So I tell them, 'wherever you spent your summers, you spend your winters.' Benito says he'll remember me in his heart. I say, 'I wanna you remember me in your wallet.'"

Again, he laughed so hard that his whole body shook, and he had to catch his breath.

"You remember that, Johnny. Also remember, if you want to keep your friends, never ask them for money. Hang out with people better than you and spend money on them. See, Johnny, that's why I am called 'The Brains.'"

Still chortling at his own homespun philosophy, Marcese, like Esposito, took Valenti's head in his hands and clapped him on both cheeks. Only this time, the experience was friendlier than when Esposito had threatened him while making this gesture.

Valenti still needed one clearance in order to work for Marcese. He would have to meet the *capo crimini* – the boss of bosses – Giuliano "The Butcher" Monteleone who controlled organized crime in the U.S. and in parts of Europe from his villa in Cinisi, Sicily.

"Johnny, welcome to my *famiglia*. You go to Cinisi sooner than expected."

CHAPTER 8

BEFORE TAKING VALENTI TO Cinisi, Marcese had an idea. He needed help with an Irish mobster and if Valenti solved his problem, The Butcher would be impressed when he met his new employee. The Butcher was a fussy guy who did not like to depend exclusively on recommendations about the talents and potential of new hires. He figured achievements were better evidence of competence than performance during interviews.

Marcese's dilemma was embodied in one Patrick "Blackjack" Doherty who had turned into a pain in the ass for The Butcher and, as a result, for Marcese and the other New York families. Doherty acquired his nickname because he spent hours at the blackjack tables in Las Vegas, and, a blackjack was his favourite weapon when death was not necessarily the objective. At times, Doherty was overzealous in its use, and in his fervour, would whack victims. Sometimes these things happen.

Doherty owned a trucking company and provided jobs along with kickbacks for Italian-American mobsters in exchange for help with reluctant and recalcitrant customers. Periodically, he used the Italians to collect debts, and rid himself of competition. He did not believe in the American credo that competition, overall, is the lifeblood of capitalism. He believed in operating a monopoly, especially if he owned it. The fewer trucking companies the better. The perfect business environment would be one in which he would be free of any competition. It remained one of his long-term goals.

The *quid pro quo* system between the Italians and Doherty had worked well for years. Both achieved the desired profitability, but it was a tense partnership.

One day, for reasons that never were clear, Doherty decided to end the relationship. He wanted to go solo. He concluded, erroneously, that he could go it alone with the help of the Irish mob. He thought he was paying out more than he was getting in return and, not fully considering or evaluating the potential consequences, told his Italian partners, "The Butcher and you *dagos* can kiss my ass. I'm tired to shelling out for nothin'. You want my money, you need to break more heads."

The Italians tried to reason with him at several meetings. Doherty held firm. All warnings that they would not sit idly by and be screwed fell on deaf ears. Worse, Doherty never looked around the negotiating table and considered, clearly considered, what his partners were capable of. They weren't patsies.

Doherty's unilateral firing of the Italians was not the most tactful way to dissolve the business venture, not that a graceful way out existed when there was substantial money involved for The Butcher. Doherty might have been more gentle, humble, diplomatic and compromising. He might have offered the Italians a little more of the pot. Perhaps, when he made his decision, he had had one too many from his bottle of Jack Daniels, his favourite booze. He should have known that the luck of the Irish was not much protection from a man who headed an organization composed of the most ruthless human beings on the planet. Not that the Irish weren't in the same class. They played hardball and were, as they say, nothing to sneeze at.

When The Butcher heard about Doherty's decision to be a lone proprietor, he told Marcese, "Eduardo, you know, when a tree no give fruit no more, it have no use. It no good. You no need it. You cutta it down."

Marcese did not like the not-so-subtle assignment. While he shared The Butcher's opinion that Doherty was, as The Butcher would say, "a prick" and of "no use," he was hesitant to assign the hit. He was reluctant to whack the guy not because he liked him and did not believe he had it coming. He was worried about starting a war with Irish mobsters, and he did not want a violent confrontation with the Irish mob to which Doherty was joined at the hip. They might believe they needed to avenge a Doherty murder. Doherty was powerful in his own right. Maybe that was why Doherty "fired" his partners, believing his own countrymen would protect him.

The Italians and their Irish counterparts had been suspicious of each other for decades ever since the Irish, who immigrated first, established a foothold on Manhattan's west side, primarily, although not exclusively, in Hell's Kitchen bounded roughly by 34th Street and 59th Street and between 8th Avenue and the Hudson River. The Italians presented an unwanted challenge after their migration from the old country. Tension always prevailed through the years, but the two co-existed relatively peacefully.

Ignoring Marcese's complaints, The Butcher would not relent. Doherty had to go. It would send a terrible message if he let him off the hook. What if word got out to his other "partners" that they could just quit with no consequences? How would he keep others in line? His whole empire could fall apart. Didn't Marcese understand? Wasn't Marcese called "The Brains?" Maybe he needed a new nickname.

"Eduardo, this-a no good for us. Others find out and I gotta more problems. You gotta no choice. I gotta no choice. You do this, okay?"

"You do this, okay?" was not really a question. It was an order and Marcese took it as such. He delayed in developing a plan and its execution, waiting for the appropriate time. With Valenti on board, the time had come.

Marcese briefed Valenti on "the problem." As they discussed Valenti's first assignment, they decided strategically to assure that Doherty's body should never be found. With no body, the Irish could not definitively accuse the Italians of the murder. They might be suspicious – Marcese and Valenti expected them to make accusations – but with no evidence in the form of a body, they might not retaliate. At least, that is what Marcese and Valenti concluded. If Doherty disappeared like the rabbit in the magician's top hat, an all-out war might be avoided.

Even in the legit world, prosecutors usually failed to win convictions when they had no body to show jurors. Pretty hard to argue that the suspected murderer murdered someone when the "murderee" could not be found. Of course, the standards for mobsters were a little different. They did not need hard evidence such as a body since all of them, when necessary, were very talented in the art of making bodies disappear. When they permitted a body to be found, it was usually a deliberate strategy to send a message to others guilty of the same sins the deceased had committed.

Doherty's disappearance would create a little doubt that might allow Marcese and Valenti to avoid a head-to-head deadly confrontation. They assumed the Irish would likewise want to avoid the inevitable death toll if the two powers clashed on New York City streets. After years of relative peace, a killing spree would also be a blow to their public relations image in the Big Apple. Those in public officialdom who profited, politically and financially, from peace among the mobsters would not be happy, and might need to take some actions inhibiting the mobs' businesses. So a gangster war, or war among the gangsters, was a lose-lose situation for all involved.

With the "no body" strategy in place, Valenti followed Doherty wherever he went for several weeks. He became an expert on Doherty's schedule and studied his every move. As he stalked his prey, Valenti searched for the appropriate place to kidnap Doherty. When Valenti was ready – his reconnaissance was impeccable – he laid out his plan to Marcese who approved the proposal while admiring the professionalism.

On the chosen night, with Marcese driving his Lincoln and Valenti a passenger, the two waited outside Doherty's office. At 8:30 p.m., as usual, Doherty came out and drove away. Marcese and Valenti followed at a safe distance. Twenty minutes later, at 8:50 p.m., Doherty stopped at a party store, as he did every night in preparation for the next day. When Doherty went inside to buy his daily six-pack of beer along with a bottle of Jack Daniels and cigarettes, Valenti got out of the Lincoln, climbed into Doherty's car, and hid in the back seat.

Doherty returned, started his car, and drove no more than a half mile when the barrel of a revolver was pressed against the back of his head.

"Follow the Lincoln that's pulling out in front of you."

Doherty did not say a word, nor did he show surprise. While he tried to control his emotions and appear calm, his heart raced, and he felt sweat in his armpits. His hands shook visibly on the steering wheel. He looked in the rear view mirror. He did not recognize the man holding the gun against his head.

Valenti noticed Doherty trying to place him. "Just keep your fuckin' eyes on the Lincoln," he warned.

They drove for a half hour with Doherty fifty yards behind the Lincoln that suddenly left the highway, and turned onto a dirt road. After another twenty minutes, they reached their destination, an isolated, abandoned farm.

"Get out," Valenti ordered, and Doherty obeyed. He

still had not said a word. There was not much to say. It was too late to rescind his earlier, somewhat hasty business decision. Even if he were in the state of mind to make some kind of offer, it was too late. All he could do was pray, but he was out of practise.

He also knew it would be a waste of time to beg for "mercy." As a pro, he understood the decision on his future, or more accurately, ending his future, had been made at top levels. Under similar circumstances, Doherty, if he were in charge of this assignment, would not succumb to pleas for "another chance," and he understood appeals by him to those carrying out orders would be futile.

"Move," Valenti told his captive, pointing to a barn.

They reached the barn. It was closed. "Open it," Valenti told his captive, and as soon as Doherty did, Valenti fired two .45 calibre bullets into his captive's back. Valenti could have killed Doherty at his home or at the party store, but he would have had to deal with the body. At the barn, he had help. Valenti always planned ahead.

Inside the barn, two of Marcese's men threw the body into a pickup truck and drove five miles to a man-made five-acre lake created by the operations of a defunct sand and gravel mining company. The men put the body in a small boat and rowed to the lake's centre where they tied chains to the victim's legs. They connected the chains to steel handles embedded in fifty pound concrete blocks. After checking all the connections, they tucked Valenti's revolver in the victim's belt, and threw the body overboard. Within minutes, it reached the bottom, about a hundred feet below the surface.

While he did not realize it at the moment, Valenti had just broken two promises. The one he made to himself that DeSante would be his last hit, and the other he made to Esposito that he was getting into a new line of business. If going back on his word were ever to occur to him, which it never did, he would handle it.

Within twenty four hours of Doherty's disappearance, Marcese received calls from Doherty's Irish mobster cohorts demanding an explanation about Doherty's whereabouts. Convinced that the Italians had retaliated for Doherty severing his business relationships, they threatened vengeance. Marcese played dumb, swearing that none of the New York families was involved in Doherty's disappearance.

"Maybe he run off with a broad," he suggested. "He no be able to keep it in his pants."

The "broad" explanation was not credible but Marcese thought he would give it a try. The Irish, prone to periodic infidelity, were experts at covering up their philandering. Frankly, at times, they did not even bother to hide their extracurricular sexual activities from their wives. And the wives accepted it. So Doherty had no reason to "run off with a broad."

Unable to convince them on the telephone of his innocence and that of other *Mafia* families, Marcese agreed to a meeting to which he invited several other shooters – "shooters" as in important decision-makers – from the families for support.

All sides argued back and forth without making any progress. Compared to these negotiations, it was easier to settle differences between Hanoi and the U.S. in the aftermath of the Vietnam War some five years earlier.

With both sides steadfast in their positions, Marcese produced a witness, a young Irish hoodlum. He called in the witness who had been waiting in another room. The witness "testified" to the group (not under oath, not that an oath would have given his words greater credibility) that some of Doherty's competitors – Irish competitors at that – hated Doherty and blew his brains out. He described the shooting in some detail. He "testified" that he did not know what happened to the body.

The Irish mobsters listened to the story sceptically. They had lots of questions. Who was this guy? Was it coincidental that he was Irish? Did Marcese produce an "Irish" witness to increase the credibility of the story? How was it that the witness witnessed the shooting? Where and how did Marcese find him?

In short, the Irish were not convinced but could not challenge the account without some evidence. For the time being, they "accepted" the story. Their plan was to question the witness without the Italians present. They were confident they would get to the truth. They would, if necessary, employ some foolproof, time-tested methods.

When the meeting adjourned, Marcese gave the witness five grand in cash.

"You do good," Marcese told the witness. "Maybe we use you again sometime."

"They," Marcese pointed to two of his men, "they take-a you home."

The witness, holding his money, couldn't have been happier. "Glad to be of help. Call any time. No need to worry. I keep my mouth shut."

Marcese nodded while patting the man gently on his back, and leading him to the front door.

"I no worry about you," Marcese said. "You no problem for me. I know that."

The witness, flush with self-satisfaction and staring at his packaged money, did not reflect or catch the slight implications of Marcese's confidence. Marcese never said, "I know I can-a trust you," or "I know you'll not talk." He didn't say anything like that. He just said, "You no problem for me." The vagueness and somewhat backhanded compliment should have been a little troubling for the witness. Regrettably, it wasn't.

On the driveway, the witness got into a car on the passenger side in the front seat. He was being driven on the same route used for Doherty, which confused the witness. He did not live on a farm. Within an hour, he was floating to the bottom of his watery grave, never to be heard from again.

Marcese told Valenti it was time for their trip to Cinisi.

CHAPTER 9

THE FOLLOWING WEEK, VALENTI found himself flying first-class at twenty five thousand feet to the hometown of his ancestors. Marcese was sleeping and snoring next to him.

The week had been a tense one. Marcese and Valenti, along with the New York families, waited for some sign of unrest from the Irish. It was natural to expect retaliation. The Irish were proud people, proud mobsters. The Italians were confident the bodies of Doherty and the "witness" would not be found but they worried that the Irish might launch an attack to avenge Doherty and, more important, demonstrate they weren't pushovers. They had pride. Marcese and Valenti expected the murder of a soldier or someone at that level, a low level, as a sort of warning to the Italians that the Irish did not believe in the Italians' innocence.

If that happened, the Italians would have to retaliate to uphold their honour and indicate they didn't like being called liars, and that could prompt another *quid pro quo* from the Irish. Before cooler murderous heads could prevail, the situation could spiral out of control. Just like in the world of the rule of law.

In this case, nothing happened. Perhaps the Irish, like the Italians, wanted to avoid bloodshed. Maybe they decided that Doherty was not worth a fight, or that Doherty had "sinned" by arbitrarily ending the business partnership. Or they might have wanted to keep the doors open for future partnerships with the Italians. Marcese and Valenti, obviously, had no hint as to why the Irish did not strike back.

Whatever the reason, all was quiet, leading Marcese and Valenti to conclude it was safe to make the trip to Cinisi. If things changed, they could always hurriedly return to New York. If the Irish launched an attack, being in Cinisi with The Butcher would make the development of strategy and tactics simpler. It also would be safer thousands of miles away.

With some nervousness and anxiety, Marcese and Valenti left for Cinisi. Marcese explained to Valenti that before he could be officially added to the payroll, he would need the approval of The Butcher. Valenti had been hired, no need to worry. The blessing from The Butcher, while a minor technicality, was required because The Butcher always wanted to shake hands with those working for, and near the top of, the organization, particularly if they were to assume the kind of sensitive position that Valenti would fill.

The Butcher had control over the Marcese empire and, in effect, governed over all six of the crime families in New York. He ruled directly over the Marceses but, given his power and absolute commitment to use whatever violence was necessary, disputes between him and the different organizations usually were resolved in The Butcher's favour.

As he sat periodically glancing at Marcese, Valenti became ambivalent. Maybe he was making a mistake. He did not like what he had heard about The Butcher, and while the passenger next to him was not an ideal boss, he could tolerate his shortcomings. He did not know or like that he would have The Butcher looking over his shoulder. Being second-guessed, and suffering the consequences associated with second-guessing, were not particularly attractive to him. He never liked being micro-managed. However, it was a little late to turn back.

Valenti's thoughts and misgivings about his decision were interrupted when a flight attendant told him and his fellow passengers, to, "Fasten your seat belts and put tray tables in their upright positions." They landed at Palermo's International Airport at Punta Raisi some twenty miles northwest of Palermo.

Valenti was on home turf, the turf of the *Cosa Nostra* and Sicilian *Mafia*. Those were the majors and, a host of minor teams existed as well. Through the years, he had heard many stories about the long history of organized crime in Sicily, and stories galore about all the bosses and their accomplishments. Thus, he was a little in awe when they landed on this sacred ground. He felt like a little kid visiting baseball's Hall of Fame in Cooperstown. He was, indeed, home.

They rented a car and drove from the airport to a villa located in the midst of beautiful rolling land on the outskirts of Cinisi. While Valenti was not one to appreciate and reflect on the beauty of nature – the last time he so-called smelled the flowers was when he gave his mother a bouquet stolen from a florist on Mother's Day – he recognized that the scenery was magnificent.

They turned off the main highway onto a dirt road that led them to the villa that was inside an electrically charged fence. At the gate stood two guards with automatic weapons. The Butcher did not believe in subtlety.

The guards waved Marcese and Valenti out of the car and checked them for weapons. After the guards concluded their search, they picked up a telephone and reported their findings, their lack of any findings. After receiving approval, the guards instructed them to drive to the front of the villa where the guests would be checked again. The Butcher worked on the principle that you can't be too careful, especially when you were such a desirable and tempting target.

The villa, built in the Middle Ages, offered a panoramic view of the countryside. The grounds featured cypress trees that dated back hundreds of years. Some wine was produced on the premises, not so much for the income – The Butcher had other revenue sources – but more for nostalgia. While not sentimental, he liked watching the workers and drinking the wine from his own vineyards. The Butcher thought producing wine on the premises gave him some respectability, some status.

The villa featured thirty five rooms, including eleven bedrooms, six bathrooms, four fireplaces, a poolroom, and a workout room that collected dust. The Butcher didn't like to work up a sweat. The mansion also housed some valuable artwork. The Butcher was not a connoisseur of art but, like the production of wine on his land, he believed the artwork provided evidence that he was culturally sophisticated.

After additional security checks at the front door, Marcese and Valenti were ushered into the foyer where they waited … waited … and waited. While agitated, they showed the good sense not to complain.

After about an hour, The Butcher appeared. The wait had been designed to give his guests a message. He was *the* boss. He would come when he was ready.

The Butcher, at five foot nine and about two hundred and eighty pounds, was all fat and rotund. He had bulging eyes, a boxer's smashed nose, and with a pockmarked red complexion. He looked like he was continually blushing.

Even by the mobs' standards, The Butcher's penchant for violence was over the top. He inflicted pain and death at the merest slight. His reputation was legendary, and he understood the value of being feared, knowing that fear helped him maintain control of his operations. The implication of The Butcher's nickname pissed off Sicily's butchers. It made them look bad.

Yes, Valenti and other of *Mafiaso* hit men killed people, but they acted out of principle. They went after rats, those who skimmed off the top and others who violated the organization's unwritten and hallowed rules, or abused relationships. They also went after public officials who gave them a hard time, those interfering with operations. That violence, even deadly violence, was invoked and justified because important principles were involved.

The Butcher, on the other hand, used deadly force for the sake of it. He lived by the Machiavellian code, "It's better to be feared than loved." Absolutely nothing stopped him from ordering the severest punishment to avenge even small missteps.

As if to make up for his looks, The Butcher was immaculate. He wore very expensive tailor-made suits, expensive shoes, shined to a mirror-like finish, and specially made white shirts and flashy ties.

He wore his suits from the time he woke up in the morning until he went to sleep. Should he get a spot on his suit, shirt or tie, he immediately changed the respective stained clothing. And he smoked very expensive cigars imported from Cuba.

The sixty five year old Butcher was born in a poor area of Sicily, where most residents lived off the land. At an early age, recognizing the intense and tiring labour involved to survive and to make a living, The Butcher decided that he did not want to be a farmer, let alone a poor farmer.

He did not like watching his parents barely eke out a living, always worrying where the next meal would come from. At school, overweight and pimply, he was constantly bullied, and he learned to defend himself very effectively. The bullies discovered that The Butcher Jr.

could take care of himself. His defensive tactics and strategies produced results, and soon he bullied the bullies. Perhaps his success could be attributed to the use of knives and guns, or whatever else worked.

To earn a buck and assist the family financially, he tried his hand at traditional jobs for teenagers – delivery boy, shining shoes, working on farms. He believed he made too little money for too much work, at least by his goals, which even at a young age were ambitious.

Examining his environment, he noticed businessmen in the community who always seemed to call all the shots. They were influential and had everything he wanted: money, respect and, most of all, they were feared in the community as The Butcher wanted to be.

Understanding at a young age that it's not what you know but who you know, he made the right contacts and won an apprenticeship with these businessmen. He became a driver for the *Mafia*. He learned much by listening, overhearing and eavesdropping, on conversations in the car. He used that information to win promotions, promotions earned after many of his passengers disappeared. He was not the typical chauffeur who could be trusted. If only his passengers had known.

Periodically, he was assigned jobs outside of his responsibilities as a driver, like setting fires, robbing stores, collecting protection money. He was very successful and his bosses recognized his talents, rewarding him accordingly. His performance reviews, taken after every job, not necessarily annually, were generally excellent.

Slowly, he worked his way through the ranks. He held almost every position, among them:

Piciotto, lower-ranking soldier; s*qarrista*, foot soldier;

caporegime, lieutenant; *contabile*, financial adviser; *capo bastone*, underboss, second in command; and, *capo crimini* – top dog or boss of bosses.

Thus, he learned all phases of operations, and studied the organization inside out. His on-the-job experiences helped him immensely when he became CEO or the boss of bosses. Nothing like starting at the bottom to gain experience. It was no easy task reaching the top. It took The Butcher about thirty five years of manoeuvring, intimidating, deceiving, lying, cheating, not to mention killing.

Through the years, he was arrested more than fifty times without ever being convicted. Parties involved in his cases, such as judges, prosecutors, jurors, always seemed to accept his defences as the truth.

Those that appeared reluctant to give him, the defendant, the benefit of reasonable doubt either disappeared, ended up in the hospital, strangely contracted amnesia, and some, the lucky ones, suddenly became rich.

No conviction is not quite accurate. He had one for drunk driving. The Butcher did not fight the charge believing it was strategically helpful to have a conviction on his record to show that the system did not treat him any differently than others. His clean record, just one conviction, would prove that he was a law-abiding citizen. Always thinking.

If he had compiled a resume, it would have included some of the following:

Experienced in arson, robbery, racketeering, prostitution, drug trafficking, corruption, money laundering, and related businesses.

Accomplishments include some fifty murders; he would not be able to say exactly how many. Increased revenues annually; never had a down year. Managed a diversified portfolio to assure that if one sector of the enterprise suffered losses, others would make it up.

Expanded business from Sicily to the U.S. and South America. Made inroads into other parts of the world.

Career objective: to keep growing, particularly in drug trafficking to take advantage of ample opportunities for growth.

Personal strengths: will stop at nothing to achieve success.

Marcese and Valenti did not know all of The Butcher's history. Despite their lack of knowledge, they were impressed by the information they had. They fully appreciated and understood his ruthlessness.

"So, welcome to my villa," were The Butcher's first words. "Come in, come in. Sit down."

The Butcher led them to one of the dining rooms. A bottle of wine and three glasses were on a table. The Butcher poured from the bottle, asked his guests to raise their glasses and shouted, "S*alute*. You like the wine? Made right here."

Marcese and Valenti expressed their appreciation. At that moment, they would have preferred a straight shot of whiskey or moonshine. Irish whiskey might have been appropriate given the successful Doherty mission.

The Butcher took out an envelope from the inside pocket of his jacket and handed it to Valenti. "For Doherty. Eduardo said you do good job. I like good jobs."

Valenti took the envelope and without opening it, put it in his pocket. "Thanks," is all he said. Later, Valenti would find five grand inside the envelope, the same amount given to the witness that claimed he saw Doherty murdered. The Butcher had budgeted the mission perfectly. It did not cost him anything extra since the five grand was not deposited in the lake with the witness. That would have been very foolish, and The Butcher was anything but foolish.

The payment for Doherty was intended to make his new employee feel welcome and appreciated. The five grand was like a signing bonus for an athlete, except that Valenti had already performed, and performed well.

"So, Johnny, we gonna do business, heh? Eduardo, here, tells me you're the best. True?"

Valenti hesitated, not just out of modesty. How do you agree that you're a pro, among the best, at wiping people off the face of the earth? It might be true, but Valenti had trouble acknowledging the fact.

"I do my job."

"You do it good, Eduardo says," The Butcher persisted.

"Yeah, I guess."

"You did some time, eh?"

The Butcher honed in on what he considered failure – jail time – to see how Valenti would react, and how he would explain it. The Butcher did not like failure.

"Yeah…took care of the problem that cost me a few years."

"DeSante?" Valenti was thunderstruck. He worked not to show his surprise. This guy was on top of his game. Obviously, his tentacles reached far and wide. He had very informed lines of communication and excellent human intelligence. Valenti ignored the question, hoping

The Butcher would not pursue it.

The Butcher didn't. Instead, he suddenly yelled out, "Ricardo, come on in."

When Richard "The Scumbag" Martino entered the room Marcese's revulsion was evident. He had been alerted by The Butcher that Martino would join them.

Martino, who lived in Cinisi, was Marcese's brother-in-law. "Scumbag" was not an official nickname but one Marcese had bestowed on him because that was exactly what he was. A scumbag. He beat Marcese's sister and the hookers he used. And he bragged about it, making him a pig in the eyes of The Butcher and other mobsters. He engendered only disdain, and many wondered why The Butcher tolerated him.

Valenti shook hands with Martino while Marcese avoided doing so. The Butcher watched the interplay with some amusement.

"Come, I show you my horses," The Butcher said.

The Butcher loved horses, owning twenty three. He raced a few at the local track and his horses had never lost in years. Never was not an exaggeration. Horse racing aficionados, those in the know, when checking racing forms did not make their betting decisions on the records of the horses, other statistical information or the jockeys. All they sought to find out was who owned the horse. If it was The Butcher, they bet on it.

In the stables, The Butcher stroked the horses and fed them apples from buckets hanging by the stalls. When he reached one of the stalls, he went inside. Marcese, Valenti and Martino thought they heard voices coming from the stall. After a few minutes, The Butcher came out with a woman and an eleven year old boy.

As the three approached Marcese, Valenti and Martino, it was obvious that Martino was uneasy. He began wringing his hands and wiping his brow. He coughed nervously as if aware of the events that were about to unfold.

"This is Sophia and her son, Tony," The Butcher said in making the introductions. "Ricardo, I think you know them, no?"

Nervously, Martino acknowledged he did. The woman was the widow of a mobster and the kid, was one of many Martino had supplied with drugs. Lacking sufficient brainpower, he never considered the risk involved in selling drugs to the son of the widow of a former fellow gangster. Yes, you were supposed to sell drugs, lots of them except to *famiglia*. Here in the stables, Martino began to recognize the errors of his ways. Just a little late.

Valenti looked at the boy who was continually moving, tapping his foot, licking his lips and running his hand under his nose. It was obvious, the kid, at eleven, was a junkie having already graduated from marijuana to cocaine.

The Butcher had his arm around the boy when he asked Marcese, "So, Eduardo, what do we do about this? Young boy like this. Break his mother's heart. I no wanna my daughter doing this stuff."

Valenti wondered about The Butcher talking about his daughter. Was he married? Who could be attracted to him, climb in bed with him? The vision of The Butcher screwing repulsed him while, at the same time, he found some humour in it.

He looked at The Butcher's left hand and there, embedded deep in the pudgy ring finger, was a wedding band. The ring fit so tightly it looked like someone had wrapped a tiny tourniquet on the finger.

As Valenti was speculating about the physical appearance of The Butcher's wife and trying to visualize The Butcher in bed, the woman screamed at Martino, "You piece of shit. You son-of-a-bitch."

The Butcher signalled the mother to stop her attack. He looked at the boy, asking, "You seen him before?" referring to Martino. When the boy didn't answer, his mother slapped him several times.

"You talk. You understand? Tell him. Everything!"

Unfortunately, for Martino, the boy confirmed what The Butcher had learned.

Not another word was said. The Butcher reached his arm out to the mother who opened her purse and produced a Colt .45 calibre ACP revolver. She gave it to The Butcher who handed it to Marcese who passed it to Valenti. They followed the chain of command – downward.

Martino could have used a sniff from his cocaine. In panic, he looked around for an escape route. There was none. The Butcher's men had been alerted to guard the doors. The decision he faced was to be killed by the revolver held by Valenti or the bullets from the guards' semi-automatic rifles. Not much of a choice.

Valenti inspected the weapon. He would not need a silencer on The Butcher's property. He held the Colt at his side with the barrel pointed to the floor. He waited. He looked at The Butcher, then Marcese.

When he turned his eyes to Martino, he recognized the fear he had seen many times, the fear of death. Martino's face was ashen. Tiny beads of sweat were on his forehead.

His lower lip trembled, and his nose was running. His eyes were wide open, and appeared as if they might fall out of their sockets.

The only sound in the stables, besides the noise coming from the horses shuffling in their stalls, was the whispered word, "Please ..." That came from Martino who was stammering, and for good reason. He repeated the word several times. Then he dropped to his knees, and cried.

After what seemed an eternity to Martino, The Butcher did nothing but raise his eyebrows to Marcese. Marcese, elated to avenge the beatings his sister suffered and get some justice for the drug-addicted boy and his mother, signalled Valenti with an almost imperceptible nod.

Valenti lifted his right arm slowly, and aimed the revolver at Martino who, on his knees, looked plaintively up at Valenti, and sobbed uncontrollably. His eyes pleaded for mercy to no avail.

With his arm as steady as if it were supported to keep it from quivering, Valenti squeezed the trigger. The bullet hit Martino in the forehead, exited from the back of his head and splattered his brains.

The party of five – The Butcher, his two guests from the U.S., the mother and her son – did not say a word. They just looked at the body, concluding that they had just administered justice. Decisive and warranted justice. The world was a better place.

No one reacted one way or another. They stood and watched as if Martino had tripped over some straw. Even the eleven year old boy watched impassively. Perhaps it was the drugs.

The only ones to react were the horses, not to Martino's death, but to the shot. They neighed, kicked the walls of their stalls and reared on their hind legs. The Butcher hurried to calm them by feeding them apples.

When he returned to the group, he was pleased to see Sophia, holding her son by the collar of his shirt, spit on the body. She faced The Butcher. She did not say anything, but her eyes thanked him. As she passed Valenti, she ran her hand affectionately up and down his arm very quickly, and disappeared out of the stables.

The Butcher, not one to hand out compliments, said, "You done good job, Johnny."

The Butcher was impressed, very impressed. He had not witnessed such professionalism in a long time. His orders had been carried out decisively, effectively, quickly, coldly, and brutally. The Butcher said do "it" and "it" was done. No questions asked. What more can a boss ask for?

He addressed his men guarding the doors. "You see that? I give orders to the Americans and it's done. I ask-a you to do something and I gotta answer a thousand questions. Maybe I should send you to U.S. for some training."

He laughed so hilariously he frightened the horses again. "Yeah, I send them to U.S." He thought his idea to be so funny, he could hardly control himself. Valenti and Marcese considered giving him an apple.

In addition to getting rid of Martino, The Butcher had also used the occasion to test Valenti. Was Valenti as effective as Marcese said? Would he hesitate? Did he follow orders without equivocation? The Butcher got his answers. Given Valenti's performance, he made The Butcher's honour roll. Despite The Butcher's outstanding evaluation, Valenti would not receive another bonus.

In the bargain, he had also tested Marcese. Were his

recommendations solid? Did he know what he was talking about? Was he a keen judge of character, bad character? Was he a dependable reference? If he judged by the mission they had just completed, The Butcher, as they say, had nothing to complain about.

Ready to celebrate, The Butcher invited his guests to "go to the races." They would be able to build on their joyous mood since his nags always won. Why ruin what had been a good day?

As he left the stables, he ordered his men to clean up "the garbage."

CHAPTER 10

THE BUTCHER PROUDLY LED his guests to his box at the Palermo-Cinisi Race Track. As they trudged along, fans nodded in respect, and out of fear. It seemed everyone knew him, or at least of him. All moved aside to let him pass. No one dared block his path. He was royalty, criminal royalty, and The Butcher bathed in it.

The Butcher had three of his horses in different races that day. He told Marcese and Valenti which ones to bet, and, not surprisingly, being good businessmen, they followed his advice. They had heard a little about the sure bets.

The three were in such a good mood one would think that the shooting in the stables only a few hours before had happened years ago. They smoked expensive, thick, long cigars while sipping drinks. The Butcher did not have a horse in the first race. He did in the second and it won easily.

Then, for the first time in years, something unusual happened in the third race that also featured one of The Butcher's horses. His horse was in the lead as it raced around the last turn and headed into the home stretch. To the surprise on everyone, a competitor in second place was catching up. The fans shouted in excitement. This was not something that had ever happened when The Butcher's horses competed. It was unusual, very unusual.

The Butcher's smile faded from his face. The second place horse was two lengths behind, then one length, then a half length. The Butcher's jockey heard thundering hooves behind him, a sound he had never heard before, at least, so close. From his position on the rail, he saw a sight he had never seen before: a horse's head at his right shoulder. Oh, shit. His horse was spent and, if his challenger continued at the present pace, he would lose.

The jockey wished that the track was straight and he could keep riding into the sunset. Unfortunately, the track was oval and it would take him right back to The Butcher to be held accountable. It was not something he looked forward to.

In the stands, about two hundred yards away, the owner of the challenging horse, was beside himself. He panicked, and screamed at the top of his lungs for the jockey to rein in the horse.

"Tienilo fermo, bastardo. Tienilo fermo, bastardo."

Over and over again, he yelled at the jockey to hold him back, to rein him in. The jockey, the *bastardo*, was hardly able to hear the horse's owner, and continued to whip the horse that reacted as expected and continued to gain on the leader. The unconventional instructions from the owner, who in his panic obviously was not thinking clearly about the implication of his appeals to the jockey, confused some of the fans. Wasn't he supposed to cheer? Along with confusion, came suspicion. Could these races be fixed? This strange, unorthodox scene did not do much for the reputation of the track.

And then it happened. The horse in second place defeated The Butcher's horse by a half length. This had never occurred before and probably would require a meeting of the powers-to-be. Fixing would need to be fixed.

The winning jockey, obviously a newcomer to the track, held up his whip while trotting a victory lap. The owner buried his head in his hands.

The Butcher was grim. He did not show his emotions. He was angry, very angry. He told Marcese and Valenti to stay put.

As The Butcher waddled his overweight body to the

winner's owner, fans parted in front of him like the Red Sea for Moses. On the way, he caught the eye of his jockey, still on his horse, and gave him a wave that said, "I no mad at you." The Butcher did not run his thumb across his throat. Understandably no one at the track was happier than this jockey. Not even the biggest winner that day could match the jockey's delight, his relief.

The Butcher reached the victor, alone in his box, who was almost in tears. The Butcher put his hand on his shoulder.

"Congratulations. Two things. Tell-a your jockey he never ride here again, and you owe me eighty five grand. Three days. You know-a where to send it. Congratulations, again."

The Butcher rejoined his guests from the U.S. He was still pissed. He just didn't like being screwed. The novice jockey may not have known the rules, but like in the law-abiding community, ignorance of the law was no excuse. He ought to have done some homework before getting in the saddle. At the least, his boss should have briefed him more thoroughly.

The Butcher consoled himself in the fact that he'd get the winning purse of sixty five thousand dollars, within three days, with an extra twenty grand he'd jacked on. He figured the added twenty thousand was like a fine for late payment of a traffic ticket. The owner of the winning thoroughbred should consider himself lucky. Some of the other penalties that The Butcher assessed when crossed were more painful, some deadly.

The Butcher could not forget his humiliation. That night he ordered Marcese and Valenti to go to the track and work with the blacksmith, who was on The Butcher's payroll, to put heavy shoes on all the horses except Uccelino, The Butcher's horse.

"Those-a shoes will slow them down," The Butcher snickered.

Marcese and Valenti were reluctant, worried about the horses. The heavier horseshoes might cause injuries. The Butcher was adamant. He was not going to lose again.

The two American visitors, their misgivings notwithstanding, executed their task at night in the stables with the help of the paid-off blacksmith, and The Butcher had the opportunity to test his devious scheme the next day.

(Uccelino was not the favourite in the race, at least according to the racetrack's official odds. That judgment really did not matter. Fans who knew the ropes, usually wagered on the unofficial favourite, especially if it was owned by The Butcher.)

The favourite was a horse named Big Shot. Big Shot led for about half the race. Then he suddenly slowed and seemed to be labouring. The extra weight of the shoes was a burden, causing pain in the horse's ankle and shins. The jockey, sensing that his horse was in trouble, reined him in and dismounted in the middle of the track. Uccelino won.

The Butcher beamed, slapping both Marcese and Valenti on their backs. "I gotta good ideas, no? You do good-a job. You should become shoemakers." His guests did not share The Butcher's enthusiasm.

The next day, the local papers reported that Big Shot had suffered broken bones and had to be destroyed.

"We are responsible for this," Valenti told Marcese. "We done that to the horse."

Marcese and Valenti spent the next few hours as if they were in mourning. They had a difficult time accepting that they helped kill an innocent horse. Had someone suggested it, they might have considered setting up a memorial fund.

Before Marcese and Valenti had fully recovered from their part in aiding and abetting in the death of Big Shot, The Butcher invited them to a tour of his grounds. All three hopped into a golf cart, and The Butcher drove about a quarter of a mile into the woods, stopping in front of a sprawling one-story building. It was huge, about a hundred and fifty thousand square feet.

When they entered the building, Marcese and Valenti could not immediately digest the scene. Before them was a huge workforce making, processing and packaging heroin. The workers managed several assembly lines so efficiently that Henry Ford would have been jealous.

Some of the workers used a chemical process to change the sap from the poppies, smuggled into Sicily, into morphine blocks. Another chemical procedure turned the blocks into heroin. Others were packaging heroin that had arrived as finished product. All of it came, via a complicated and sophisticated smuggling operation, from Afghanistan that was just beginning to fully take advantage and reap the economic benefits of its poppy fields. It had learned from Turkey and other neighbours who for many years provided the world with this narcotic, courtesy of people like The Butcher. The Turks used the Sicilian and Corsican *Mafias* to send their product to the West for distribution by their sister *Mafia* chapters in the U.S.

The Afghans needed entrepreneurs like The Butcher to assist them, and they learned quickly. To their surprise and delight, business just continued to grow, grow literally. It was not manna from heaven; it was manna from the ground. The supply was endless, limited only by the acreage available to grow poppies. Efforts to control it were, overall, futile. Burn the plants, and the poppies would just pop up somewhere else. They were appropriately named.

The Butcher's production facility was camouflaged in the forest. It really did not need to be. He paid a handsome price for public officials to look the other way, and most did. His payroll was quite extensive.

If some public officials decided to take a stand in the interest of principle and a little thing like the law, they might just disappear. Or they would be found with multiple holes in their bodies as a reminder to others that they had a choice. Reap non-taxable income or suffer a similar fate. It was really a no-brainer and not surprisingly, most took the money.

While highly sophisticated, there was only one problem with The Butcher's operation. Some of the employees would "sample" the product and many were not able to complete an eight-hour day. So their pay was often docked and shift changes were required frequently. If the plant had been unionized, The Butcher might have been faced with pickets and strikes. No need to worry. As was the case of public officials acquiescing, The Butcher encountered no employee relations issues, not that he would not have been able to handle them.

The Butcher showed his guests the laboratories where trained personnel chemically altered the poppy sap to morphine and then to heroin, the storage facilities, and how the final product was shipped to its destination, hidden in a variety of packaging. Not that the system was perfect. Inspectors at the ship docks, airports and freight train stations periodically found some of the heroin, but that was the cost of doing business. The Butcher and other drug traffickers considered loss of product to authorities expected overhead. The percentage of heroin discovered, moreover, was very small.

As a matter of fact, The Butcher welcomed these seizures. Periodic losses implied police were doing their jobs and that little of the product was making it through. The facts were otherwise. Thus, it was a win-win situation: police authorities received some credit and publicity for their successes, and the drug traffickers wanted the world to believe they were having trouble transporting their product.

"You guys, pretty good, huh?" The Butcher asked proudly.

"Some operation," Marcese said, complimenting his host. Valenti echoed Marcese with a sophisticated, "Holy shit."

"Thanks, yeah, pretty good," The Butcher said. "Come in the house. I wanna talk to you about what we're gonna do. I gotta big, big plans."

In one of his living rooms, The Butcher sank into a soft, large couch. The couch creaked and it appeared The Butcher would be gobbled up in the soft cushions. It looked like he never would be able to get up again. He launched into an hour-long monologue on how he wanted to expand the business in the U.S.

"I want you guys to get the families together and work out a deal," The Butcher said. "Everyone gets a piece of the action. I getta the biggest piece. It's-a my business."

Marcese and Valenti were sceptical, given the politics and jealousies of the *Mafia* families in and around New York. For obvious reasons, they did not state or even try to show that they had reservations.

Carefully, Marcese offered, "Ain't gonna be easy."

"I no care if it is easy. We all gonna make millions.

They gotta understand. I no like 'no' for an answer. They don't want to fuck with me. Right, Johnny?"

Valenti, who was not any happier than Marcese about the assignment, said, "We gonna try when we get back."

"Not try," their host insisted. "Try is no good. You gonna do it. Understand?"

Valenti nodded. He understood. It did not take a lot of brains to acquiesce. Given the choices before him, he agreed.

What The Butcher did not understand, or foresee, was that someday he would regret and pay a heavy price for having hired a professional killer like Valenti, especially one with such outstanding talents.

CHAPTER 11

BACK AT SOME THIRTY thousand feet heading home, with "understand" echoing in their heads, Marcese and Valenti understood all too well. They understood a lot of things. They got a shitty assignment; they did not want to fail The Butcher given the price they may pay; the New York families would not be very happy with the "order;" and, worst of all, they could not get out from under The Butcher's dictum.

Valenti also understood very clearly, perhaps for the first time, that the decision he made to change families and, thereby, work directly for The Butcher might not have been such a good idea. It was too late to put the cards he had dealt to himself back in the deck.

This time Marcese did not sleep on the plane as he had on the trip to Sicily. Instead, he and Valenti discussed strategy. They argued whether it was best to approach each family separately, and try to find support with which to approach the next one. Or, would they have a better chance of success calling a meeting of "The Commission," the ruling body comprised of members of the six families charged with making decisions on major policies? Its rulings were law, like the U.S. Congress, except it was much more effective. The Commission was able to enforce its edicts, to act with resolve and to do so quickly and, most important, unlike the representatives in the nation's capital, it was able to punish those that violated its decisions. Washington, indeed, could learn a thing or two from this governing body.

By the time the wheels of their plane hit the runway, the two had decided to ask for a meeting of The Commission, and a week later they were sitting in a hotel conference room in the Catskill Mountains, also known as the Borscht Belt because it was a resort area frequented primarily by Jews, particularly in the late 1950s and the '60s. Baker, Valenti's former Jewish neighbour in the hotel he lived in when he got out of prison, would have strongly endorsed the choice for the Commission's enclave.

Only the top honchos of the respective families were admitted to Commission meetings, and while Valenti did not have such status, he was allowed to attend since he was present when The Butcher described his ambitious business venture. Valenti, admittedly, was a little intimidated by the power represented. He was sitting with those who ran much of New York, with all due respect to the state's governor, mayor and other public officials.

Around the table sat Esposito, Valenti's nemesis, Antonio "No Compromise" Mobilia, Romano "Hard Nose" Vitale, Tony "Hot Shot" Mancini, Arturo "Fat Fingers" Manzella, and Marcese. None of the families was involved with drugs, except, Marcese, the only Sicilian in the group. The other five families were engaged in horse racing, prostitution, gambling, garbage collection and payoffs for protection.

As Esposito walked by Valenti, he grabbed his former employee by the nape of the neck, and gave it a squeeze, hard enough to cause a little pain.

"Didn't like what you did to me. No hard feelings. It's alright. You no worry."

While he tried to hide his anger, Esposito was not much of an actor. His disdain was evident. He remained very pissed off.

As Valenti massaged his neck, he smiled weakly at Esposito, knowing that his former boss was not one to forgive or forget. If and when Esposito had the opportunity, he would not hesitate to get his revenge.

Valenti would not let his guard down. He would watch his back, front, and sides.

After the six exchanged greetings, slapped each other on the back and asked about each other's businesses, Marcese took the floor. Describing his meeting in Cinisi, he outlined The Butcher's proposal. "I aint' gonna talk long," he assured his colleagues. Time, after all, is money.

He spoke for about thirty minutes describing The Butcher's factory, how he smuggled raw materials from Afghanistan to produce heroin in his laboratories, and how he distributed it to various parts of the world. Marcese was lavish in his praise of The Butcher's sophisticated operation, telling the group how impressed he and Valenti were by the complexity of business, and its profitability as described by The Butcher.

"He wants to expand with you guys here in New York and in other states. Whatta you guys think?"

No one said anything immediately. They exchanged sceptical glances around the table. They did not have to say a word. They were not enamoured by the business opportunity. Esposito, clearly angry, spoke up.

"No," said Esposito. "No deal." While the others remained silent, it was obvious they agreed with their unofficial spokesperson. They let Esposito speak for them.

"Don't need that shit," he continued. "Our soldiers start selling drugs, they end up using the stuff. Junkies turn into ratters. We ain't buying in. I hate ratters. And turncoats."

He added "and turncoats" for Valenti's benefit. So much for moving on. Valenti pretended he did not hear the remark.

Esposito represented the prevailing view which was that junkies when they're arrested, sing, rat, and talk some more. They are more than willing to tell tales out of school in exchange for reducing a twenty-five year sentence to ten. They had seen it happen over and over again. Cops squeezed junkies, at times offering free drugs, to open up a potential rat. "It ain't worth it," Esposito said, and his fellow Commission members agreed.

Marcese gave it one last half-heartedly try, like a football coach giving a pep talk to his team that is losing 57-0. The coach knows the game is lost, but he has an obligation.

So the meeting adjourned without a formal vote. Had one been taken, it would have been 5-1 with the one vote in favour coming from Marcese who dealt in drugs and was The Butcher's proxy. Valenti was not eligible to vote.

Marcese and Valenti did not look forward to a very difficult part of the failed mission: delivering the bad news to The Butcher. While oceans apart on the telephone, they could feel The Butcher's anger.

The Butcher ignored Marcese's report, stating, "We don't need 'em. We need guys with square balls. Square ones are bigger than round ones. Don't think those guys got any."

He told them about one that did. That was one Tomaso "Tommy Boy" Galente.

"You work with Tommy Boy. He's got 'em. Right Johnny?"

Valenti had been surprised when The Butcher implied at their meeting that he knew Valenti took care of DeSante. He was again impressed that The Butcher was able to identify Galente, who Esposito had recently named to replace DeSante as his lieutenant, as a possible ally, and that Valenti was his friend.

The Butcher not only knew him but also that there was bad blood between Galente and Esposito. While Galente despised Esposito, he accepted the number two spot, hoping that he might wield more influence over policy, and one never knew when something might happen to number one. Indeed, something was about to happen.

The truth was Galente had been waiting in the wings for a long time to "get" Esposito. He considered Esposito a cheapskate, giving his troops "only crumbs ... trying to get a fair share was like trying to squeeze juice out of a rock. You get nothin'." So Galente was prepared and anxious to join The Butcher even before hearing about the heroin proposal.

The bad blood between Galente and Esposito went deeper than Galente just considering Esposito a skinflint. They clashed continually on many issues. They never saw eye-to-eye on anything. Moreover, Esposito was creating serious morale problems among the troops. When Esposito's men complained to Galente, he would use gallows humour to diffuse their anger, telling them, "The whipping will stop when morale improves." The men laughed at the axiom they had heard many times. It did little to soothe their discontent.

Several times, Galente sought help from The Butcher, asking him to make changes, but he was always turned town. Each time Galente approached The Butcher, he was told, some other time. The Butcher said he had other major sensitive political issues confronting him which, at the time, were more serious. Only so much a man can do on any one occasion.

With Esposito sticking it to The Butcher in refusing the drug deal, the timing could not have been more propitious. So The Butcher became a big believer in

Milton's assurance that they also serve who only stand and wait. He had waited, and he was served with Galente who was ready to help, and do so gladly.

"Tommy Boy got my okay for Esposito," The Butcher said. "You tell him I said okay.

He do this right and he takes over. He moves right up."

The assignment to give the assignment to Galente was to be Valenti's responsibility because he had a warm, long-standing friendship with Galente.

Valenti was not offended that he had not been asked to put Esposito away. He did not consider it an insult or that The Butcher did not think him up to the task. He understood motivation, i. e. that Galente wanted to get even, and motivation went a long way into assuring success.

Valenti and Galente met in a small pub on New York's west side. For the first forty five minutes or so, they lied about all the broads they laid in school, the cars they stole, the cops they conned when arrested and later paid off as they grew into their teens, and all "the good times" they had in the good old days. After a bit of chitchat, they came to the subject that brought them together.

"The Butcher says okay," Valenti said, "Okay on Esposito."

No more needed to be said. Galente accepted the order like a starving man being offered a piece of bread. He had been waiting for a long time. His patience was rewarded.

"Glad to hear it," said Galente. "You tell him I say okay to his okay."

The "where, when and how," was for Valenti and

Galente to figure out. For the next two hours they worked on a plan like an army preparing for an invasion. The major objective was to get rid of Esposito. They also wanted to send a message to other Commission members that The Butcher's plan for expanding the heroin drug smuggling operation into the U.S. was not a question of "if" it was going to happen but "when" -- with or without their backing. The Esposito "incident" was designed to suggest that it was better for them to support the proposed program than not. Or, at least, step aside when increased smuggling began so as not to inhibit a smooth-running business.

The decisions were made.

Where: In the men's room of Leonardo's, one of Esposito's favourite haunts. Leonardo's was an Italian restaurant that, in Esposito's opinion, served the best pasta and steak in New York City. They decided that Esposito would meet his fate in the men's room for a very good reason. When still on good terms with Esposito, they had learned that he had paid to have an escape tunnel built behind a door in the panelling next to his favourite table. Just in case. In the men's room, Esposito would have no escape route.

When: on a Saturday night when Esposito usually had dinner in the restaurant with his entourage.

How: an Uzi submachine gun. Admittedly, much more fire power than was needed for the job.   They worked on the premise it was better to be over prepared than under prepared. It would be a little hard to hide, but Galente would solve the problem by wearing a long coat under which he could hide the weapon.

Escape: Valenti would be nearby in a car. No one else would be involved.

In keeping with their plan, Galente and Valenti ate dinner at Leonardo's the following day and did some reconnaissance, particularly making sure the back door was kept unlocked during business hours. The plan was for Galente to hide outside the restaurant while waiting for Esposito to arrive. When he did, Galente would enter by the back door and head straight for the men's room.

As soon as Esposito arrived, Galente would hide in one of the stalls, crouching on the toilet so his feet would not be visible. He would have a good view of the urinals through the crack between the hinges on the door jamb, and when Esposito unzipped, it would be the last time he relieved himself. If Esposito were accompanied by one of his stooges, he would be sprayed as well, but not with urine. Galente hoped that Esposito's kidneys would demand relief shortly after drinking his favourite beer, that he would not have to wait long while crouching on the toilet seat. Only so much a man could take.

On the chosen Saturday night, Galente hid in the shadows along one side of Leonardo's. The weapon was hidden under a long overcoat. When Esposito's car pulled up to the front door of the restaurant, Galente slipped into the restaurant through the back door, and headed for the restroom where he taped a sign, "out of order," on the door of the stall. He picked the stall that gave him the best view of the urinals. He locked the stall, and climbed on top of the toilet. He had no idea how long he would have to wait, but he and Valenti had estimated it would be about one hour. The hardest part would be the stiffness suffered while crouching on the toilet. Every job has its downside. To pass the time, he continually inspected his weapon.

The ambience in the john was not very pleasant for Galente. At one point, hearing panting from the stall next to him, he assumed some guy was relieving his sexual frustrations. He was repulsed but also a little sympathetic, concluding that the guy's date rejected him because she had a headache.

Galente tried to ignore the environment while concentrating on his objective. If he achieved it, enduring the restroom atmosphere would have been worth it. He could not understand how bathroom porters in fancy restaurants could spend an entire day in the john handing out towels. That was more distasteful to him than cutting a guy down with a submachine. Everyone has different likes and dislikes.

Just as his wait approached a little more than an hour, he saw one of Esposito's henchmen enter. He looked around, checked under the stalls, but very superficially. The goon read the "out of order" sign and accepted it at face value.

Concluding the men's room was safe for his boss to do his thing, the henchman left and returned a few minutes later with Esposito. Both stopped at the sink where Esposito looked in the mirror to adjust his tie and comb his hair before using the urinal. As Esposito ran his comb through his hair, he heard the stall open behind him. He took no notice until he saw, in the mirror, Galente pointing a very dangerous weapon at his back. The bodyguard saw the same vision in the reflection. It was too late.

Before Esposito could take evasive action, not that there was much he could have done to protect himself against a weapon that was rated at firing more than six hundred bullets a minute, his back was riddled with bullets as was his underperforming employee. If the bodyguard had survived, he would have been charged with dereliction of duty.

Galente did not even wait to see his victims hit the floor. With the submachine gun under his coat, and a chauffeur's cap pulled down over his eyes, he ran out of the restroom, and pushed his way through several employees rushing in. The employees, anxious to find the source of the *rat-a-tat-rat-a-tat*, did not realize until interviewed by police that they may have been able to stop the man that created such a mess in the restroom. Admittedly, there would have been some risk if they had tried.

Galente was in Valenti's car within three to four minutes, and they were a good mile or so away when they heard sirens. About an hour later, they stopped at the East River to deposit the Uzi for safekeeping. For Valenti, Galente, and others in their business, the river was like a safety deposit box at a bank. Unlike a bank, the river was free and, most importantly, they considered it more secure than a bank's vault.

After ridding themselves of indicting evidence, they called to report the news to The Butcher, news that would make his day.

"He's history," Galente said curtly but somewhat proudly.

"You done good, Tommy," The Butcher said, not even asking for details. "I'm gonna take care of you. You'll see."

Having given his word, The Butcher would make Tomaso "Tommy Boy" Galente the head of the temporarily headless Esposito *Mafia* family. Valenti would remain an employee of the Marcese family but Marcese, who was into drugs, would work closely with the Esposito organization which, given the demise of its leader, would require a new name. The fact that Valenti was a pal of the boss-to-be of what had been a rival organization gave Marcese a level of reassurance.

With Galente as head of one of the six families, The

Butcher now had two strong allies for his plans to expand his drug trafficking business. Who knew what the future might hold? He put his hopes in expanding his New York alliances as well.

CHAPTER 12

THE BUTCHER REMAINED PISSED at the decision of the New York families. He did not like anyone saying "no" to him but he took some consolation in the fact that he would eventually get his way. Always did.

He understood salesmen don't succeed in every pitch. Indeed, the rule of thumb was that the ratio of successful sales to sales calls was about three in a hundred. And The Butcher's record was much better than that for several reasons. He was not really cold calling, and his methods of persuasion were more effective than those of traditional salesmen. Understanding the consequences of slamming the door in the faces of The Butcher's sales reps, potential buyers were inclined to accept offers, even if the contractual provisions may not have been particularly attractive or very profitable

Even when rejected, The Butcher came away with something. The "something" was, at times, more valuable than the sale. That was true in the pitch to the New York families. This time the "something" was the demise of Esposito. That would make things easier when he decided to approach the families again. Plus, he got rid of someone he never really liked. A little bonus.

"He was-a little prick," The Butcher said when informed that Esposito never left the men's room.

Meanwhile, the world was large and there were plenty of other territories in which to expand. The Butcher's strategic plan, his master plan, was to create a worldwide organization, and he would be at the top to run it. He would make McDonald's look like a mom-and-pop operation by comparison.

He had a stronghold in Sicily and in a few other parts of Europe. Plans for expanding in the U.S. were in the making, particularly with Galente and Marcese in place. The Butcher also had his eye on South America, particularly Brazil, where a former Sicilian mobster had made his home.

Thus, Galente's first assignment from The Butcher was to make sales call to Domenico Giannola who lived on the outskirts of Rio de Janeiro. Galente might have hesitated in accepting the assignment had he known the whole story about The Butcher's relationship with Giannola.

Giannola, before fleeing to Brazil, had his operations in Sicily. He frequently butted heads with The Butcher. The two did more than butt heads. They had a war with high casualties, particularly for Giannola. He not only lost several of his top men in assassinations but also members of his family, his real family. The fatalities included a brother, a nephew and a cousin.

The bitter rivalry between Giannola and The Butcher had its genesis in land deals Giannola and his brother, Frederico, had worked out with their connections in government. Officials would tip him off to land in Sicily's coastal regions, the value of which would increase dramatically after yet undisclosed plans were approved, and made public.

These plans included the construction of infrastructure, highways, and other improvements, all of which would more than triple the value of the land.

With this insider information, the Giannolas would gobble up the property at ridiculously low prices. Then, they would build large developments, giving them huge profits, and government officials, the Giannolas' benefactors, would receive very healthy kickbacks. Officeholders would also benefit politically because they bragged to their constituents that the new developments provided much needed additional tax revenue.

It was a win-win for everyone, but The Butcher was not very happy. He had helped Giannola with strategy and offered tactical support, but took offence because he believed he did not receive what he considered was a fair share of the profits. His revenues from this arrangement did not make him very happy. He wanted a larger piece of the pie. Maybe a little more than a piece. Let's say half.

Despite his unhappiness, The Butcher was available when Domenico Giannola reached out to The Butcher, asking him to "take care of" government troublemakers that Giannola's identified as "problems." These officials, for some strange reason, thought the arrangements "unfair" and even "illegal." They did not consider what amounted to insider trading as serving the public interest. Periodically, they would complain to the media but, aware of the risks they were taking, they were usually identified only as "reliable sources."

Giannola's network generally was able to identify the culprits. It was very easy. They simply asked the reporters. The reporters, recognizing the power of the inquisitors and the consequences of not cooperating, were more than happy to surrender whatever protections they believed they had from revealing sources. The Sicilian equivalent to the U.S. Constitution's First Amendment principles, if it even existed, was worthless.

Worried that the spoilers could upset a very nice, profitable arrangement, Giannola recruited The Butcher for help, and The Butcher, happy to be of service, took the assignments with some relish. He went on a killing spree, and he did so for several reasons. He thrived on violence and killing, and he wanted to display his power to Giannola and the government. He also assumed, given his significant efforts to assure Giannola's business success,

Giannola would reciprocate with a higher share of Giannola's take. Hardly unreasonable for The Butcher to expect greater compensation for his work which involved murdering government officeholders. This was risky business, and in any endeavour, when risks go up, so do the financial rewards. At least, they should. Giannola ignored this long-standing and generally accepted business formula.

An additional insult came when The Butcher asked Giannola to help him expand his drug business. "Don't want no part in drugs," he told The Butcher. "We got a very nice land business, and some other businesses. Drugs are trouble and will just screw us up." He did not explain why The Butcher did not deserve more revenues from the real estate business.

The Butcher was humiliated, and humiliation bred retaliation. He declared war, killing many of Giannola's men and relatives, and The Butcher did not forget about the politicians who worked with his mobster enemy.

"They fuck with me, I fuck with them," he told his assassins.

The Butcher's brutality, especially the murder of numerous public officials, even attracted the attention of the Pope. In a special encyclical, one aimed at a very small, limited audience (The Butcher) but not one that would make papal history, the Pope pleaded for an end to the violence along with repentance. He would have settled for the former and accept the fact that he might have to forget about repentance. Only so much the Holy Father could hope and pray for even if he was the head of the Catholic Church.

Giannola, who attended church regularly, was very pleased with the Vatican's position paper. His reasons for ending the violence were somewhat different from those of the Pope.   The Pope was speaking from a moral standpoint. He thought rampant killing, any killing, was wrong.   Giannola worried about preserving an infrastructure in which to operate a profitable real estate business.   The Pope's motivation did not concern Giannola. He welcomed the support. Each week, to show his gratitude, he made very generous contributions in church when the collection plate was passed.   Church officials and ushers were very grateful and, like Giannola, they did not care about motivation.

With the Pope on his side, Giannola, on his own, tried to reason with The Butcher. Regrettably, Giannola did not consider that if the Holy Father was unsuccessful in his public pleadings, he certainly wasn't going to convince The Butcher to change his ways.

The Butcher recognized that Giannola loved his family, and for The Butcher that was considered a personality trait to be exploited, not an attribute to be admired.   Anything that could be exploited was a weakness.

Giannola's brother was the first fatality.   While usually extremely careful, Frederico Giannola, left the home of his brother late at night believing, after a few drinks, that he was safe.   With only a couple of bodyguards in his car, he drove no more than a mile on a quiet stretch of highway when their car was blocked by one from the front and another in the rear.

It happened quickly, and before Frederico Giannola could even open the door of his car, the vehicle was machine gunned from all sides. Police reported Frederico Giannola and his two men were each hit with about ten bullets. There was no need for an autopsy to determine the cause of death.

Next came Frederico's sixteen year old son, Nicolo,

who pledged to avenge his father's death. The boy thought telling people of his plans would prove, while still a boy, he was a man of honour. The boy wanted justice and in his youthful innocence and naiveté talked a little too much, too loudly and to too many people.

Loose lips sink ships, and they sank the boy. Word reached The Butcher quickly and without hesitation he ordered the assassination of Nicolo Giannola. He did not care whether Nicolo was a real threat, whether the boy would or could carry out his self-appointed mission. Nor did he reflect that Nicolo was only sixteen years old. The Butcher gave the order.

It was hardly a challenge to The Butcher's assassins. Given his youth, Nicolo was very careless and The Butcher's men found him alone one day, only a month after his father's murder. They kidnapped him, shot him, and tossed the body as a warning to the family on the sidewalk about twenty yards from the Giannola home.

After those hits, The Butcher's men went after Giannola's cousin, who just disappeared. The question was not whether he was murdered. The only question was how, but Giannola would never find out. That's how The Butcher wanted it. A little mystery. Thus, Giannola took stock of his losses, surrendered, and fled to Brazil.

The Butcher somehow "forgot" to tell his emissaries from the U.S. about this history. In assigning Galente to pay Giannola a visit, The Butcher told him to tell his former rival to let bygones be bygones. Not good to hold grudges. They cause ulcers. Had The Butcher been more eloquent, he might have added that Galente remind Giannola that to err is human but to forgive divine. Not that The Butcher was one to forgive, or to believe he ever erred. What is good for the goose is not necessarily always good for the gander. Sometimes double standards serve a useful purpose.

Basically, he instructed the two to tell Giannola, "It wasn't personal. It was business. He gotta understand. No hard-a feelings."

Appreciating that Giannola might not want to see his representatives, The Butcher had the meeting scheduled by an intermediary, a supposedly neutral third party. He learned that strategy from world diplomats who used such tactics as having non-involved parties set up "unofficial" meetings, for instance, between bitter enemies like the Arab countries and Israel, and the Protestants and Catholics of Ireland. If it was good enough for world enemies to agree to meet through intermediaries, it was good enough for The Butcher, and The Butcher did not expect Giannola to object.

So Galente, with only superficial knowledge of The Butcher-Giannola history, asked Valenti, after getting permission from Marcese, to join him, for the trip to Brazil. He would have a valued companion along, one he could trust, and who knew, he might need the expert services of his skilled friend. Didn't hurt to have a hit man nearby since one never knew when he might be needed.

Valenti, for his part, had not realized when he signed on with Marcese that so much travel would be part of his job. First, Cinisi, Sicily followed by Brazil. Not that he minded, but he wished he had the opportunity to see more than airports, conference rooms, or stables.

What he could not foresee was that this trip would change his life forever. For the first time, a woman would touch his soul, evoking emotions that he did not know existed. A hit man, a murderer, a man who killed without a second thought, would be moved as he had never been moved before.

"Good to work with you, Johnny," said Galente as they sat on the plane taking them to Brazil. "We go back a long way."

"Way back," Valenti replied. "Never thought I'd buy you a beer in Rio."

"You buying? That's a first."

They both laughed as the plane landed, shaking them slightly in their seats.

After an overnight stay at the airport hotel, they drove in a rented car to Giannola's estate located about thirty miles from the airport that served the area in the lakes region of Rio between the towns of Ponta Negra and Marica. It was a beautiful setting, with the Atlantic Ocean on one side and several lakes on the other. While breathtaking, the scenery was starkly different from The Butcher's property that featured meadows and wineries. Giannola had to settle for sights of the ocean and women in bikinis. The property was on no more than ten acres. Giannola had to cut back after losing to The Butcher. He had only one security guard at the front door.

Galente and Valenti, after a thorough security check, were permitted to enter the house. Giannola had agreed to the meeting reluctantly, and only because he was told it might get him back into the big leagues. In Brazil, he felt like a baseball player who had played at Yankee Stadium but was demoted to the minors, and had to ride dirty buses and eat in fast-food diners in small towns no one ever heard of. Admittedly, Giannola's pay was still better than that of a third baseman playing in the minors in Toledo.

Giannola was shooting pool in a spacious recreation room when his guests arrived. The wood-panelled walls were covered with photographs taken during happier years, photos of him and dons, all smoking what appeared to be foot-long cigars.   When he was particularly depressed, he would scan the photos and reminisce about the years gone by, the good old-a days. Giannola was a nostalgic guy.

"Welcome, you're welcome in-a my house."   He stepped between the two and grabbed each by his elbow.

"Come, I show some pictures."

For the next half hour he told them, in some detail, about his relationship with the people in the photographs and how he missed all his friends. He did not mention the loss of big bucks that hurt him even more. There were no photos of The Butcher on the walls.

Recognizing that perhaps he was boring his guests, he took them to a family room to discuss business that might give him the opportunity to add more photos to the panelled walls.

"So, tell me, why you come all this way from the U.S. It's a long way, no?"

Galente was about to answer when the front door opened and a woman passed quickly by the family room.

"Gisele, come in here. Meet-a my American friends."

Giannola introduced the daughter of his brother, Frederico. His niece was gorgeous.

Gisele Giannola, twenty-five years old with long black hair reaching her waist, was curvaceous and wore a short skirt that revealed her beautiful long shapely legs. She had high cheekbones, full lips, a perfectly sculpted nose and black eyes which seemed bottomless.   Her skin was tanned, smooth without any imperfections.

She extended her arm to shake hands with Galente and Valenti. When Valenti shook her hand, he felt the softness of her skin, and he did not want to let go.

"My niece. I take care of her. I buy house for her next to my home. She nice, beautiful, eh?" Giannola asked rhetorically. "Gisele, we see you later. We need to talk-a business."

Gisele left the room but her image did not, at least for Valenti. He was captivated. He had had many beautiful women, but this one was different. He was experiencing strange sensations that were new to him.

This must have been the kind of woman Antonio Carlos Jobim had in mind when he wrote the song, *"The Girl From Ipanema."* This was Ipanema country and Gisele Giannola was, as the first line of the song said, "tall and tan and young and lovely …"

As Valenti tried to sort out and understand what was happening to him, Galente outlined the reasons for the visit. He was just warming up in his presentation when the light bulb went on for Giannola.

"That *bastardo* Monteleone sent you, right?" he shouted.

"Hear me out," Galente implored. "Let me tell you the plan. I think you'll like …"

"You crazy! He killed my brother, my nephew, a cousin, many men. You wanna me to forget? I saved Gisele. That's all I got-a left. You think I can forget?"

"Listen. He's our boss. He asks us to see you, and we do it. That's it. It's business, you know."

"Let-a me ask you, I kill your brother, you still work with me?" It was hardly an unreasonable question.

The citing by Giannola of the murder of his family members by The Butcher was news to Galente and

Valenti. They were surprised, although they did not show it. They wished they had known a little bit about this history. Salesmen should have as much information about their prospective clients as possible to prepare effective sales strategies. The Butcher's emissaries did not have a ready answer. They were a little tongue-tied.

Galente ignored Giannola's logic, and tried to convince Giannola to let him finish explaining the plan that could lead him back to the big time. Giannola would have none of it.

"I gotta nothin' against you," Giannola said, signalling the end of the conversation. "You my guests and did nothin' to me. You go back to Monteleone and tell him from me, to stick it up his ass. You do that for me."

Galente surrendered, recognizing further arguments would be a waste of time. It was, obviously, a lost cause. He and his friend had travelled a long way for a ten minute meeting, but those frustrations and inconveniences were part of the trials and tribulations of travelling salesmen.

Galente stood up and prepared to leave as did Valenti who had only heard parts of the exchange between the two. His mind had wandered back and forth from the meeting to a long-legged woman that had him mesmerized.

"You no forget," Giannola repeated. "To go to hell. You tell him from me."

In the cab back to their hotel, Galente noticed his friend appeared to be preoccupied. Valenti had hardly said a word.

"Johnny, don't worry," Galente reassured him. "Ain't our fault. The Butcher killed his brother and says it's just business. I don't blame Giannola."

Valenti did not appear to have heard Galente. His mind was racing and, overall, he had never felt so good and agitated at the same time. It was weird.

Galente and Valenti sat for several minutes with neither saying a word before Galente's patience wore out.

"Johnny, what the hell's wrong with you?" Then it hit him. "The broad?"

Valenti was angered at the description of Gisele Giannola as a "broad." The woman he had seen did not qualify as a "broad."

"Look, if you're horny, we hit the bars and get lucky. Or, we get a couple of Spanish hookers." Galente was never any good at geography. Spanish, Brazilian, what was the difference? They all sounded the same, especially if you didn't understand the language. When in foreign countries, Galente figured all he had to do was to show them the numbers on his American dollars, starting with a fifty dollar bill.

"They speak Portuguese not Spanish here," Valenti advised his friend.

"Who gives a shit? I ain't hiring them for language lessons."

Back at their hotel, they had a drink at the bar, but Valenti was not very talkative or good company. After about a half hour, Galente had it with Valenti's sulking.

"I'm goin' to bed. You're a pain in the ass."

In his room, Valenti paced. He was extremely nervous. He turned on the TV and turned it off. He looked at a couple of Brazilian magazines and newspapers which he could not read. He brushed his teeth. He tried to sleep.

After debating with himself, he made his decision. He would go back and try to see Gisele. He remembered that Giannola said she lived adjacent to his house. It was worth a try. He might not succeed but nothing ventured, nothing gained.

He went back to the bar, downed a shot of straight bourbon, hailed a cab and ordered it to take him to the Giannola estate. He had the cab driver drop him off about a block from the Giannola complex. He explored his surroundings. He saw only one other building on the block, and he hoped it housed Gisele Giannola.

It was 12:35 a.m. when he pushed the doorbell with less trepidation than might be expected. He waited a few seconds and tried again. To his surprise, a very pleasant surprise, the door was opened by Gisele Giannola who was in a bathrobe that made her look all the more desirable.

"I'm sorry … I know it's late … but I wanna talk to you," he stammered. "I don't have much time. Goin' back to the U.S. tomorrow. Okay?"

Gisele, appearing almost happy to see Valenti, invited her unexpected guest into the house. "Come on in. Don't tell my uncle."

Valenti looked at her in awe. Without makeup and her hair wet from just having showered, she was even more beautiful than he remembered. As he walked next to her into the house, he could smell the fragrance of her body. She led him to the living room where she sat on a couch while he was seated in an adjacent chair.

For the next hour, Johnny Valenti talked to Gisele Giannola. That alone was a new and strange experience for him. Throughout his life, when he was with women, it was not much more than "How ya doin'? Wanna a drink?" and "Let's do it." If for whatever reason, they did not want "to do it," he would recite an amended surgeon general's warning that went something like this: "Saying no may be more hazardous to your health than the cigarette you're smoking." Upon hearing this admonition, his "dates" generally, actually always, wanted "to do it."

His only relationship had been with Fiora, and that was more a matter of accommodation than passionate love. Yes, they were probably on their way to marriage if DeSante had not altered their plans, and while Valenti treated her with respect and really liked her, she never really touched his heart.

This was different, very different. They talked until three a.m. when Valenti rose from his chair and sat next to her on the couch. He moved very close to Gisele and kissed her.

She liked Valenti and did not hold back. Soon their tongues increased desire, and, before long, she removed her robe and he undressed. Naked, they slid to the floor.

After he had explored her with his hands, she parted her legs to let him enter her. As he did, he felt a surge of emotion unlike anything he had ever experienced. He had screwed lots of women but, until Gisele, he had never made love before.

As they increased each other's passion, he hoped it would never end. But end it did and, as he lay on his back, this man who made his living killing people, tried to understand what he was feeling. Love, understandably, was an alien emotion to a professional hit man.

At about five a.m., he indicated he had to leave because he wanted to be back at his hotel before Galente discovered his absence. Valenti assumed Galente would harass him mercilessly if he found out he had spent the night with Gisele.

"I'm comin' back," he told her.

"Is that something like 'I'll call you'?"

"No, it ain't. You'll see."

She would, later that day. When Galente met Valenti for breakfast, Valenti told him he was staying for another week.

"The broad?" Galente asked, repeating the question he asked in the cab the previous evening.

"Tommy, I ain't in no mood for your shit. I'll be back in a week or so. You can tell Marcese and The Butcher about Giannola. If they ask about me, tell them I'm on vacation."

Galente did not argue. He was happy for his friend. What worried him was that a serious relationship might soften Valenti and leave him unable to fulfil his professional obligations. Could Valenti handle love and the demands of his job? Galente and the other bosses had no use for a mushy, lovesick hit man.

Galente didn't have to worry. He would find out that Valenti would be adept at multi-tasking and compartmentalization. He could separate his professional responsibilities from his love for Gisele Giannola.

CHAPTER 13

BACK IN HIS VILLA in Cinisi, Sicily, The Butcher was not a happy camper. Nothing but bad news in the last month or so.

The Big Six (really the Big Five since Marcese supported The Butcher's plan) in the States had rejected his plan to expand drug sales, and Giannola, in Brazil, could not overlook the killing of family members and friends or understand "it was just business." How petty can a man get? It happened so long ago. How long can a man hold a grudge?

In addition, he had troubles in Harlem, the black enclave in New York City. While reviewing balance sheets, he discovered, to his dismay, that drug sales were down dramatically. That bothered him not only because of the reduced revenues, but it raised questions of trust. Was someone ripping him off? Was Marcese playing some financial hanky-panky?

He decided to address the Harlem problem, and for help he called on his son-in-law, Luciano "The Punk" Cusumano. Cusumano thought that his nickname was intended as a compliment. It wasn't.

His greasy hair was combed back straight on both sides. He wore gaudy suits, and ties that were so flashy, onlookers had to squint to look at them. As to brains, it would be fair to say he had few, if any. If it weren't for the fact that he was The Butcher's son-in-law, he would be working with a pair of pliers adjusting slot machines to lower the returns they spit out to gamblers in the casinos.

Ignoring Cusumano's lack of professional talents, The Butcher decided to send Cusumano to the U.S. to investigate the business climate and the potential for expansion in Harlem. He wasn't happy about having his dimwit son-in-law as an envoy, but he thought he might be able to do the job.

The Butcher also chose Cusumano for the Harlem assignment because he shared his son-in-law's racist views. He had developed his impressions of blacks mostly from movies in which blacks were usually portrayed as druggies and/or alcoholics. He should have done more homework before choosing Cusumano for what would be a very sensitive role. Cusumano was not known for finesse, and as The Butcher was to discover, tact and diplomacy, which his son-in-law lacked, would have proved useful for this mission.

In any event, he had hope because hope springs eternal even when it involves punk sons-in-law.

First, before Cusumano left on his voyage, The Butcher had a personal problem that was extremely troubling. It involved his twenty three year old daughter, Rita, Cusumano's wife.

"You sure?" The Butcher asked Cusumano who was wearing a pink shirt, bright yellow tie and a double-breasted royal blue pin-stripped suit. He was smoking a fat cigar, the kind The Butcher enjoyed as well.

"She's been screwing some bastard," Cusumano answered angrily, using language not particularly appropriate when addressing the father of a daughter who has been unfaithful to her husband. "I'm telling you what I know."

The Butcher, the father, listened carefully as Cusumano told him more than he really wanted or needed to know. Pain was obvious in his face. His insides churned. The Butcher's daughter, who was having an affair, was dishonouring the Monteleone name, his name. The name of his ancestors, the name "Monteleone" that was revered, indeed more feared than revered, by everyone in Sicily.

The Butcher could not live with that. To the man who had people killed in various parts of the world at the slightest indiscretion nothing was more important than honour He would not allow anything or anyone to besmirch the family name, not even his daughter. How could he live with himself knowing people were whispering behind his back about his unfaithful daughter? How could he look people in the eye when he thought they gossiped about Rita Monteleone cheating on her husband? When they gossiped, they would invoke the Monteleone name.

Monteleone paced the room as Cusumano watched, not fully aware of the chord he had struck in his father-in-law. Cusumano, puffing from his cigar and blowing circle rings, had no idea of the thoughts running through The Butcher's head. The Butcher made his decision.

"Before you go," he told Cusumano. "We take care of your problem." He did not mean "your" problem. He meant "my" problem.

Cusumano did not ask "how?" Nor did he fully comprehend the full extent of the "hurt" he had inflicted on The Butcher with the story about Rita Monteleone's infidelity. Even with his lack of brains, Cusumano was optimistic the problem would be solved because, above all, The Butcher was a problem-solver. He had confidence in his father-in-law though he could not envision the solution.

Rita Monteleone's boyfriend was a high school history teacher in Cinisi who either did not think about the risk he was taking or concluded that he was prepared to have an affair with the wife of a mobster – of all people the son-in-law of The Butcher – regardless of the risks in exchange for Rita's love. Like so many others, male or female, who are unable to think clearly when love overtakes reason, he had made a very serious mistake. As a history teacher, if only he had studied the lives of lovers throughout the centuries who suffered dreadful fates because they were blinded by passion. Tragedy generally followed when the heart trumped intellect, reason and good judgement.

Similarly, Rita, who had confided in her mother, ignored her mother's fervent pleas to end the affair. While Maria Monteleone shared her daughter's revulsion for Luciano Cusumano, she objected to the illicit liaison not only on moral grounds but because she was all too aware of what her husband, The Butcher, would do should he find out that his hallowed family name had been dishonoured.

After questioning Cusumano for as much detail as possible, including details about his daughter's schedule, The Butcher asked his son-in-law to pick him up on the day Rita Monteleone was expected to be at her lover's home.

On the appointed day, The Butcher did not say a word on the half-hour drive. He sat stoically next to Cusumano on the passenger side. His expression was totally blank during the entire time. He did not move a muscle on his face. Periodically, he would stick his hand in his right suit pocket, fumble with something and then remove his hand.

When they arrived, he made no attempt to hide. He let Cusumano park the car in front of the house. Again, that right hand slipped into his suit pocket. Each of The Butcher's movements was decisive – his walk, his orders – yet there seemed to be a slight degree of hesitation, indecision. It was not noticeable because The Butcher hid well whatever second-thoughts he was having.

"Wait here," he told Cusumano, while picking up a crow bar from the floor of the car. The Butcher got out of the car, walked slowly to the house, and found the front door locked. He pried it open.

The house was quiet. No one was in the living room. The Butcher headed toward the back of the house. In the hallway, on his right, he stopped in front of a closed door. He steadied himself before opening the door. Regrettably, he saw what he never imagined he would ever see nor wanted to see.

He saw his daughter in bed with a man, but he was not her husband. The naked man next to Rita was in shock. He immediately recognized The Butcher. In panic, he jumped out of bed and ran full speed through the glass door wall, curtains and all. The Butcher paid no attention to him. He just stared at his daughter.

Lying in bed, Rita grabbed the sheets and pulled them up to her neck. Tears flowed almost immediately. She watched her father frightfully, her eyes reflecting shame, embarrassment, panic, but most of all terror. Rita Monteleone knew her father, and that knowledge fuelled her fear. Her entire body was trembling uncontrollably.

The two looked at each other. Each was traumatized but for different reasons. One was consumed by fear and terror and the other by disdain, anger and humiliation. Neither was able to fully comprehend the moment.

"Rita ...," The Butcher started. He quickly stopped. He decided against saying anything. What was there to say? How could he explain what he was about to do? What was the point of offering an explanation? Would his words make a difference?

After a few seconds, The Butcher reached into the right coat pocket in which he had fidgeted all the way to this house. His hand rested there for a few seconds. When he withdrew it, he had a black .38 calibre revolver in his hand.

Rita rose to her knees, and naked in front of her father, she rocked back and forth on the bed. Her arms were crossed in front of her as she tried to cover her breasts.

"Please, Papa, please … please, Papa, please … please, Papa, please …"

Over and over she pleaded for her father's mercy, rocking continuously. Tears covered her face and ran down her neck. Her face had lost all its colour. Her voice quivered as she pleaded in desperation knowing only too well the futility of her appeals.

"Please, Papa, please ..."

Her pleadings of "please, Papa, please" were interspersed with, "I'm sorry … very sorry …"

The Butcher said nothing. He blocked out her pleas. He pointed the revolver at his only child, twenty three year old Rita Monteleone. He held his arm steady for a few seconds. The seconds ticked away – one, two, three. Nothing. Another two seconds – one, two. Had he changed his mind? Why was he hesitating? Was this only a threat? Did he just want to scare her? Was he trying to prolong the moment to make her suffer?

The answers to these questions came suddenly. The Butcher squeezed the trigger with resolve and purpose. As he did, he closed his eyes. The Butcher had closed his eyes. He did not see the bullet hit his daughter's forehead and exit in the back. He did not see her fall onto the bed, or the blood splatter on the white sheets. He did not see any of that because he did not open his eyes until he turned around to leave the room. He never looked at his dead daughter. He did not want to live with such a scene in his memory.

Mission accomplished.   Father had killed daughter. The besmirching of the Monteleone name had been avenged. He could feel proud. He could hold his head up high.   No one could ever say that Giuliano Monteleone was not a man of honour.   He had solved what he had described as Cusumano's problem.

When The Butcher got back to his car, Cusumano had a prisoner. He was holding a naked man whom he caught running from the house. Cusumano had a gun pointed at his head. The Butcher did not even look at him.

"Let him go," The Butcher said.

The lover, confused, grateful, panicky, headed back toward the house. He had taken about four steps when a bullet hit him in the back of the head. The Butcher put his revolver back in his right pocket. Neither even gave the man a second look.

On the way back to his house, The Butcher was as stoic as he had been earlier on the way to his mission. The only change was that he no longer stuck his hand into his pocket. Cusumano noticed that The Butcher had a slight nervous tic under his right eye. Periodically, The Butcher

would rub the spot trying to make it stop. He was not successful. Ultimately, The Butcher stopped rubbing his face, deciding the twitch would fade as quickly as it had developed.

At his villa, it was time for The Butcher to face his wife of some twenty-eight years. He entered his home, and found his wife near the kitchen. As he approached her, Maria Monteleone caught her husband's eye. They said nothing but seemed to communicate. There appeared to be a mutual understanding. Even before her husband spoke, Maria Monteleone's eyes welled with tears, and her face revealed her excruciating pain. Her body shook, and she grabbed a door jamb to steady herself.

Her eyes pleaded with her husband not to tell her the news she expected, news she – any mother – could not bear to hear.

"We no have a daughter no more."

Rita Monteleone's mother fainted even before she heard the last word – "more."

The Butcher told one of his maids to assist his wife as went to his study and closed the door. He sat in an overstuffed chair. He stared into space. He felt sweat in his palms and tears form in his eyes. He fought hard to keep the tears from coming. He stood up, paced the room briskly, desperately working to suppress unexpected and unwanted emotions. He was The Butcher, the main man, the head of *Mafia* families, a leader, a killer. He would not surrender to softness even following his daughter's death caused by his own hands.

He would not play Shakespeare's King Lear, whose ego incapacitated him from differentiating good from evil, leading to the death of his daughter, Cordelia, who loved him dearly. Even after he became mad, Lear knew his vanity had caused her death and, bereaved by what he had done, the once powerful king would die heartbroken in full recognition of the fateful and deadly forces he had unleashed.

Contrition was not part of The Butcher's psychological makeup. What's more, Lear's problems emanated from a tragic mistake. The Butcher, a Monteleone, perhaps more powerful than kings, was not guilty of error. He was defending honour. The price was high, indeed, but the price had to be paid. What else could he do? There was no other choice. The Monteleone name would not be tarnished. Thus, he would not go mad. He would not mourn. He would not even let himself cry.

He had been successful because, above all, he always protected the Monteleone name. This was a time for pride not weakness or mourning. Tradition had been upheld.

It was, for him, in the end, all a matter of honour, of living by a code that had been followed and revered in Sicily for centuries. *Onore* – honour. That trumped everything.

CHAPTER 14

HARLEM WAS NO STRANGER to organized crime that was principally involved in numbers, prostitution and drugs.   Over the years, the illegal activities of this primarily black section of Manhattan evolved as the population changed and grew.

In the 1920s, black gangsters ran the numbers racket while Jewish and Italian mobsters operated nightclubs patronized primarily by whites.   Forty years later, in the 1960s, drugs became more prevalent in Harlem.   They plagued Harlem to a higher degree than the rest of New York, and the nation as a whole.

The Butcher was concerned because sales in Harlem, where he had a foothold, weren't as good as he had planned.   They did not meet his financial goals.   He wanted greater profits, and he wanted to expand.

In the short term, he had raised prices on heroin, but still the returns on his investment were not what they were supposed to be, or what he wanted.   Worse, the price increase backfired.   The druggies could not afford the higher prices and, as a result, bought less.   Or they diluted the product to make it last longer.   Druggies can be ingenious.   Capitalism doesn't always work the way one wants or expects even when one makes most of the rules as The Butcher did.   So he sent his son-in-law to meet with those who ran the illegal drug trade in Harlem.

Luciano "The Punk" Cusumano arrived in New York about the same time Johnny Valenti returned from Brazil following a week-long tryst with Gisele Giannola. Cusumano was dressed in technicolour.   Marcese and Valenti wondered whether he wore his sunglasses to protect his eyes from his clothes.

"The man," as the cock-sure Cusumano referred to

himself, told the two that he could "handle the niggers. Leave everything to me."

The plan was to develop what in the law-abiding world was called a joint venture with each party sharing a percentage of the profits. How the pie was divided would be based on the support provided by the partners. They would take in account such resources as security, enforcers, salespeople, bookkeeping, bribes and other essentials needed to run a sophisticated illegal drug operation.

To have any chance of securing a joint venture they would have to convince The Rev. Willie "Diamond Fingers" Johnson, a formidable figure in Harlem. Indeed, when he walked the streets, he engendered the same kind of reaction The Butcher did strolling in Cinisi.

People got out of his way, tipped their hats, or crossed the street to avoid even possible eye contact. If he encountered some of his customers drugged out on the street, he would stick a twenty dollar bill in their pockets to help them over the hump. Big hearted guy. He considered his gesture analogous to the distribution of coupons in the Sunday paper, understanding twenty would get him a hundred or more. He was helping to keep them hooked.

The Rev. Johnson had his main offices in the First Baptist Church on West 130th Street, hence the reference to "The Reverend." He was not really a clergyman, but he was a major supporter of the church. Should the real reverend need help, financial or otherwise, he could always count on the occupant on the second floor in offices right above the altar. The real reverend's prayers were always answered, if not by the Almighty or divine intervention, then by Willie Johnson. The real reverend bestowed "honorary reverend" status on Johnson, wanting to do a little something in return.

Johnson was extremely grateful because the title and the site of his office gave him a degree of respectability. Respectability was important to Johnson. Being addressed as "reverend" always raised Johnson's spirits. He beamed at the sound of the word. And Johnson's family, not knowing all the details of how he earned a living, was very proud.

As Johnson requested on the telephone, Marcese, Valenti and Cusumano made the appointment for a Sunday. Willie Johnson liked being in his office on Sundays because he loved gospel music. The revelry and passion from the congregants moved him while conducting business. He thought more clearly hearing the prayers, and it was good for his soul.

When the trio arrived, Johnson was sitting behind his desk with two very large men standing by each of his shoulders. They looked very serious as did Johnson. That is they were serious until they saw Cusumano. It required all their self-control not to burst out laughing at the sight of Cusumano's multi-colour outfit.

"Well, will you look at that dude," the Rev. Johnson said addressing his men. "My, oh, my. Ain't we just pretty." The reverend's men stifled their laughter.

Johnson and his bodyguards were dressed in very conservative and expensive suits. They wore white shirts with gold cuff links, and red-black striped ties. The only sign of ostentation came from four diamond rings on Johnson's fingers, two on each hand. Thus, the nickname. In any other setting, they might have been mistaken for lawyers or investment bankers.

Johnson was sipping cognac. Never too early to savour good liqueur. He was confident the real reverend would not mind a little responsible drinking in his church, even during Sunday morning services.

The meeting on the joint venture began almost at the very same time as the real reverend pleaded with his congregants to *"give your souls to Jesus."*

"I will," "Tell me more," "I ain't gonna sin no more," "Yeah, Jesus," all filtered into the office as Johnson asked his guests about their proposal.

Marcese took over and described a plan that involved aggressive sales of heroin in Johnson's territory, translating into high, very high profits.

"I don't need no partners," Johnson said emphatically. "We's doing all right, no?"

The somewhat rhetorical question, the "no?" was addressed to the men protecting his flanks. They nodded in agreement. No, no need for partners, they agreed.

On the first floor, the organ started to play and vibrations shook Johnson's office. The congregants swayed, clapped and interjected their individual feelings as the choir began the Sunday gospel program.

Johnson held out his hand, indicating he wanted quiet so he could concentrate on the congregants appealing with their harmonious voices to the Almighty. He was always moved by the sincerity of the churchgoers. Oh, how could He not listen? He had an obligation to respond to such pleas.

Then Johnson turned to his guests. "Done pretty good witout you so far. Don't need partners. Don't want any."

"We can double your take," offered Valenti.

"We's in a church and the Lord says not good to be greedy," said Johnson as the congregation below belted out, *"That's the truth. He always tell the truth."*

"Look," said Johnson, "You from Italy. I don't even know where that is and don't give a shit. You in Harlem and you don't know nothin' about black folks. Like any business, you gotta know your customers. I know nothin' about your mother fuckers and you don't know mine. I ain't interested in no deal."

From the first floor came, *"That's right. He speaks the truth. He never lie. We's better listen to Him."*

Cusumano, who had sat restlessly on a couch, had enough. He should have reflected on the advice that sometimes it is better to hold thy tongue, in or out of church.

Addressing Marcese and Valenti, he said, "Let me talk to these niggers. Who they think they are? They're niggers...that's all. Niggers."

At the same time, the congregants below confessed, *"I've sinned, O Lord, I've sinned. I's sorry I sinned. Tain't good to sin. I's prepared for Jesus."*

Marcese and Valenti were stunned. It was too late to give Cusumano a lesson in race relations, to warn him to temper his racism, or just shut up. Even they were offended by their colleague's bluntness and crassness. Given the suddenness of Cusumamo's outburst, they were powerless to remedy an extremely sensitive situation.

Johnson got up from the chair behind his desk, cognac in hand. He walked to the couch and threw the cognac at Cusumano. Cusumano, trying to appear unfazed, took a handkerchief out of a pocket, and used it to absorb the liqueur. He did his best to appear nonchalant.

"What you niggers think you're doing?" Cusumano said, compounding a delicate situation. "You don't know who you fuckin' with."

Before launching into his not-so-diplomatic tirade, Cusumano could have used more information on his adversaries. He should have conducted some background checks before confronting the Rev. Johnson. He would have discovered that the Rev. Johnson was a man of little patience, especially when he was insulted, and the target of racism. Cusumano would have learned much about what happened to those who crossed Johnson.

Johnson stood over his visitor only a foot away. He stared coldly at Cusumano before turning to his men.

Looking at his bodyguards, Johnson said, "This honky mother fucker comin' in here calling us niggers. Can we let that go? In church?" The two men shook their heads. No way. Not in our house, a house of God.

The congregants meanwhile asked for, *"Mercy, dear Lord, show me mercy. I's sinned but show me mercy. I don't know what I do."*

The organ blared while Valenti, absentmindedly and subconsciously tapping his foot to the music, was only half aware of what was going on around him. He watched the bogus reverend, but did not fully comprehend the scene as his mind centred on making love to and with Gisele. While the real reverend would have been offended by Valenti's thoughts in a house of prayer, the honorary reverend probably would have identified with his guest and his thoughts of love.

Almost on cue with a chord from the organ, appropriately a sad minor chord, Johnson pulled out a .38 calibre revolver which had been tucked in his belt. He seemed to wait for the organ below to hit a loud crescendo while playing *"Just A Closer Walk With Thee"* – a walk Cusumano was about to take – before firing three shots into Cusumano's abdomen. When he fired, the revolver was only inches away from Cusumano, causing Cusumano's clothes to catch on fire. The cognac and heat of the bullet were not compatible.

"Oh, Lord, I's a comin'... I's a comin' to you. I's a comin' into Your arms. Do not forsake me."

Johnson coolly asked his assistants to douse Cusumano with the fire extinguisher on the wall before the smouldering Cusumano damaged the office. He did not want to have to redecorate.

"Don't want to hurt the church's furniture," Johnson said as he tucked the revolver back into his belt.

If The Butcher had been at the meeting, he would have been confused. He never saw blacks act that way with whites in the movies. They were always subservient. Perhaps he should have done more scholarly research before sending Cusumano as his emissary.

With Cusumano's clothes emitting smoke, Johnson told his other two guests, "We'll take care of your bro'. Get your white asses out of here. You know what I'm sayin'? If the Italian mother fucker wants war, he'll get it. You know what I'm sayin'? We'll throw all of your asses out of Harlem. You got no right to be here anyway, no how. You know what I'm sayin'?"

Which was greeted from below by, *"Yes, we's understanding you," "Hallelujah,"* and *"Amen."*

Hearing Johnson's not so subtle message, Marcese and Valenti did not argue. They realized that not all business proposals are agreed to on the first try. Sometimes many attempts are required as well as long and deliberate negotiations. It also takes a little more tact than had been demonstrated at this meeting. Racial insults are not conducive to convincing the targets of the bigotry to join you.

"Maybe another time," Marcese offered lamely. "I know-a how you feel. We'll talk-a again. I'll call-a you."

He got up and pointed at the body while shrugging his shoulders. He was asking, "Should we take him?"

"As I said, we'll take care of your honky mother-fuckin' bro'. You're guests. Least we can do."

As they left, each took a last look at Cusumano's body. His colourful clothes were a mess.

At their office, Marcese and Valenti placed the necessary phone call to The Butcher. They did not know if he would be more disappointed at having lost a son-in-law or a business deal.

"Ain't got good news," Marcese started. "They don't wanna deal."

The Butcher said nothing when Marcese added, "One more thing. Luciano ... there was-a some trouble. He didn't make it out."

"I gotta lot of problems," The Butcher said. "Gotta no time to think about him. Maybe later."

To which the congregants in the First Baptist Church would have responded, *"I don't worry ... Jesus is awaitin' ... He don't forsake no one. Amen."*

CHAPTER 15

ADMITTEDLY, MARCESE AND VALENTI were somewhat shocked by the Rev. Johnson's decisive action. He was not intimidated by The Butcher, nor did he fear the potential consequences. He acted quickly and firmly. No hesitation. While surprised and a little pissed, they also were impressed by his take-charge attitude.

"That guy don't-a fool 'round," said Marcese with admiration in his voice. "If he was white and Italian, we could use-a him."

"Yeah, nothin' we can do about that," Valenti said.

"I like-a what I see, but I don't understand. He gotta do that just because he called a nigger? The nigger a little too sensitive?"

"Who knows?" answered Valenti. "Never understood them. He don't understand, he could make a lot more money."

They tried to put the incident behind them. These things sometimes happen. Can't be helped. No use wasting energy on what could not be changed.

To assuage their grief, Marcese scheduled a trip to see Benito "The Money Maker" Ferrari in Florida, the financial adviser to the Marcese and Galente families.

Galente would join in this regularly scheduled foray, and they invited Valenti along, sort of a bonus for having witnessed the Harlem episode. Help him forget.

Marcese and Galente had between one and three million to play around with, but the traditional and legal interest rates hardly fulfilled their desired financial objectives. At those rates, they felt cheated. Nothing but chicken feed.

Ferrari was what might be called a "financial guru." He had the golden touch. He always made money. He was the New York mobsters' key adviser on investments, and he earned fortunes for them. Some of his recommendations, a few, were legal while others involved complicated financial entanglements that clients like Marcese and Galente did not understand. Legal, illegal, they did not care as long as the return on their investments was in double digits.

Even the government that periodically audited Ferrari could not figure out all his shenanigans. He was cheating, no question. They just did not know how and couldn't prove it.

While extremely anxious to see their money grow, they nevertheless hated meetings with Ferrari, whom they considered, in the words of Galente, "a complete asshole." He was endured but not embraced by the mob.

The issue with Ferrari was that while Italian himself, he showed little, if any, respect for his Italian mobster clients or their culture. He insulted them by innuendo, gossipping about some, and was generally terribly infuriating. He did not realize how he was alienating the very people to whom he should have been solicitous. He did not consider that he might be endangering himself with his more than boorish behaviour. In short, he was arrogant, and obnoxious.

If it weren't for his financial talents, he either would have had his arms and legs broken, or worse, and he would never have been allowed to work with *the* families. Given Ferrari's financial skills at making money, his insults were ignored. A man could take a lot of verbal abuse when he knew the rewards are millions of dollars. Money soothed a lot of hurts and, as Marcese said when he anointed Rossini a mobster, money even makes stuttering acceptable.

"I don't know how much of that shithead I can take," said Galente on the plane to Florida. "He really is a shithead."

"Tommy Boy, sometimes you need-a patience," Marcese said, playing the elder statesman. "You no wrong but he make-a us money. For lots-a money, he can call me names. He no make-a money, that's another matter. Then, Tommy Boy, you and me talk."

They arrived at Tampa International Airport, stopped for something to eat before driving to an isolated area on Sanibel Island where Ferrari lived in a huge, rambling white ranch-style home. Statues of Italian heroes and religious figures were all over the grounds. The property totalled fifteen acres and had a couple of short golf holes on which Ferrari practised.

The forty three year old Ferrari was alerted to his guests' arrival by a secret security system, and he met them at the front door. Not only was he obnoxious but he was sloppy as well. His shirts were never tucked in, his ties always had spots on them, and he drooled continually. If that was not enough, he scratched his crotch constantly even in the presence of others, including women. Always unshaven, his hair was never combed and he looked and smelled like he hadn't bathed in weeks. He probably hadn't.

"Welcome," he shouted from the front porch as he massaged his testicles. "Welcome. You gonna go home richer than you came."

After the usual handshakes and short embraces, very brief given Ferrari's body odour, the three were invited to Ferrari's family room where he had drinks and cigars waiting. They made small talk for a few minutes, and it did not take Ferrari long to brag about his achievements and criticize the Americanization of his Italian guests.

"I got a new wife," Ferrari began. "She's twenty five, big tits, tight ass. And she's Italian."

He got out of his chair and with his hand motioned them to join him at the door wall. He pointed to the Olympic-size swimming pool where his wife – wife number four – was standing in her bikini. She was beautiful. Jewels, furs and fancy, expensive cars had provided Ferrari with a trophy wife. After the first few weeks, she hardly let him touch her.

There was a reason Ferrari scratched his groin.

"I don't know what you think, but Italians should marry Italians," he continued. Within a half hour of the visit, he had insulted Marcese and Galente because both had married American women. "I say something, she listens. She does what I say."

He also did not reflect that Marcese and Galente might have some feelings for *famiglia*, that despite occasional and sometimes not-so-occasional infidelity, they might just care for their wives and children.

As if he had not said enough, he added, "American women are pigs and whores." Uncharacteristically realizing that perhaps, just perhaps, his visitors might be married to American women, he quickly added, "not all American women."

Galente, visibly angry, told Ferrari, "Whatever happens in America happens in Italy, too. Ain't no different. The world the same everywhere."

Ferrari, showing rare sensitivity, started to "explain" when Marcese interrupted him.

"We no have lot of time, Benito," said Marcese,

anxious to avoid what he considered an unnecessary confrontation. "Let's do business."

"How much you got?" Ferrari asked.

"About two million. Could get another mill or so, if needed."

Ferrari excused himself, saying he needed some papers. When he left, Galente could not restrain himself. "This guy is a real asshole"

Always the philosopher, Marcese – The Brains – countered, "An asshole who make-a us money without risk from them feds. You have-a thin skin."

Having heard the Harlem story, Galente was tempted to call the Rev. Johnson and ask him to make a quick trip to Florida.

When Ferrari returned with a briefcase, he asked them all to join him in his office in another room at the back of the house. Valenti demurred from joining them, saying "If you need me, I'll be by the pool." Valenti recognized he could not help with complicated financial negotiations. What's more, he did not see any stables on the grounds.

Valenti opened the door wall and walked out. He spotted Ferrari's wife sunning herself on the other side of the pool and slowly sauntered in her direction. She was topless, lying on her stomach with her head facing Valenti. He stopped within five feet of her, pulled up a lawn chair and introduced himself.

"I'm Leona," she said.

As they made small talk for about an hour, Valenti thought he saw interest in him in her eyes. She was exquisite. Valenti asked himself, how the fuck could she fuck that slob?

"You here for long?" she asked.

"Only as long at the meeting lasts," Valenti said.

"Well, we'll have to hurry. Put some of this on my back, will you?"

Valenti squeezed suntan lotion into his hands, and knelt down beside Leona. He applied the lotion to the top of her shoulders and slowly inched his way down her back. Ever so slowly. He continued his downward path, expecting her to protest but she didn't.

He hesitated. Suddenly, he remembered Gisele, but his desire was too powerful to cool his lust. Anyway, he rationalized, this would be a quickie, not even a one-night-stand. What's more, Gisele was thousands of miles away and would never know. And, thus far, Gisele was not a sure thing. Yes, he wanted Gisele. Who knows? Lots of things could still happen. Leona would be forgotten by the time he boarded his plane. So, what the hell.

His thoughts of Gisele were interrupted when Leone turned over. She took his hands and placed them on her breasts. He did not object, and he massaged her breasts gently. He could hear and see her breathing increase. He kept one hand on her breasts while he moved the other down into her bikini. When he reached between her legs, she gasped and whimpered.

She could see the bulge in his crotch. She reached to touch him and stroked him through his pants. Periodically, she would look toward the house over Valenti's shoulder, wary that her husband, or someone else, might see them. She did so half-heartedly.

Overall, neither seemed concerned that Ferrari might, at any moment, return from his office and catch them getting acquainted. If Ferrari did, Valenti certainly wouldn't give a damn although Leona might have been in danger of becoming the "former" wife number four. She didn't seem to care about that either.

Deciding that some privacy might be in order, she got up from the chaise longue and, with him following, went to a nearby cabana. They entered and he closed the door. He ripped off her bikini and she knelt down before him, arousing him with her mouth, tongue and fingers. He let her continue for a few minutes before he pushed her onto an air mattress where he returned the favour by putting his head between her legs and used his tongue to please her. He could hear Leona moaning.

He tore off his clothes, got on top of her, and thrust himself inside her. She dug her nails so deeply into his back, inflicting scratches and cuts that bled, that if it weren't for the pleasure, he would have complained about the pain. He had his answer. It was clear to him she had not screwed the slob, at least in some time.

She cried out in concert with his thrusting, raising Valenti's concerns that they might be heard. And he was right to have worried. About five minutes of rhythmic thrashing, the door suddenly opened. Standing before them, just as beautiful as Leona, was her sister-in-law, Juliet, also in a bikini.

"Oh my," said Juliet facetiously and flirtatiously. "My brother would not like this."

"So let's not tell him," Valenti said mischievously. "And if you join us, you'll also have a secret from your brother."

With a look on her face that said, "You got to be kidding," Juliet turned around and left. Apparently unable to forget the image or resist the invitation, she returned within a few minutes. She closed the door, removed her top, stepped out of her bottoms. She reached for Leona.

Valenti, naked, stood aside as they plunged their tongues in the other's mouth, sucked on breasts and used their fingers to probe each other.

Watching was interesting but not especially satisfying. Valenti concluded that sex was not a spectator sport. He helped Juliet onto her back and entered her as Leona straddled her sister-in-law's head, facing Valenti. Valenti massaged her breasts while she kissed him as he tried to rouse Juliet to an orgasm.

After a few minutes, he did the same with Leona. He switched so often that had he been asked whom he was screwing, he probably would not have been able to answer. He was inside of Leona when he reached his climax almost simultaneously with her. She shrieked so loudly that he was more than fearful that someone else would hear them. He was not interested in a third woman joining them.

"That's not fair," said Juliet watching the two in the afterglow of their climaxes.

"You're right," said Valenti, and, ever the gentleman, he worked on Juliet with his tongue and finger until she was similarly satisfied.

"You're pretty good," said Juliet. "Who are you?"

It was a paraphrase of the question posed by those who were the beneficiaries of the Good Samaritan work of the Lone Ranger. After defeating the bad guys in his fight for justice, the Lone Ranger would gallop off into the sunset with those he saved, asking, "Who was that masked man, anyway?"

The Lone Ranger never answered, and Valenti was similarly reluctant to offer much information about himself. Hit men don't like to talk about themselves, or reveal details about their lives. They sure don't want to give their names to strangers. Under the circumstances, Valenti, being a fair man, thought it was a reasonable question posed by his beneficiaries, at least one of them (Leone had not asked). After all, they just had quite an introduction.

Agreeing Juliet had a right to some identification, Valenti gave a brief, but vague, explanation, put on his clothes and promised that he would see them again. The women did not know that it might be six months, maybe longer or, most likely, never. It all depended on the financial markets.

He returned to the meeting and listened as Marcese, Galente and Ferrari made financial decisions, none of which he understood. The meeting lasted for another three hours. He realized he could have spent more time with Leone and Juliet.

"That should do it," said Ferrari. "I'll keep you informed. These investments are as good as gold."

As they prepared to leave, he asked, "You want to meet my wife? She's very beautiful."

Marcese and Galente demurred while Valenti, smiling, shook his head, stating, "We already met." He added for good measure, "I met Juliet too."

In the car, Marcese expressed his pleasure on what he thought had been a successful, productive trip. "I think we make-a lots of money quickly. He smart fella."

"He's a pig," said Galente.

Changing the subject slightly, Valenti volunteered, "Tommy Boy you were absolutely right that the world is the same everywhere. He don't know he got whores in his house."

Marcese and Galente did not know what the hell

Valenti was talking about. They looked at him puzzled. Valenti teased them but did not expand on his philosophical observation about whether any country has a monopoly on whores. Ultimately, he relented and described his *ménage à trois.*

At first, they did not believe him until he offered, and not very delicately, very specific details of the episode. They believed him. This was a man they trusted with more sensitive information so why should he lie about screwing two women? He had no need to lie. Valenti did not need any reinforcement for his image as a man. He was secure with himself.

The two laughed uproariously. They could hardly catch their breath. Tears rolled down their eyes.

"You do both?" Marcese asked through his laughter. When Valenti nodded, his boss said, "You do good by American women. Johnny, you uphold their honour. You honourable man."

American women might not have interpreted Valenti's actions in the same way. But then, Marcese was the only one who counted. He was the boss, the one who signed the checks or, rather, distributed the cash.

CHAPTER 16

THE BUTCHER'S PROBLEMS CONTINUED to pile up. He had been rejected by mobster families in New York and by the guy in Brazil, and then he suffered the unkindest, and most unexpected cut of all: he was snubbed by blacks in Harlem. Blacks had stuck it to The Butcher! He'd had just about as much as he could take.

He would have his revenge against any, and all, of those who turned on him. He had to face some troubling and difficult strategic questions. Which one to go after first? Whom should he whack to send a message to the others? Should he open more than one front? Could he fight them all at one time? Was any of it necessary? Should he be happy with what he had?

He was even worried about those on his side, especially Johnny Valenti. The guy was there when all the proposed business deals went down. Coincidence? Maybe not. He learned that Valenti was in bed with the guy in Brazil. That was not quite accurate. He was in bed with the guy's niece. The question was did he have a reason to be concerned? Would Valenti sell him out in Rio, for instance, if his relationship with Gisele Giannola were at stake? He'd have to keep an eye on him. Oh yes, he'd also lost a son-in-law. Admittedly, he wasn't much to write home about but he had been, regrettably, *famiglia.*

Along with business pressures, his daughter weighed heavily on him. It was not easy to forget. He constantly reminded himself that he had a duty. He had to protect the family name. He did what any honourable Sicilian would do. Others in the world lived by the same code. He was not alone, not that it mattered. In some Muslim countries adulterous women were buried with their heads above ground and stoned to death. He found that a bit barbaric, but identified with the mission's objective. Along with some misgivings, he was proud at being able to do a deed that others would consider unspeakable, beyond comprehension.

Despite all these clouds hanging over his head, The Butcher was not too depressed because he lived by the creed that it never gets darker than midnight. And, for him, it was midnight. So, since it could only get lighter, he was somewhat optimistic about his future. He was looking forward to the dawn.

His many organizational and personal problems notwithstanding, The Butcher was very clear about his next step. All his efforts and resources had to be devoted to a new pain in the ass in the form of Henry T. Hawk, the recently appointed head of the FBI. Other issues paled against what The Butcher believed was the threat, a potentially fatal threat, from Hawk. This guy, The Butcher concluded, was to be feared.

Why? Hawk was just like The Butcher except on the law-abiding side of society. Hawk would do anything to succeed; his ambitions had no limits. The Butcher recognized these traits in Hawk although he failed to see the similarities to his own personality. Hawk, a fifty six year old career FBI agent, had worked his way up through the ranks. About a year before The Butcher's business crises piled up, the President of the United States, with much fanfare, had named Hawk director of the FBI. At the press conference announcing Hawk's appointment, the President described the traditional objectives he expected Hawk to pursue, and he made a special point of wanting his new director to go after the mob, to wipe it out or, at least, force it to set up shop elsewhere, somewhere other than the United States. Let them create off-shore operations. Just get them off U.S. soil.

"Let me be perfectly clear," the President had said,

"one of the primary objectives of my administration is to get rid of organized crime, once and for all, in the U.S. The crime syndicates have weakened our moral and social fibre and it is time, indeed, it is long overdue, that we put them out of business. And I believe Henry T. Hawk is the man for the job. I have complete faith in him, and he will have all the resources he needs to complete this mission. "

Hawk beamed as the president spoke so highly of him. He seemed to be drooling. He was "Brutus-ly" ambitious and he had played hardball politics to be appointed top cop. True, he did not stick it to anyone as Brutus did to Caesar, but his political tactics were very effective. He left many an agent politically wounded. Marcus Antonius, more commonly known as Marc Anthony, who did not think much of Brutus, would not have considered Hawk an honourable man either. Indeed, one reason the President anointed Hawk was that the President admired his no-holds barred approach to getting the job. The President identified with him. After all, the tactics and strategies needed to become president of the United States would not have been endorsed by Mother Teresa. Hawk had the kind of traits, the President believed, needed to confront and defeat the underworld. He possessed a sort of killer instinct, so to speak. Couldn't have any namsy-pansies in and around the White House.

"Thank you, Mr. President," Hawk said in appreciation of the President's accolades. "This is a very special honour, and I am humbled by your faith in me. Let me state emphatically, I will do all in my power to eradicate organized crime in our country. Mr. President, I share your passion and commitment to this objective."

With such a pledge to live up to, Hawk launched his tenure with a bang not a whimper. In the first year, he arrested dozens of organized crime figures. He seized millions of dollars worth of illegal drugs, broke up prostitution rings as well as gambling and money laundering operations. He was on the front page of a major daily newspaper at least once a week, and he was featured on the covers of several magazines, including *Time* and *Newsweek*. Hawk was more successful in twelve months than his predecessors had been in the previous twenty years.

Overall, the President was pleased. Hawk was making him look good and the PR was exceptional. In exchange, he was prepared to surrender the organized crime vote. Hawk was, as The Butcher would describe him, "a ball buster." In conversations with Marcese, Galente, and Valenti, The Butcher expressed his consternation.

"He causes too much-a trouble," he said. "We gotta get rid of him. He gotta go. Nobody does this to us, to me. Nobody."

The Butcher's obsession with the FBI director was twofold. Not only was he causing The Butcher unprecedented problems, but The Butcher hated cops with a passion. Next to rats, cops were number one on his hit list.

When one of The Butcher's cousins decided to become a cop, The Butcher was apoplectic. Having a cop in the family or even socializing with one was a violation of his most revered principles. In addition, it would not help his reputation to have it known that the Monteleones had a cop in their family. It could make him vulnerable, very vulnerable. His instincts told him this would create a conflict of interest. He could not picture a cop sitting at family dinners on holidays.

When the cousin argued that it had been his lifelong ambition to put on a uniform and uphold the law, he also wisely pledged not to interfere with The Butcher's business. The Butcher ignored the cousin's impassioned promises and pleas. The Butcher was not one to support the notion that people should choose careers they find satisfying and exciting because they will spend a lifetime working in them.

Instead, The Butcher had his cousin maimed in a beating, a beating that left him with a bad limp. The physical disability disqualified him for the police force. As part of his plan, The Butcher gave his cousin a job, and the cousin, while unhappy at first, was elated when he earned more money in one year than he would have as a cop in ten. With such success, he became a cop hater as well. It all turned into a win-win for the two parties involved, and cemented the family relationship.

When The Butcher first ranted about Hawk, Marcese, Galente and Valenti, at the time, thought The Butcher was just letting off steam. Raids, confiscation of drugs and cash along with the subsequent trials, were part of the cost of doing business. It was called overhead. The Butcher seemed to become more paranoid about Hawk as time passed. The more they heard, the more they thought he was out of control. He was becoming obsessive, believing in his own invulnerability.

When Marcese raised a mild objection, The Butcher looked him in the eye, and said, "You give my soldiers fifty percent of whatta you got, and we forget about Hawk." Marcese fell silent. The Butcher had made his point.

In their respective jobs, Hawk and The Butcher were all too aware of each other's objectives. The Butcher was on Hawk's agenda, at the top. Hawk knew that The Butcher knew he was doing business with a target on his back. The Butcher knew that Hawk knew he knew. The two were involved in a deadly cat-and-mouse game. Ultimately, the game would be fatal to whoever became the mouse.

The Butcher, in analyzing various anti-Hawk plans, could have proceeded with the most common approach. That would have involved killing individual FBI agents to intimidate others, and to dissuade their boss from continuing his crusade. The cops might consider the potential death toll too high a price to be paid. He could bet his cards on the supposition that they were not prepared to sacrifice lives, that political pressure would force them to stop their anti-mob campaign. That the public, appalled by the carnage, would not stand for it.

The Butcher had misgivings. He had little doubt that Hawk was tough and prepared to lose some men, many men, to achieve his objective. Military generals always consider the prospective fatality toll when going to battle. They weigh the value of the goal against the expected deaths. The Butcher figured Hawk had done the same. The tit for tat, he murdering FBI agents and the feds killing his men, could go on for years, as in the past, with no meaningful results. The Butcher did not want to engage in a futile war that might not achieve his desired results.

Thus, only one anti-Hawk tactic would work. He would have to whack the FBI director. An ambitious goal, indeed, but he thought he could pull it off. If he were successful, it would send a message to the most powerful man in the world, the President of the United States, while putting the rest of the world on notice. No one would ever challenge him again, including those in organized crime, without thinking twice. He would be the unquestioned king.

In one intercontinental telephone call, The Butcher told Marcese, Galente and Valenti, it was time. When they asked, "Time for what?" he seemed hurt by the question.

He had told them over and over about his plans to whack Hawk, and they had the nerve to ask, "Time for what?" Weren't they listening? They got problems hearing?

"What's-a matter with you?" he shouted with irritation. "I tell-a you many times we gotta whack Hawk. That's the time."

While wanting to argue against the Hawk mission, they recognized that it would be futile. It was evident The Butcher had made up his mind. He had given the assignment to a special unit, a sort of Green Beret-Special Forces outfit that he had organized with the best, most brutal and cold-blooded soldiers in his underworld empire. He told his three-man U.S. delegation its job was to provide strategic and tactical advice if such support was requested by his special team.

"He's gonna get us all killed," Valenti told his two bosses.

As The Butcher's hostility toward Hawk grew with each drug bust and arrest, Valenti was becoming more and more disillusioned with The Butcher. The Hawk mission, he thought, was a hare-brained idea. The tension between him and The Butcher was increasing. He suspected that The Butcher did not trust him and Valenti believed that his relationship with Gisele Giannola probably had added to that mistrust. While a dedicated hit man, he could not support The Butcher's random violence and killings. Inevitably, someday the tension between the two would explode. They were two star-crossed mobsters.

Meanwhile, he put his reservations about The Butcher's plans for Hawk and his mistrust of the boss of bosses on the back burner. Not much he could do in any event. Perhaps fate would intervene and somehow derail The Butcher's anti-Hawk strategy.

Valenti had a more immediate interest, a burning interest, to visit Gisele Giannola.

CHAPTER 17

JOHNNY VALENTI WAS PANTING next to his lover. He had been back three weeks, the best three weeks of his life. He was infatuated with Gisele Giannola, and most of the time, when not making love, he was trying to convince her to marry him, and to return with him to New York.

He had forgotten, totally, about The Butcher. If someone had asked him about The Butcher, he probably would have asked, "Who?" Gisele Giannola was a very effective anti-Butcher antidote.

Gisele Giannola liked, perhaps even loved, Valenti but she had misgivings. Her reservations resulted from suspicions, suspicions about his work. She did not know exactly what her boyfriend did for a living, although she suspected that his work might not be legal. Similarly, she never asked her uncle about his business, but the signs were all too apparent that he earned his money from less than wholesome activities.

Valenti, while not confessing his speciality, did not try to hide the fact that his work would not win any Good Samaritan awards from fraternal organizations. He was also convinced that telling her "I kill people for a living" would not help convince her to become his wife. True, Gisele Giannola was an understanding woman who would want her husband to be happy in his work, but she had limits.

Without being explicit, he promised her, "I can change." From what, he did not explain. He argued persistently that he could achieve a Dr. Jekyll-Mr. Hyde transformation. In his case, it would require a change from Mr. Hyde to the good doctor, and he would have to do it without the secret potion.

"If no one believes that I love you. I can hardly believe it. It is because they and I never thought it was in me. I swear this even surprises me."

Valenti's exclamations of his love for Gisele were not the most romantic. If spoken in a play or movie, they would hardly evoke tears from even the most emotional of women. They were heartfelt despite coming from an ex-convict who had murdered people and was on a payroll to kill more.

"I need to think," said Gisele Giannola, not too unreasonably. "Go talk to my uncle."

Valenti half expected it would come to that. Gisele Giannola owed much to her uncle; indeed, he had saved her after her father's life was taken by The Butcher. While pursuing Gisele, Valenti had started planning his strategy to get Giannola's blessing. It would not be easy.

"No," is all Giannola said when Valenti made his pitch. "You work-a for The Butcher. He kill my family. Put me out of business. No."

Valenti was reluctant to use the "It was just business" approach. He may not have been the brightest of hit men, but he decided against that argument. He liked Giannola and thought the man was justified in his beef. Despite his profession, Valenti had a sense of justice. He had no hard feelings toward the survivors of those he killed who might feel animosity toward him. He understood their anger and desire to get even. Only natural. He followed what some might consider a weird set of ethics, but at least he had one.

Valenti was persistent with Giannola. In making his argument, Valenti went into a long monologue on how he told The Butcher that while in Brazil to woo Gisele, he would try to convince Giannola to join The Butcher in his drug distribution business. Taking a risk that Giannola would not sell him out, Valenti confessed that he had misgivings about The Butcher.

"Too powerful, if you ask me," said Valenti, surprising Giannola.

Valenti spent most of his time trying to assure Giannola that he would treat his niece with respect. He would protect her from his professional environment and all its entanglements.

"She'll never know," he said. "She will be my wife and a mother."

Giannola was torn. Giannola had heard his share of bullshit. He prided himself in being able to see through con men. Despite his ambivalence, he thought Valenti meant what he said. Giannola believed Valenti. Valenti's criticism of The Butcher helped. The proverb which held that "the enemy of my enemy is my friend" had it right. While Valenti was hardly The Butcher's enemy, at least, not yet, Giannola was affected by the criticism of the Sicilian mobster king. It was about time someone understood why he was angry at the slaughter of members of his family. Too long in coming.

"I think about it," he told Valenti as the latter returned to his intended for another night of love-making.

"You'll be my wife," Valenti assured Gisele and, as he predicted, a month later Gisele Giannola became Mrs. Johnny Valenti, the wife of one of the most effective and successful hit men in the Big Apple, or elsewhere. Whatever misgivings she might have had, she was now the wife of a man considered at the top of the field. She had married the best, and she was content as she flew with her new husband to a new world in New York.

Valenti was anxious to begin his life as a "family"

man. He was returning to a scenario in which his boss – *the* boss – was making plans to kill the director of the FBI of the United States of America. Sometimes problems pile up while you're away. At times, it hardly pays to go on vacation.

While Valenti, Marcese and Galente worried about The Butcher's obsession and plans for Hawk, they resigned themselves to the fact they were helpless. If they objected too strongly, they would become targets. It was no fun worrying whether your car would explode when you turned on the ignition or having bodyguards constantly circling around you. Regardless of the security measures they might implement, ultimately, someone like Valenti would eventually be successful. It would only be a matter of time. So they accepted the inevitable and hoped that somehow The Butcher would come to his senses. He would not.

Valenti spent most of his time with his new bride. One of the advantages of being a hit man was that the hours were good, very good. There was little travel, unless the contract involved taking out someone in other parts of the country or overseas. On most days, he would be home for dinner. What more could a newlywed ask for?

During the first year of his marriage, he only had two jobs and they did not require a major time commitment. Both involved low-ranking soldiers. One was a rat and the other was caught skimming from the top.

He whacked the rat in the living room of his home. Nothing gave Valenti more satisfaction than taking care of those who sang to the cops. No one was lower on his rating scale than a rat. He made sure other potential rats got the message by shoving a canary into the mouth of his victim. He made no attempts to get rid of the body because he, and his bosses, wanted the word to go out via the media which would report that the victim was found choking on a canary. They always hoped the media would publish photos of the victim with the canary. That would really help deliver the message. But even the tabloids considered that in bad taste.

Valenti had skipped the canary ceremony in the execution of DeSante when he avenged being framed for murder because he wanted no trace or even a hint, at the time, that he might have been involved. He would have been a suspect because it was no secret that he wanted to get even.

As to the swindler who tried to swindle the mob, Valenti killed him while he was fishing so disposal of the body was easy. Sometimes one gets lucky on the job.

Other than those two jobs, Valenti had lots of time on his hands. Gisele never asked how he managed to have so much time off while making a considerable amount of money. Not that she was not tempted to ask about her husband's work. What wife would not want to know? She intuitively concluded it was better not to ask.

He was the perfect husband, catering to his wife's every whim. When she became pregnant, about a year after their marriage, Valenti was even more attentive. If Gisele had cravings for particular foods, Valenti would get them for her, at any hour. He would go to stores to buy the food late at night or early in the morning, regardless of the weather.

Admittedly, he did not just do this because of his love for Gisele or to prove that he was a responsive and caring husband. Valenti acted because he shared the belief of many Italians that if the cravings were not fulfilled, the baby would be born with birth marks, marks that would be the colour of the desired food.

Thus, Valenti in trying to satisfy his wife's unusual requests for unusual foods at unusual hours, he was also trying to ward off unwanted evil spirits. Some hit men have strange quirks.

Just about the time Valenti's wife gave birth to twins – Little Johnny and Lucia – he heard from Marcese and Galente that The Butcher was coming to New York. They feared the worst, and they were not wrong to worry. It – the anti-Hawk program – had taken more than a year to plan. The Butcher was ready. He had the Hawk in his sights. The strategy, planning, and tactics had been studied countless times. Nothing would be left to chance. The Butcher and his special team were prepared for the execution of Operation Hawk. They were confident of success. In their estimation, it could not fail. If only President Kennedy had prepared as comprehensively for the Bay of Pigs invasion in Cuba only three months after his inauguration in 1961.

For the plan's execution, The Butcher had reserved the entire top floor of a forty story hotel at the outskirts of New York City. This very special occasion could be attended by "invitation only." The hotel faced neighbouring Newark, about thirteen miles west in New Jersey.

The Butcher requested the honour of the attendance of Marcese, Galente and Valenti. For the three, the invitation presented one of those very ticklish political problems, like deciding whether to attend the wedding of a relative not particularly liked. As with the relative, they would have preferred to have shunned the party. Given the politics involved, and the credibility problem of all three calling in sick, they accepted the invitation but kept their feelings to themselves. Wisely so.

Marcese, Galente and Valenti car-pooled and were

heading to the hotel when Valenti, the driver, noticed in the rear view mirror, that they were being followed. In their business, checking the rear view mirror was a natural and inseparable part of their jobs. Indeed, when new drivers were hired, they were watched to see if they were watching.

Quickly, Valenti swerved into a parking garage. After stashing the car on the fifth floor, they took a staircase down to the first floor, and raced to a subway station. Fairly certain that they had lost the feds, the three jumped on a train headed for Newark.

While always sensitive to the possibility of being followed, they were on high alert that day primarily because The Butcher had told them to be extra cautious. He was worried that, despite all his careful planning, word might have leaked out that he was in town for a "special project."

Given modern, sophisticated technology, the feds had exceptional eavesdropping capabilities. To avoid possible eavesdropping, on many occasions, whether in their homes, cars or restaurants, the mobsters would communicate with *pizzini*, little bits of paper that they would destroy after reading them.

Shortly after the trio sat down on the subway which was only about half filled, a uniformed cop collapsed about ten feet from them. The tension in the car was evident with no one knowing exactly what to do. Marcese and Galente looked down at the cop and stepped away as did some other passengers. Valenti did not. Instead, he ran to the cop. He undid the cop's tie, unbuttoned his shirt, checked the pulse and opened the cop's mouth to make certain that the airways were clear. As Marcese and Galente watched in shock, Valenti started CPR and mouth-to-mouth resuscitation.

Marcese bent over Valenti. "Whatcha doin'? This is a pig."

When Valenti ignored Marcese, Galente interceded, "You put your mouth to that pig? He goes, we got lots more pigs in New York. What's the big deal?"

Marcese tried again. "Make-a New Yorkers happy, Johnny, let him die. We got too many pigs anyway."

Valenti paid no attention to either of them. When they reached the next stop, Marcese and Galente pulled him aside inside the subway station.

"What's wrong with you, Johnny?" Marcese asked on the platform. "Goin' soft on me?"

Valenti explained, "He don't do nothin' to me. He's just a cop making a living. If he was gonna come after me, that's another matter. I would go after him like I do rats, deadbeats and cheats. I go after them guys with no honour."

Marcese and Galente accepted a little of Valenti's philosophy, the part about rats, deadbeats and cheats. They made no distinctions when it came to cops. All of them were fair game.

Given the pressure to make it to The Butcher's special celebration, this was not a time for a philosophical debate with Valenti on bad cops, who deserved whatever came their way and more, and good cops, assuming there were any. They would save that for another day.

When Marcese asked Valenti if he were getting soft, there was more substance to his question than he realized. He did not know about the results, or lack of results, on a hit he had assigned to Valenti a few weeks earlier.

The contract involved a fifty seven year old owner of a dry cleaning store in Brooklyn. A compulsive gambler, he owed twenty five grand and most of that resulted from a mind-boggling interest rate. He had missed deadline after deadline. Marcese ran out of patience and ordered, Valenti to take care of the problem.

Valenti was greeted at the store by the sound of the bell that rang when customers opened the door. The owner looked up to find Valenti, whom he had never met, standing in the doorway. Given Valenti's demeanour, the store owner, even without an introduction, understood, understood fully, the man's mission.

He turned pale, and trembled. He looked at his wife who, seeing distress in her husband's eyes, immediately knew something was wrong, terribly wrong. She watched helplessly as her husband and Valenti left the store without ever saying a word.

"Drive," Valenti told his hostage when they reached his car. The man followed Valenti's orders, and his instructions on directions. They drove for a few minutes before he addressed his captive.

"How much you owe?" Valenti asked.

"I think twenty five grand," the driver stammered in a quivering voice. "I can get it by tomorrow," he lied.

When Valenti ignored the promise of payment, the man continued, "I got a wife, kids. Please, I pay tomorrow. I'll throw in another grand."

The man's pleas were futile. Valenti had heard these desperate promises many times under these circumstances. Still, Valenti looked at the man with more interest than he did all his other victims. He saw a man about five foot six, bald with greying hair around the side of his head. He was wrinkled, and his complexion was flushed. He wore clothes that were soiled and he appeared much older than fifty seven. This guy obviously did not have a pot to piss in.

Why was Valenti evaluating his whackee-designate? He had never done that before. Why was he taking inventory, taking a measure of the man? Why did he even ask how much he owed? The circumstances should and did not matter; they never had before. He always approached his assignments with the philosophy that he was a professional and had a job to do. Kids, no kids, did not matter. Married, unmarried, who cares? Sick or injured, not his problem.

This time, for the first time, it was different and Valenti did not know why. He could not explain his ambivalence, hesitancy, even sentimentality. He could not understand his mood.

When they reached their destination -- isolated woods about forty miles from the store -- they got out of the car. At gunpoint, Valenti ordered the store owner into the woods.

"Stop," is all Valenti said after a fifteen minute walk. He told the man, who was facing him, to turn around.

The command was unusual. Never before had he showed any signs of sympathy toward his victims by not forcing them to watch him at the moment of death. He received some pleasure on seeing the eyes of his victims usually fixated on the barrel of the gun.

Then it happened. He hesitated. His arm was outstretched and ready. He did not squeeze the trigger. After a few seconds, he lowered his arm and brought it up again. Again, nothing happened.

Exasperated, Valenti approached the store owner, and turned him around. The man was shaking and drenched in sweat. Valenti could almost hear his teeth chatter.

"You disappear," Valenti instructed. "You call no one, no one, got it."

The man nodded so hard he easily could have suffered a whiplash.

"You don't call your wife, kids, anyone for six months. Then you can call and have them disappear with you. No one better be able to find you, especially me."

The man fell to his knees and grabbed Valenti around his hips, continually repeating, "Yes, thank you, yes, thank you … yes, thank you …"

"Get up," Valenti shouted. He stuck the revolver in the store owner's mouth, warning him, "I hear anything about you, and I'll come back and blow your brains out." The man seemed to understand.

Believing he had made his point, Valenti left the man in the woods, and drove off, admittedly somewhat confused about himself. What was happening to him? What the hell was wrong?

He had saved the man's life and probably cured him of his gambling addiction. Indeed, Gamblers Anonymous might consider Valenti's treatment. It was fast, inexpensive, and provided a sure antidote for gambling and other addictions. It was guaranteed to work.

Why was he unable to do his job? Was he going soft? Was he through? What had happened? Why would he risk his own life to save a deadbeat son-of-a-bitch he did not even know?

He had all these questions but no answers, only worries, as he headed back to the city. Maybe it was just one of those days. Everyone has a bad day on the job. He would worry about it if and when it ever happened again. He doubted it would. He would just have to wait and see.

Neither Marcese nor Galente had any idea that Valenti had faltered. If they had, Valenti would not be car-pooling with them. Even in the *Mafia*, you were judged on the company you keep. Moreover, they would have had to inflict some punishment, probably the one Valenti was unable to carry out. They never found out. The store owner did an excellent job following Valenti's instructions. He had a very good incentive to avoid making any mistakes.

The three did not discuss the cop incident as they continued to their meeting where The Butcher would implement his plan to kill the nation's number one cop, the director of the Federal Bureau of Investigation. If The Butcher were successful, and The Butcher was confident he would be, CPR, the kind Valenti used on the cop in the subway, would not help the FBI director.

"Welcome to my party," said The Butcher as he greeted Marcese, Galente and Valenti. "I will show you power today, my power."

The three tried hard to hide their concern and opposition to taking on the full power of the United States government. Not only did they believe the entire idea was crazy, they did not comprehend how The Butcher intended to whack Hawk. Because of his cause, going after the mob, Hawk was probably the most protected public official in the U.S., not including the President. He had a motorcade consisting of about six cars in front of his and another six behind. The cars were bullet proof, and he was followed by helicopters in the air. Days before his arrival to any destination, security personnel checked the grounds and surroundings for any potential dangers.

It seemed to Marcese, Galente and Valenti that it would be impossible to get near Hawk or assassinate him with the most sophisticated long-range rifle. Security was just too tight.

In the room with them were more than thirty other guests, including members of The Butcher's special team. On a table next to a wall were numerous pairs of binoculars.

"Have a drink, *salute*," The Butcher said. "We still have about a half hour."

At about the time The Butcher was entertaining his party, Henry T. Hawk landed at Newark International Airport. Followed by an entourage of security personnel, he made his way to the tarmac toward microphones set up by the media.

"Thank you ladies and gentlemen for coming out to the airport," Hawk started. "I want to announce to you today that we have in custody Tony "Scar Face" Celleni, one of the leaders in the *Mafia*. Mr. Celleni has been indicted on fifty one counts, including murder, arson, money laundering and illegal gambling.

"This is a big day for the U.S. His arrest is a major blow to organized crime in this country. I am proud of the work of the FBI and many other agencies that assisted in the investigation and arrest of Mr. Celleni. I want to assure everyone this is not the end of our mission. We will continue our efforts to tirelessly hunt down other *Mafia* bosses like Mr. Celleni until we rid ourselves of organized crime in the U.S. Thank you very much."

Hawk left the microphones and headed toward his car that was parked in the middle of his long motorcade. Helicopters flew overhead as Hawk drove off toward the New Jersey Turnpike.

Under normal circumstances, The Butcher would have been very pissed at Hawk's announcement of the arrest. Even had he heard it, he would not have been upset because this was, for him, a very special day.

About twenty minutes after Hawk left the airport, The Butcher checked his watch and told his guests to pick up a pair of binoculars and join him at the windows facing Newark. Peering through binoculars, the guests look liked bird watchers searching for a rare species or fans at a race track. They followed The Butcher's instructions but did not know or understand what they were supposed to see. They did as they were told. No one complained.

The Butcher looked at his watch again. "You need-a patience. Don't worry. About three minutes," is all he said. He continued checking the time as he peered through his binoculars toward the Newark airport. Exactly three minutes later, The Butcher and his guests heard what they thought was thunder, and then saw several columns of smoke rise in the distance.

The Butcher beamed and indulged in nothing but self-satisfaction. He had achieved his objective, and revelled in the fact that he was the only one who could have pulled it off. No one else in the world would have even tried what he had accomplished. The Butcher was pleased with himself, very pleased.

He turned to his party. Holding a drink, he bragged, "We do good job. No more Hawk."

Then he downed his drink with one swallow.

Without any explanation from The Butcher on what had happened, all seemed to understand that Hawk had been murdered in some kind of explosion, a massive one. Even though miles away, they heard the blast and saw the smoke. It had to have been a huge operation.

The guests, all seasoned tough gangsters, were awed, many of them letting out gasps. No one asked any questions. The Butcher did not have to explain details.

The guests, intuitively, grasped what had happened. Whatever they thought about The Butcher's determination to get Hawk, developing and carrying out the plan took ingenuity.   Yes,   criminal   ingenuity   but   ingenuity nevertheless. They were impressed.

What The Butcher's men had done was to bury very powerful explosives under a quarter- mile section of the turnpike. At the appropriate moment, The Butcher's team set off the explosives by remote control. Timing was essential, the key element in the operation. With the help of moles in U.S. agencies, they managed to obtain Hawk's schedule. The media also helped by publishing much of the director's itinerary, and giving the time the FBI director would make a major announcement at the airport that morning.

The explosion not only killed Hawk but seventeen security personnel and eighteen civilians driving on the other side of the turnpike. More than sixty people were also injured.

"I'm a going home to celebrate in Cinisi," The Butcher said. "We no gonna have trouble no more. No one screws with-a me. No one."

The guests applauded, including Marcese and Galente. Hardly enthusiastic, they were fulfilling their obligation as invited guests to this special event. Valenti did not share in the excitement. He was aghast. He could not hide his disdain, anger, frustration, and The Butcher noticed. He did not like Valenti's lack of enthusiasm at the completion of such a successful mission. Here he was celebrating and Valenti demurred from participating. Not nice. It was another black mark against Valenti. The Butcher made another decision on the spot. He would have to address his "Valenti problem" sooner or later, probably sooner. For the time being, he put Valenti out of his mind. He wanted to savour the moment. He would put Valenti on his "to do" list.

As to the assassination of Hawk, if only The Butcher had read a little history. He might have pondered over the observation of the commander of the Japanese fleet, Admiral Isoroku Yamamoto, who after the attack on the U.S. Naval fleet at Pearl Harbor, said, "I fear all we have done is awaken a sleeping giant."

That is exactly what The Butcher had done. He awakened a sleeping giant, a giant that would torment him and his crime syndicate as never before.

CHAPTER 18

THE SLEEPING GIANT AWOKE with a start.

"This brazen, heartless and vicious attack will not go unpunished," promised the President of the United States as he spoke to the nation on television. "Those responsible will be brought to justice. I make that pledge to the American people.

"Further, I call on the entire civilized world to join us. I ask that the United Nations make the eradication of organized crime a major strategic objective. I implore the UN to help the U.S. in finding and punishing those responsible for this hideous crime."

While the following remark was not exactly politically correct, the President added, "I call on the officials of Italy and Sicily to join in this crusade. And it is and must be a crusade. Organized crime, regrettably, has a long history in that part of the world, and some of it has been exported to the U.S. and other countries. Those are not the kind of imports we are looking for.

"We have no quarrel with the people of Italy or Sicily. They are our friends. While a proud, law-abiding, loving people, they must face the fact that organized crime has deep roots in their countries. They must help stamp out this insidious disease in our society."

At the press conference following his speech, the President elaborated on his remarks.

"This attack was not only an attack on the U.S. but the entire civilized world."

Reporter: "Do you know what the objective was?"

"Absolutely. It is all very obvious. It was to murder a man, Henry T. Hawk, who was making progress in destroying the *Mafia,* and ridding us of this plague. They decided to kill him. The objective is very clear to me. Mr. Hawk gave his life for this country and his death will be avenged."

Reporter: "How do you know he was the target?"

"I can't go into all the details, obviously. We have absolutely no doubt about the reason for the attack. Let me make one thing clear to those who carried out this senseless murder. We are only more determined in our efforts. We will work even more diligently. Our memorial to the hero, Henry T. Hawk, will be the arrest, conviction and sentencing of those responsible for this crime."

Reporter: "Specifically, do you know who is responsible?"

"We have some leads which I would rather not discuss. These are good leads based on reliable intelligence. We will have more to say about that sometime in the future."

Reporter: "My sources told me that a powerful figure known as The Butcher in Sicily is involved. Can you say anything about that?"

"I really don't want to get into specific names or suspects. I hope you can understand that. We will keep you informed as well as we can without jeopardizing the investigation."

"What can you tell us about The Butcher?" the reporter followed up.

"Well, we are still investigating," the President offered. "As I said, we don't want to jeopardize the case with premature disclosures."

A reporter from the Italian-American Weekly shouted from the back of the White House press room: "Why you insult the Italian and Sicilian people? Why you call us criminals?"

"If I may, I said no such thing. I have the utmost respect for the people of Italy and Sicily. Some of my best ... What I mean is that many members of my administration are of Italian descent. They are a great people, and we value the immigrants who have made their home in the United States. They are part of our historic melting pot."

While a little politically insensitive in blaming Italians and Sicilians, he apparently wanted to teach a little history about the origins of the *Mafia* in Italy, and how it spread to Sicily.

Overall, the President had a point. The *Mafia,* actually the *Cosa Nostra,* had its roots in Italy where it was started as a secret criminal society in the 19th century. As the organization evolved, "*Mafia*" was used but had different meanings to Italians, including love, respect, honour.

Some scholars and historians maintained "*Mafia*" was an acronym for "*Morta Alla Francia, Italia Anela*" ("*Death to France. This is Italy's Cry)*," that reportedly was first invoked during a rebellion by Sicilians against oppressive French rule in 1282. Others considered that a myth.

Whatever the history of the *Mafia* or *Cosa Nostra*, as the President tried to defend what the Italian scribe considered to be an ethnic slur, the President was helped by another reporter whose job it was to end the press conferences after a half hour or so by saying, "Thank you, Mr. President." The reporter carried out his responsibility during this sensitive exchange, and the President replied, "Thank you." He meant it, not wanting to extend his discussion about his reference to Italians and Sicilians, and left.

The Butcher followed news reports of the President's speech and press conference not with concern, but with pride. He especially liked the question about his possible involvement. How about that? He was making headlines. Not at all bad. His colleagues did not share in his interpretation of the political scenario.

Like the Italian reporter, The Butcher did take some umbrage at the President automatically twinning organized crime with Italians and Sicilians. His "hurt"' notwithstanding, he was sufficiently sophisticated to know that the President was not sacrificing many votes with his disparaging remarks. Non-resident Italians and Sicilians were not eligible to vote in U.S. elections. He was also confident that the President would work to make it up to Italian and Sicilian voters in the U.S. He would bet on it.

As to the politics of the situation, the President's staff had checked the numbers before he gave his speech and they assured him he did not get many votes from the Italian/Sicilian community in the election that took him to the Oval Office. Thus, they counselled him, he could do whatever he thought was right. In this case, he could stand on principle if he believed it helpful to the overall objective and cause.

The Butcher was not able to bask in what he considered his success for long. The President came at him with a vengeance. The FBI, supported by other federal agencies, went on a rampage, arresting suspects, seizing drugs, cash, and arsenals of weapons, while closing gambling and prostitution operations throughout the country.

Organized crime operations in New York, Chicago, Los Angeles, Las Vegas and other cities suffered major setbacks as their leaders and soldiers were arrested in the nationwide sweep. At the same time, other countries, in a show of support, launched similar crackdowns.

Italy and Sicily also conducted a series of raids. The Italian president expressed support for his American counterpart while trying to placate his constituency. Although he shared the views of the Italian-American reporter at the U.S. president's press conference, the Italian president did not make any reference to the ethnic slight. Instead, he said:

"We sympathize with our good friends in the U.S. We will work tirelessly to arrest and prosecute whatever factions of organized crime in Italy that had a part, if any, in the carnage at Newark Airport.

"At the same time, I want to emphasize to the world that Italians are peaceful and respectful people whose values are no different than those of our friends in other countries."

The Pope joined in as well, sending his condolences to the American people, and like the Italian president, he made no public reference to the U.S. President's political error, if it was an error. He offered the following holy words:

"We pray at this moment. We pray for the victims and for all Americans who are grieving at this moment. We pray for those who carried out this deed. May God have mercy on their souls. All Italians, a proud and just people, cry out for justice. This is a sad day for them."

With the Italian president and the Pope speaking out, Sicilian officials had no comment.

The Butcher read all the public statements carefully. He thought that the Italians and Sicilians got the better of the PR.

The Butcher could take little solace from the political

jockeying. There was no respite to be had as the U.S. and other countries continually increased their pressure on organized crime.

The Butcher's operations in the U.S. and elsewhere along with competitive crime syndicates throughout the world, suffered dearly. Hundreds were arrested, and organized crime was becoming very disorganized with its ranks in disarray.

On the bright side, with top echelon leaders in jail, out on bail and/or preoccupied with court appearances, the crisis offered opportunities for advancement for middle-managers, even soldiers. Lots of openings. Not that anyone was looking for promotions with the cops after anyone with even a little authority.

While The Butcher was blamed for igniting fires that many, like the Marceses and Galentes, worried would consume organized crime, The Butcher did not see it that way. He believed he had done the right thing, that the fires would burn themselves out and the *Mafia* would be rejuvenated and, ultimately, be stronger than ever.

In fact, he had done significant damage to his organization and many mobster families.

CHAPTER 19

"HE DID-A WHAT?" The Butcher asked while on the telephone. "He make-a deal?"

In a telephone call from the U.S., The Butcher learned that one of his men accused of second-degree homicide was ready to accept a reduced charge in exchange for surrendering some names.

The Butcher's mole inside a federal organized crime unit that gave The Butcher valuable, high-quality human intelligence, informed him that one of his men was ready to violate a sacred principle by making a deal to reduce his jail time.

"That prick ever hear of *onore*?" The Butcher asked. "He no know you don't talk, you stand up, keep-a your mouth shut? Maybe I do him a favour so he won't ever do any time."

Then came the follow-up blow. He was told that Johnny Valenti, having done eighteen for a crime he did not commit, had advised the accused to take the deal which included squealing.

"You sure?" The Butcher asked, feeling his blood pressure rise. "They always tell me Valenti never violate *omertá*." Assured of the accuracy of the information, The Butcher slammed the phone down on the receiver. He had just about enough of Valenti.

The Butcher had been stewing about Valenti for a long time. He couldn't put his finger on it, but he just didn't like the guy. The fact that Valenti was married to Giannola's niece did not help. The Butcher gave no credence to the axiom that love is blind and sometimes leads to unexpected and unwanted relationships. He had not read *Romeo and Juliet* nor did he know that the tragically doomed lovers had lived in Verona, Italy. Not that it would have made a difference.

He was furious about Valenti, believing that he was a rat. He could not forget Valenti's less than enthusiastic reaction to the explosion that killed Hawk. While most of those attending the "celebration" congratulated him and applauded the event, Valenti stood by silently. It was evident to The Butcher, Valenti was not a team player.

On top of all of Valenti's previous sins came the news that he advised the accused murderer to cozy up to cops, prosecutors. For what? A measly reduction of maybe five to ten years in jail.

He stalked around his villa breaking everything in sight. "Fuckin' Valenti," he swore out loud. "They told me he doesn't sing. He's gonna regret the day he was born."

Valenti was giving The Butcher headaches not to mention possible ulcers. He thought about him day and night, deciding he would – had to – take care of the problem. Even if he were wrong about Valenti, he would be happier with him gone. At this point, guilt or innocence was not really important. Valenti was keeping The Butcher up at night, and The Butcher didn't like it.

All his troubles with the feds in the U.S., he believed, came from rats. Whacking Hawk had nothing to do with the pressure. Rats were the ones responsible for the increased business for bail bondsmen, and defence attorneys. He was convinced he was not paranoid; someone really was after him. And Johnny Valenti, he thought, was rat number one.

With the latest intelligence from his mole, The Butcher reached his decision that would let him sleep better at nights. He would not have to worry about Valenti . He'd be gone, history.

The Butcher called Marcese and Galente, telling them he wanted Valenti to whack a guy in Chicago. He did not reveal his ultimate objective which was to whack Valenti. It wasn't so much a matter of trust, but why take chances. Frankly, it was a matter of trust.

"He owe too much for too long," The Butcher explained about the target. "Tell Valenti to take care of it." He added, "He do good job, I pay double for contract."

He gave them all the details Valenti would need, address, occupation, description of the debtor and other details, and set a deadline, saying that Valenti needed to complete the job within two weeks.

"I can-a wait no longer," The Butcher told Marcese and Galente.

Marcese and Galente were not particularly enthusiastic about the assignment. They had never liked The Butcher and believed they were suffering needlessly given The Butcher's Napoleonic lust for power that led him to take on the world.

The last thing they needed at this time was a hit that would only increase the pressure from police authorities. The cops would get a shot of investigative adrenalin even if they thought the victim got what he deserved. It gave them an additional excuse, as if they needed one, to go after the mob, and another opportunity for much-valued publicity in the media.

Marcese and Galente wanted to lie low and wait until the pressure eased. When they attempted to protest, The Butcher cut them off, stating, "I no wanna hear it."

Reluctantly, they transmitted the orders to Valenti who hardly jumped for joy. True, he hadn't worked for a while but, given the circumstances, the temporary layoff suited him just fine.

"This is crazy," he said, "We got too much heat. The Butcher is nuts. He's a man of no peace."

Marcese and Galente did not disagree. They just looked at Valenti with an expression on their faces that seemed to ask, "So, whatcha want us to do?"

Valenti did not blame them. They were as helpless as he was. Orders were orders. As he tried to cool his anger, he was seething. He realized he had made a mistake when he joined the Marcese family and came under the control of The Butcher. He remembered his misgivings to and from his first trip to Cinisi. His fears had been confirmed. Ah, hindsight.

He always cringed when he heard The Butcher say of himself, "I am a killer and a man of honour." Valenti could accept and identify with the first part of The Butcher's motto, but men of honour do not kill innocent people. Even hit men have their boundaries, their limits.

As he pondered his assignment, he had lots of questions. The Butcher certainly was not dumb, so why would he order a hit at this time? Did he have some other objective? Why this guy in Chicago when there were other deadbeats? How much did the guy owe to warrant whacking? How long had he owed the money? Why not just break a leg or two? Or, if necessary, throw in both arms. That kind of convincing usually assured payment. What was so special about this deadbeat, anyway? In short, the whole idea stunk.

Valenti was particularly bothered by The Butcher's offer of a financial incentive if "he

do a good job." He had done good jobs before. He wasn't bragging, it just happened to be true. He had never qualified for a bonus. The Butcher was hardly a generous man, and what's more, he had the power to order Valenti to do the job without special compensation. He could use the extra money like any family man, but was it designed to blind him to an ulterior motive?

He smelled a rat and not the kind that violated *omertá.* He would have to be careful, very careful.

With his instructions and a description of the target in hand, he made his travel plans to the Windy City. He gave as few details as possible to Marcese and Galente. It was not that he did not trust them. He worried that if The Butcher asked about his plans, specific details, they would not have any choice but to tell him.

After arriving in Chicago, he staked out the home of his prey in suburban Skokie for a few days. Unfortunately, he never saw anyone. Frustrated, uneasy, and suspicious, Valenti decided that while he had not spotted his intended target, it was time to make his move. He would do the job at about eight on the night just before the two-week deadline. As he made his decision, he questioned, for the first time, the need for a deadline. This was only a debt. It was not a "time sensitive" problem. Even if it were not accomplished by a certain time, The Butcher would not suffer serious consequences.

On the night he had chosen, Valenti, with binoculars around his neck, sat in his rented car about one hundred yards from the house. He was early, about an hour before he intended to approach the house. Periodically, he would drive away so as not to raise concerns of neighbours who might report a "suspicious" person in front of their house. He would return quickly, parking in another spot but always where he would have full view of the house.

It was almost eight p.m. A few minutes before the self-appointed deadline, a car drove up and pulled into the driveway. The driver got out and appeared to be carrying a pizza. With his binoculars, Valenti could see it was a deliveryman in uniform. At the front door, the man rang the doorbell. Within seconds, the door opened, and the pizza man appeared to have been yanked inside. Strange, thought Valenti. Why didn't he just hand the pizza to the customer, as is usual, and wait to be paid? Why would he go into the house? And so quickly.

Valenti waited patiently, periodically checking his watch. Five minutes, ten, fifteen. Still no pizza man. About a half hour later, the front door opened. Two bulky men, holding a slumping pizza deliveryman by the elbows, led him back to his car in the driveway. They deposited him in the back seat. One man got behind the steering wheel while the other went into another car. The two drove off probably to deliver the deliveryman to a vacant lot. They would not leave a tip.

It was apparent that the pizza man had been beaten, beaten for information, a suspicious Valenti concluded, about him. They had worked on the poor man until they were confident that the pizza guy was really a pizza guy. Talk about being at the wrong place at the wrong time.

It was obvious to Valenti that The Butcher's henchmen had been waiting for him, and suspected the pizza man might be on a reconnaissance mission, that he played some role for Valenti in the hit proposed by The Butcher. They pulled him into the house when he delivered the pizza. That would explain why he disappeared so quickly. He was, most likely and understandably, terrified. He should have asked for hazard pay when he took the pizza delivery job.

Valenti's suspicions were confirmed. On every job throughout years, he always checked and rechecked his information and analyzed every aspect of his assignment. His wariness and caution increased in direct proportion to his experience.   What served him well was that he had never trusted The Butcher. He was suspicious of him from the start.

He was never happier about being extremely cautious, so much so that some might have accused him of paranoia. Yes, he felt a little bad for the unluckiest pizza deliveryman in Chicago or elsewhere.

Whatever sympathy he may have had for the pizza man was overshadowed by the glee he experienced at outfoxing The Butcher by having ordered the pizza.

CHAPTER 20

VALENTI SAT IN HIS car for a few minutes savouring his success. He had dodged a bullet, literally. His instincts had served him well. For a brief moment, he was almost smug. He did not engage in self-satisfaction for long because the question before him was, "Now what?" That was not an easy question for him to answer.

The Butcher would be furious. Not only had the mission failed, but his ego had been bruised, and nothing enraged The Butcher more than having his self-worth impugned. He was The Butcher with the emphasis on "The." He would unleash all the power necessary to get even. He would have his revenge, no matter how long it took.

In preparing for this moment, Valenti had considered the circumstances and made some preliminary plans. He had packed some extra clothes in his suitcase and taken more cash than he needed for the trip to Chicago. He was faced with executing a disappearing act. He had thought about hiding out, going on the lam, and he did not look forward to it. He had no choice.

He had some indirect experience with the exercise since he had tracked down several individuals who had tried to disappear and whom he had been hired to find. Well, not only find. So he could learn from their mistakes. And they made many.

He was concerned primarily with the safety of Gisele, Little Johnny and Lucia. What would happen to them? Who would take care of them? When, if ever, would he see them again? These questions he had not faced. As he pondered his dilemma, small beads of sweat broke out on his forehead. Protecting his family was his major objective. He would do whatever it took. Nothing was more important.

Luigi. Yes, he would call Luigi, the only person he could trust implicitly. He drove to a nearby gas station. Using the public telephone, he called his lifelong friend, and when Giancamilli answered, Valenti unburdened himself, relating the entire pizza episode to his friend.

"You done good, Johnny," Giancamilli said trying to offer support. "You pretty smart guy."

He sensed doubt and uncertainty in Valenti's voice. He had never heard Valenti so tentative. If Valenti was scared, and he was, it was because of the risks faced by his family. The Butcher had no boundaries he would not cross, but neither talked on the phone about The Butcher's total commitment to unlimited cruelty when he considered it necessary. They blocked it out.

"Johnny, you don't worry," Giancamilli said, "I'll take care of Gisele and the kids. You stay away for a while. I'll get some information, and we'll see what the bastard does."

Valenti was not particularly reassured. "Yeah, thanks Luigi. I appreciate that. I'll stay in touch. You make up some story for Gisele. Tell her not to worry. I'll be back soon."

He hung up and returned to his car. He did not move for about a half hour before making his decision. He would head for Vegas. Using a phony name, he would get "lost" in the nation's gambling mecca. He'd seek a job in a casino or bar, and keep a low profile. Nothing big. Just something to make a few bucks until he could return home, pick up his family and disappear forever.

As Valenti headed West, The Butcher raged in Cinisi. He ordered the two men to whom he had assigned the Valenti hit to Cinisi and berated them mercilessly. He called them every name in the book while pacing furiously in front of them.

"Who you think you work-a for?" The Butcher asked. "Some shit head don't know what he's doing? You tell-a me you eat pizza while Valenti sticks it to you. Where your brains?"

The Butcher paced faster, continually, ranting, "Pizza, pizza, pizza, pizza." He looked at the two men. His faced was flushed, and he was sweating.

"Get out-a here. I no wanna to see you again." The two turned and headed to the front door. Before they could open it, The Butcher retrieved a .38 from a desk and shot them both in the back.

"I no have to pay you for the pizza," he said, looking at the bodies.

He called in another two-man team and gave them the assignment the two lying a few yards away had failed to carry out successfully.

"I want Valenti," he told them. "Those two," he continued while pointing toward the bodies, "No do the job." The Butcher's not too subtle point was not lost on their replacements.

He had left them lying there assuming the bodies would give his new team the needed incentive to succeed. He let them know that failure would mean more than the boss filing a bad performance review. The Butcher sat down with his two lieutenants and for the next hour they discussed Valenti, where he might be headed, his closest friends, and his family.

Nothing appeared to interest The Butcher more than Valenti's family. His wife, Gisele Giannola, was the niece of one of his enemies, and they had two kids. That might be Valenti's Achilles heel, his weakness.

"You get me information about his *famiglia,*" The Butcher ordered. "You call me when you have anything. Anytime. Understand?"

The two, periodically looking at the bodies near the front door, assured The Butcher they would not fail. They expressed total confidence that they would be successful, no doubt about it.

As they left, The Butcher shouted at them, "No more pizza."

The Butcher was taking no chances. He called two more of his men and gave them the same assignment. It might not be good employee relations, but he did not worry about the politics should the two teams run into each other. All he wanted was success, and success was defined as a dead Valenti.

Once more he emphasized that while they were developing leads to find Valenti, they also focus on his family.

The Butcher was preoccupied with Valenti, his family and pizza. Thoughts about Valenti tortured him, and he was determined to rid himself of this plague.

As the second team left his house to head for the U.S., he mused, "Maybe I close all the pizza joints in Cinisi. Pizza. I no believe it."

CHAPTER 21

THE PIZZA INCIDENT DROVE The Butcher crazy. He had never been so angry and his anger led to frustration, rage, depression and more paranoia than he had ever experienced as the top honcho in Sicily and as head of the six families in the U.S. He was suspicious of everyone, not knowing whom to trust. He saw rats and turncoats everywhere.

He started to doubt whether he would ever feel secure again. And doubt is not a desirable psychological state for someone who ruled, and had to rule, with an iron fist. A leader cannot afford to have any doubts because they lead to bad decisions. The Butcher had to be cool, analytical, shrewd, and duplicitous. He was not the leader of a church choir or Boy Scout troop.

He began to question his all-purpose solution -- murder -- as the appropriate remedy for his problems. How many killings would he have to order to create the psychological peace he wanted and needed? Was he killing some "innocent" mobsters who were loyal to him? If so, would those killings turn others against him, weakening his rule? He was besieged from all sides.

Despite the psychological crisis created primarily by Valenti and despite a self-awareness that his judgement might be impaired given the stress he was feeling, The Butcher's suspicious mind led him to question the loyalty of Tomaso "Tommy Boy" Galente. Yes, Galente had dutifully followed The Butcher's orders to whack Esposito. Yes, he, and he alone, was responsible for appointing Galente to run one of New York's families. Yes, yes, it was all true. Whatever the facts and history, Galente worried him. He could not forget that Galente was one of Valenti's good friends.

Friendship creates strong bonds and how could The

Butcher be confident that when push came to shove, if Galente had the choice to save The Butcher or Valenti from a bullet, he would not choose Valenti over The Butcher? No such guarantee existed, leading The Butcher to err, if he was erring, on the side of caution.

After reviewing his payroll, he called on Carlo "The Hammer" Michelotti, and told him he was sending him to the States to work under Galente.

"He teach-a you many things," The Butcher told Michelotti.

The two talked about the tutorial role Galente would play, and the holes Galente would fill in Michelotti's professional portfolio.

Michelotti accepted the assignment happily. He liked Galente and always wanted to visit the U.S. He was aware of Galente's reputation as a boss who looked after his men. Just as Michelotti was about the leave, as the meeting appeared over, The Butcher snuck in a request.

"So, Carlo, when you work with him, you call me, huh, with things you see."

At first Michelotti did not understand, and he tried to indicate he was a bit confused. "I don't ..."

The Butcher interrupted him. "I need to know, you know, if he is doing what I say. He no workin' for someone else."

Michelotti suddenly understood. He was being sent as a spy. The story about him learning from Galente was just bullshit. He did not like the assignment, not at all. But what was a man to do when ordered to do so by The Butcher?

The Butcher did not give Michelotti a chance to protest. He patted Michelotti on the back while walking him to the door. "I know you do good job for me, Carlo. I know."

Two weeks later, Michelotti, the pawn in this deadly chess game, sat in Galente's office, saying The Butcher had sent him to sign on with the Galente family, that The Butcher thought Galente could teach him a thing or two. Galente did not feel one way or another about having an intern. Michelotti might be able to handle some of the assignments that did not require the talents of more experienced staff.

Michelotti called The Butcher every week or so, telling him, in effect, that he had found nothing. Galente was very faithful from what he could see.

Michelotti did not like the part he was asked to play. He felt slimy, like a snake and he wanted no part of The Butcher's duplicitous scheme. Thus, after about a month, Michelotti went to see Galente at his home and revealed his role as a Mata Hari although he was not as good looking as the World War I spy-prostitute.

"Tommy, I can't do this no more," Michelotti said, catching Galente by surprise.

"What can't you do?" Galente asked.

"The Butcher wants me to rat, spy on you. I can't do it. He has me calling him every week to tell him what I find out. No more."

Galente did not display any surprise or shock although he was puzzled and perplexed by the admission of this spy turned counter-spy. His mind raced with questions he kept to himself. Why would he tell me this? Why is he putting his life on the line? How does he know he can trust me? Didn't he consider that I might tell The Butcher of his confession? Who is the spy working for? Has he really turned into a counter-counter spy? Why did he wait so long to tell me? Would he have told me if he found what he believed was evidence of my disloyalty to The Butcher?

Trust. Whom could he trust? He remembered Valenti warning him on many occasions, "Don't talk to me about trust. You can't even trust yourself when you're hungry, because your stomach let's everyone know you're fuckin' hungry."

Valenti wasn't as eloquent or insightful as Shakespeare, Socrates, Plato, Aristotle or other historic sages, but the earthy quality of his friend's philosophy made sense to Galente.

Galente sat quietly contemplating what he had just heard. Whatever he decided to do would have to be carefully thought out. There was no room for error. He analyzed a variety of scenarios letting Michelotti sit befuddled next to him.

"How come you don't say nothin'?" Michelotti asked.

"I'm thinking, Carlo. Remember what they say in the old country, 'Talking without thinking is like shooting without looking.'"

After delivering this wisdom, he sat without saying a word for another few minutes before getting up to embrace Michelotti. He kissed him on both cheeks, and thanked him with a whisper in the right ear, "You done good by me. I won't forget this. I'll be right back."

When he returned, he said Michelotti should play The Butcher's game and continue to report on Galente's unfailing loyalty.

"Tell him you find nothing," said Galente. "Tell him I am as faithful as a new bride, not a wife of many years, but a bride," he added laughing at his implication.

He asked Michelotti to join him for a meeting with

Marcese. "It's important Marcese know you working for me. Get my car from the garage," he said handing Michelotti the keys. "I'll meet you out in front."

After Michelotti left, Galente remained seated at his desk, and he waited. He did not have to wait long. After a few minutes, he heard the explosion he expected. His car along with Michelotti were blown to bits. The man Galente had assigned to wire his car with a bomb after Galente had left his meeting with Michelotti did his job as well as the firing squad that executed the famous female World War I spy.

What if Michelotti were innocent? That is, what if he really did not like spying for The Butcher? As far as Galente was concerned, doubts were no hindrance to justify the killing. He could not take the risk. If Michelotti indeed had expressed his loyalty to Galente rather than The Butcher, well, he was, unfortunately and regrettably, a casualty of war. War, and this was war, sometimes causes collateral damage. Galente would consider Michelotti collateral damage, if the spy had not been a spy at all. Galente would accept his error like a man if he ever found out that Michelotti had turned on The Butcher by revealing his role. Everyone makes mistakes. No one's perfect.

Galente expected that The Butcher would be suspicious. He would consider that Michelotti's role was discovered or that he may even have confessed. Given that Michelotti blown to bits, and no one else was involved, The Butcher never would have his answer.

There was also another important nuance to the execution of Michelotti. Everyone would believe that he, Galente, was the target. It was his car. Even The Butcher had to have doubts that Galente was the instigator, the initiator, the contractor of this hit.

That doubt gave Galente valuable cover. The Butcher would want to retaliate but he could not be confident that whatever violence reaction he ordered was justified. Indeed, he might be attacking an innocent man, not that such a consideration had ever stopped him before. It did not stop Galente. But Galente was still the head of a major *Mafia* family and that had to be considered while Michelotti was only a soldier. Soldiers were much more expendable, like expendable infantry men vs. generals. The Butcher could not act totally arbitrarily in this case.

It was the uncertainty about whether The Butcher considered him guilty that Galente counted on to give him some immunity from revenge, if not a sense of security, at least temporarily. The Butcher would continue to probe, to try and discover the "truth." Thus, Galente would have to look over his shoulder more than he did under "normal" circumstances, not that circumstances were ever normal in his business. If he were targeted, all the precautions in the world would not protect him. He would not have been able to get life insurance if the insurers were aware of all the circumstances. They were a little fussy about pre-existing conditions.

Meanwhile, Galente would inform The Butcher of the tragedy, express his regrets if not sympathies for the loss, while conferring with Marcese on the meaning of the latest clash of violent forces.

The ultimate goal that needed to be achieved was clear to Galente. He did not know when or how or by whom. He just accepted the fact, in his organized crime soul, that The Butcher had to be whacked. That day would have to come.

The Butcher's demise would take more than just asking one of his men to wire a car. It would require ingenuity, creativity, significant resources, men they could trust – there was that word "trust" again – along with uncompromising determination and courage. He and others would have to be prepared to take on a very risky proposition. Failure was not an option for very obvious reasons.

Whatever the risks, nothing would give him more pleasure than the death of The Butcher. He was optimistic that the day would come.

CHAPTER 22

"BOURBON ON THE rocks."

"Comin' right up."

Tony reached for a bottle of Old Grand Dad. He filled a glass with ice and a shot of the hard stuff. With the customer watching, he added another half a shot for good measure.

"Here you go."

"Thanks, Tony. Appreciate you toppin' it off."

Tony, a/k/a Johnny Valenti, had gone underground in Las Vegas, the city that produced more revenue from gambling and sex than the budgets of many countries in the world. He had changed his name to Tony Genitti, without filing the required paperwork at city hall, and found a job as a bartender at the Heaven's Gate Hotel. The implication of the hotel's name was somewhat of an exaggeration. It did provide guests, as one of its perks, clean towels at least once a month. On the negative side, the creaking of mattresses at night caused by hookers plying their trade made falling and staying asleep pretty tough.

He had rented a room in a motel far from the strip that might very well have been owned by the same guy who was the majority stockholder in the hotel. The towels at the motel could very well have been the used ones from Heaven's Gate.

Given his circumstances, Valenti wasn't fussy. His living conditions were not his major concern. He had only one objective and that was to keep a low profile, a very low profile, until he could develop a master plan for a safe future. He was focused almost exclusively on his family, devoting all his time in strategizing how he could move

Gisele and his two kids to a safe haven, a place where they could all live together without fear. He respected, in a strange way, The Butcher's resourcefulness and his almost endless resources. The Butcher would not give up. He would do what was necessary to find Valenti. And if found, Valenti knew his fate.

His task would not be easy. He needed to be patient, to take his time, to think clearly. Most of all, he needed to be careful, not make any mistakes, not leave any footprints, any trail that could be followed. So he kept to himself, was vague to his employers and associates about his background, and when not working he played a little blackjack or craps at the tables, went to the movies or watched TV in his motel room. In a city where, besides gambling, sex was the prime activity, next to breathing, Valenti was celibate. The Catholic Church could have recruited him for the priesthood, if it were willing to forget about his past.

Unless fate intervened, Valenti felt he was safe, as safe as anyone could be in the world he lived in. Having been a hunter, he worked on the principle that the hunted could always be found. It might take time but a persistent and experienced hunter, if patient, will be rewarded with the sought after prize. That was the truism that bothered Valenti. Would he ever be safe again? Would he ever live another day with Gisele and the kids and not have to worry? Where would he go and what would he need to do to achieve that objective? Those were the questions that haunted him. At this point, he had no answers.

Unfortunately, fate did intervene but it was not because he had made a mistake. It was, as they say, just one of those strange coincidences that usually prompted those involved to observe, "It sure is a small world."

For about an hour, a customer at the end of the bar

stared at him. The customer, a man in his late thirties, thought he recognized the bartender. Something about Valenti struck him as familiar. He could not take his eyes off Valenti. He tried desperately to remember.

When Tony –Valenti – noticed, he asked his curious customer, "Get you somethin'?"

"Nay, I'm all set. Where you from?"

"Bounced around a lot. No place special."

"Do I know you?"

"Can't say. You don't look familiar."

"I'm pretty sure. It'll come to me. Just can't place you."

Tony laughed, reached for a bottle of the beer the guy was drinking, gave it to the customer, adding, "This one's on me."

The customer sat for another half hour, continually looking at Valenti. Valenti ignored the stares, but periodically glanced at the guy, trying to appear nonchalant. It could have been considered a silly little game except that recognition by the customer could have deadly consequences.

After finishing his drink, the customer threw ten bucks on the bar, jumped off his stool and waved at Valenti who waved back. He was about ten yards from the bar when he turned around. With a head signal, he motioned for Valenti to come over to him.

"Hey, sorry, none of my business, you ever do time?"

"Couple of days here and there for having one too many." Trying to ease the tension, he added, "Well, more than one too many. Maybe a dozen."

"I was at Ray Brook. Thought maybe you were there."

"Ray Brook? Nay, that's heavy duty stuff. Never."

"I thought …. Sorry."

"No problem. Sometimes this happens."

Valenti could feel his blood pressure rise. He broke out in a cold sweat, and his breathing became a little laboured. Shit, shit, shit. Who was this son-of-a-bitch? Would the guy remember him? Did he have contacts? Could he cause him trouble? Valenti needed a break, some fresh air. He told the other bartender he'd be back in five and went out for some fresh air. He paced in front of the hotel like a tiger in a cage.

While extremely agitated, he concluded that the guy was not the hunter. He would not have acknowledged recognizing him if he was on assignment. What if he remembered, had contacts and tried to parlay that into a quick buck. Or what if he remembered and just innocently told others, the wrong people, that he had seen Valenti? That was a most likely, very possible scenario. "It's a small world" is more than an adage. There is some, more than some, truth to it.

Valenti tried to stay calm. He told himself the odds of the guy remembering him *and* telling the wrong people was like pulling a card for an inside straight in poker. Pretty high odds and they favoured Valenti. All he could do was to be extra careful and decide, in a couple of days, if he had to disappear again.

What Valenti did not acknowledge or subconsciously refused to recognize was that at times gamblers do pull a card for an inside straight. Not often, admittedly. But it happens. He was in denial.

Fortunately, actually unfortunately, slowly his anxiety abated. Each day Valenti spent less and less time worrying about the incident until his thoughts turned to an attractive woman drinking at the bar about a month after the worrisome encounter.

She was sexy, always wearing miniskirts and low cut blouses. She engaged Valenti with small talk and flirtatious eyes. Each time Valenti looked at her, he was consumed with desire. He had been faithful to Gisele, but it was becoming more difficult. His hormones raced and raged, so much so that when he just looked at the woman he was glad he was wearing a bartender's apron to avoid the obvious embarrassment.

She appeared at the bar for several consecutive days, and Valenti gave her more than the justified drinks on the house. He had sent a message, and she picked up on it.

After a couple of free drinks, she broke the ice, asking him, "Isn't there something I can do for you in return?"

"Can you think of something?"

She got off the bar stool, walked away and every five yards or so turned around, looking at him with a stare that asked, "Well, you coming?"

Valenti surrendered to his desires. Just so much anyone can ask of a man. He threw his bar towel in the sink, told his bartending partner he'd be back in thirty minutes and followed the woman into the elevator. They were alone and when the doors closed she pressed the button numbered "7," turned and kissed him passionately. As they embraced and kissed, she suddenly pushed the "stop" button.

"You're gonna go down on the elevator," she said playfully, proud of her double entendre.

She unbuttoned her blouse and Valenti saw she was braless. She pulled his shirt out of his pants. Then she kissed his neck, and raised his desire with her tongue inside his ears. She placed her right hand on the nape of his neck and pulled him toward her. As she tried to push her left hand inside his pants, he suddenly grabbed her wrist.

Valenti was conflicted, to say the least. He had been celibate for weeks. Even before the temptation in front of him, he was having trouble controlling his desires. This beautiful woman was prepared, more than prepared, to satisfy his sexual tensions and anxieties. Within minutes, he would feel normal again. No matter how he tried, he could not get Gisele out of his mind. He thought about his wife at an admittedly very tense and embarrassing moment – only seconds away from screwing another woman. Talk about conflicts. Psychiatrists could have a field day with the collision of these sexual and psychological forces.

As Valenti tried to sort out his emotions and make a definitive decision, the woman, confused by his on-and-off-again participation, asked, "Something wrong with me? You don't like the elevator? Wanna go somewhere else?"

"It ain't you," he said. "Got some problems. Maybe another time."

"What the hell you doing in Vegas?" she woman asked, implying that if he weren't interested in sex, this was the last city in the world in which to live.

"You got a point. As I said, maybe another time."

He restarted the elevator and when it opened at the ground floor, he made one last attempt to rectify what was a very embarrassing situation.

"If you come back to the bar, another drink's on me,"

he said. He added, "Sorry."

Back behind the bar, besides feeling stressed given the elevator encounter, he was confused and embarrassed and felt some pride as well. He had been true to Gisele, although she would never know.

> *Omertá* technically related only to the code of silence – ratting – or selling people out, but Valenti's interpretation of omertá, the interpretation of a hit man, included faithfulness to his wife. He was not a strict constructionist. He did not limit his interpretation of omertá to just keeping one's mouth shut. There was more, much more, to it. *Omertá* involved honour, different types of honour. Being faithful to one's spouse was a sign of honour. *Omertá* required a man to stand up when the time demanded it. Valenti had complied with the subtleties of his interpretation of *omertá.*

He wasn't jumping for joy but was content with his decision. A cold shower – a few cold showers - would help him through his sexual crisis. It would not be easy since he was alone in a city where sex, as his partner in the elevator had pointed out, was so prevalent even the Pope would have a hard time not giving in to temptation.

In the midst of this very personal crisis, came the – *the* – phone call.

"They found your ass, and as a result we found you," said the voice on the other end of the line.

Valenti was stunned. He did not say anything for a few seconds, realizing he may just have heard his death sentence. He tried to digest the news. "How?"

"The best information we have is someone recognized you. He told someone who told someone, who told someone."

Shit, the customer at the bar. Must have been. Valenti was a victim of the "six degrees of separation" theory. Valenti probably never heard of that theory. Not much of a social or cultural philosopher, he attributed his bad luck to The Butcher drawing the long-shot inside straight.

"You sure?"

"No question," said the voice that belonged to a mole in a special U.S. organized crime division. "Tapes are good, clear."

For years, the mole had proved invaluable to Valenti. For a monthly retainer, Valenti's bosses and Valenti had been provided with inside information that helped them immensely in their business. It's always helpful to know what your adversaries are doing. Gives you time to plan your getaways, destroy evidence.

The mole told Valenti of The Butcher's plan they had picked up with their eavesdropping. The strategy was to involve him with a woman who, one night, would ask him to her home. She would lead him to a quiet street where The Butcher's men would be waiting in a parked van. While not of the same professional calibre as Valenti, the men had the same job descriptions and were more than capable to do the job.

Valenti became angry with himself. How could he have taken the risk to stay in Vegas when the customer recognized him? Dumb, dumb, dumb. Valenti was pissed at himself because he knew better. Many of his targets had made such stupid mistakes. What was wrong with him? No use kicking himself in the ass. No point to that. Time to make plans, better ones.

Out of nowhere, it hit him. The broad. Given his sexual frustrations, he never asked himself why she would sit alone at the bar night after night and pursue him when she could get laid in the hotel with anyone and everyone. His sexual desires and frustrations got in the way of asking the right questions. The real problem was he did not ask any.

Again, dumb, dumb, and dumber.

She was The Butcher's assignee, the Delilah, and Samson had suffered dearly after being seduced by her, losing more than just his hair. Valenti would have faced a similar fate if he had succumbed to his sexual drives. Valenti described his encounter to the mole, and asked, "What now?"

The mole outlined a proposal. If the woman returned and invited him home, Valenti should call him immediately. The feds would tail them through the streets. When he and the woman reached the van, Valenti should walk right up to it and warn those that were prepared to put some holes in him that if they did, they would be arrested within minutes because the feds had staked out the area after learning of the assassination plot through wiretaps.

Valenti had a million questions about the quality of the mole's scheme, but at this point he had few options. His confidence for a successful mission rested almost entirely on the fact that the mole would not want to lose his monthly retainer. Somewhat ironic. His faith – and life – rested on a member of the nation's most powerful police force.

"Think this will work?" he asked.

The answer, "It's the best we got," did not give Valenti the kind of reassurance he wanted and had hoped for but he signed on.

"I'll call." And he hung up.

The woman did not show up for several days, worrying Valenti. Just as he was about to give up hope, there she was, sitting in her usual spot, the stool at the end of the bar. From afar, he winked at her.

He would play it cool. He did want to appear in a hurry or anxious. Having made a series of mistakes, he did not want to make another, a more costly, irreparable one.

He sauntered over, asking, "Can I use my rain check?"

Coolly and seductively, she asked, "How do you know you have one?"

"Just hoping. A guy needs to have hope. Had lots on my mind the other night."

"I could tell. The rain check isn't any good for the elevator. Why don't we go to my place?"

"Meet me in the lobby. Give me a minute to check out."

He made the necessary phone call to the mole, and in the lobby, he took her hand but instead of leaving the hotel, he headed for the men's room where he tipped a bellboy and told him to bar the door, let no one in.

The bellboy, looking at the woman, chuckled. Who was he to argue with the man? Everyone has their own tastes, their fetishes. If this guy wanted to do it in the john, so be it.

Inside the restroom, Valenti told a couple of men at the urinals to "Get with it" and "Get out!" He grabbed one guy, who didn't get the message, by the collar and shoved him toward the exit. The man had not finished and pissed all over his pants while trying to zip up.

"You like toilets better than elevators?" she asked

facetiously.

Valenti looked at her with cold eyes, and slammed the woman against the wall with one hand around her neck. He squeezed her neck hard enough to turn her face red, but she was still able to breathe – barely.

"You whore. Sold me out for what? A couple of hundred bucks. If I didn't need you, I'd flush you down the toilet."

He squeezed her neck tighter and was tempted to stop her breathing. He didn't, realizing she was pivotal in the execution of the plan that was designed to save his life. So he eased the pressure.

"Until this is over, you don't say nothin'. Not one word. You just do what I tell you. Got that?"

The woman, who was barely conscious, tried to nod which, under the circumstances, proved difficult. Valenti was able to interpret that she agreed. He had no doubts.

When he let go, he gave her a few minutes to recover. She gasped, sat down on the floor, and when she was able to do so, stood up and washed her face at the sink. When Valenti saw she was breathing normally, he grabbed her hand and headed out of the hotel.

He ordered her to take him to the van. She led him through the streets, and ten minutes into their walk, she turned onto a dark side street. Valenti immediately saw it. The van was parked about five hundred yards ahead of them. He looked around and spotted his backup consisting of two black four-door sedans with two fed agents in each.

When they arrived at the van, he put his forefinger to his lips, indicating she should keep her mouth shut. Given what she had just experienced, he had no need to worry. He knocked on the van's door that opened within seconds.

All he did was point to the two sedans and said, "Feds."

"You're a scum rat," the guy at the door sneered. "A rat working with cops. Nothin' lower than that. Nothin' but scum."

"I ain't no rat and tell that bastard in Cinisi I hope he shows his ass here one day."

He held the woman tightly by the arm, turned, and headed back to a main street. Just before he reached it, while still on the side street, he hesitated about letting the woman go. Should he kill her or let her walk? Would she be a threat to him? Decisions, decisions. He concluded she had the fright of her life, and would never talk to anyone, let alone the cops, about this night.

"Consider this your lucky day. I'm feeling good. I don't have to tell you to forget about tonight. Just do your tricks and have a good life. Get your ass out of here."

Back in his room, Valenti called the mole, a man whose guts he hated because of his duplicity. He had to admit tonight the mole had earned his money.

"You owe me," the mole said. "Big time."

"Don't push your luck. You know where they're staying?"

With information from the mole, the next night at about three a.m., he took a cab to a motel along the highway at the edge of town. He had the cab drop him off a mile from his destination, and he walked the rest of the way. He spotted the van parked in the lot. He pried open a door and slid into the back seat where he waited.

The biggest challenge he faced was not falling asleep. The adrenalin rushing through him in anticipation of his objective helped keep him awake.

At about ten a.m., some seven hours later, they came out of their room. He hid behind the front seat. After they opened the car doors, one slid into the driver's seat while the other sat next to him on the passenger side. When the driver started the motor, Valenti popped up, revolver in hand.

He immediately shot the driver in the back of the head, not wanting to risk facing two men at the same time.

"You tell him I ain't no rat and to stop screwin' with me," Valenti told the passenger.

The man, his eyes opened as far as possible, nodded in fear when Valenti added, "You know somethin'? Someday, I'll deliver the message myself." Without another word, he shot the man in the face.

Valenti sat in the van for a few minutes, savouring his good fortune. Then he drove into the desert where he dumped the bodies. From there he pointed the van toward Reno to go underground again. This time he would be a little smarter, a lot smarter.

CHAPTER 23

IN NEW YORK, TOMASO "Tommy Boy" Galente
was in the headlines. The bombing at his home had once
more awakened the media to the mob. Coverage of the
underworld, after the Hawk assassination, had been sparse
without any "newsworthy" events generally defined as a
spectacular killing. Galente gave them a story, a big story.

The bombed car was still smoking when Galente, who
loved publicity, picked up the telephone to call his
favourite scribe at *The New York Gazette*. The writer was
half reporter, half gossip columnist, and Galente fed the
newsman's insatiable appetite for exclusives.

"Joe, got a big one for you," Galente started.

He set the usual ground rules. Galente would only be
identified as an anonymous source on the information
regarding the bombing but, on the record, he could quote
him as denying any involvement. Galente could not lose.

"You the only one I'm calling," said Galente. With
the stealth of Deep Throat in Watergate, he described an
intricate plan his adversaries had hatched to have him
killed.

"Cops will tell you I'm a suspect, like always, but I
ain't involved," Galente protested. "You can use a photo
of me in your files but a good one."

Galente was not exactly truthful when he told his news
contact that he would be the only reporter that he called.
He telephoned others as well but with them, he set rules
that they could not quote him by name at all. Thus, he
could not be accused of undermining his key contact. The
strategy worked flawlessly. Galente got his message out
throughout New York and, for that matter, the world
because the stories would be picked up by the newswire
services. The media helped him prop up his reputation,

and he did not have to pay any PR professionals. Official paid spokesmen could do only so much, and many times their hearts weren't in it. Galente did not want someone else telling the world what a good guy he was. He would do it himself.

The next day, *The Gazette* ran the story with headlines generally reserved for the declaration of war.

"Mobster Killed in Car Bomb, Alleged Mafia Don Denies Involvement," screamed the headline.

The story was marked "exclusive" and, because of the interview with Galente, had a copyright.

The story reported:

"The New York Daily Gazette *learned from reliable sources that the car bombing of a low-ranking 'soldier' in organized crime was part of an intricate plot to murder the alleged head of one of New York's most powerful Mafia families.*

"The Gazette *also learned that the actual target may have been Tomaso "Tommy Boy" Galente, the alleged head of one of six Mafia families who in an exclusive interview with* The Gazette, *said he narrowly escaped.*

"The victim, Carlo "The Hammer" Michelotti, The Gazette *learned, had been asked to get Galente's car when it exploded, killing him and damaging Galente's home.*

"'I barely escaped,' Galente told The Gazette. *'I feel bad for Carlo. He was a good man.'*

"Galente also told The Gazette *exclusively that 'I ain't a member of the* Mafia. *I'm a businessman in real estate and I got some retail businesses.'"*

Other media outlets had similar stories, all gushing about their exclusives gleaned from "informed sources,"

"sources very familiar with organized crime," and "extremely reliable sources." At least the reference to "one source very familiar with organize crime" was accurate.

As he read the papers, Galente was very satisfied. Mission accomplished. In a strategy that would make the PR news media practitioners envious, he had turned the story into his favour. He also looked very good in the file photos printed on all the front pages of the papers. He was in publicity heaven.

The only ones who would be pissed would be his lawyers who, like all lawyers, always advised clients charged or suspected of wrongdoing not to talk to the press. Galente refused to accept the advice for which he paid a very high price.

"If I don't talk to the press, the feds make me out to be a shit, a gangster," Galente told his lawyers. "You tell me to shut up and the papers print what the feds say. Make me look terrible. Hurts me, my family, my kids. When I talk, they read the truth."

Galente explained to the lawyers that his only objective was for the public to know the "truth." So, in keeping with his dedication and commitment to "truth," he overruled his lawyers and even invited his favourite reporter from *The Gazette* to his home for an exclusive in-depth follow-up interview.

Facing several problems, most involving The Butcher, Marcese and Galente had an emergency meeting to take stock of their position.

First, Valenti had disappeared after outwitting The Butcher in what had become known as "The Pizza Affair." That made The Butcher 0-1 in New York. This loss was followed by Galente being suspicious about The Butcher's representative, and Galente had him blown to pieces. The score: The Butcher 0, New York 2. On the business end, he was snubbed by blacks and, to top it off, they had killed his son-in-law. That made it 0-3. Frankly, he could accept the loss of Cusumano. He had called the prospective partners "niggers." But after they avenged the racial slur, surely they could have looked beyond that and proceeded with the proposed joint venture. If he could accept the demise of his son-in-law, he thought they should have been able to forget a racial slur. Business is business.

The Butcher was losing and he did not like to lose. That would not sit well with him. Eventually, he would have his pound of flesh. It may take time, but he would get "justice," The Butcher's kind of justice. That meant the pressure would build for The Butcher and, as it did, work conditions, and the overall environment, would continue to deteriorate. Marcese and Galente recognized their dilemma and they were very upset.

"He don't fit in with us," offered Marcese. "He ain't our kind of pasta."

How could they get out from under the clutches of The Butcher? He was the boss of all six families in New York. He lived in Cinisi. He was well protected in his villa. He was violent, extremely violent, but not stupid. It appeared that whatever plan they hatched, it would have to involve an all out attack. Something like an army attacking a beach front stronghold of the enemy. The target, most likely, would know the attack was coming, and the attackers would have to be prepared to take casualties, many casualties with no promise of success.

Such a tactic would take enormous resources and manpower. Many others would have to be involved and trust. the most potent and important element of such a plan, would have to be extended to forty or fifty others, maybe more.   Could they succeed in recruiting and training such a force and could they trust all its members, every single one of them, not to rat? Would somebody, who either liked The Butcher or wanted to work for him, squeal for the expected rewards? The temptation to rat in exchange for The Butcher's favours would be very tempting.

The Butcher understood that ambition helped provide him with a protective shield.   Ambition is a strong incentive to sell people out. That's how The Butcher had worked his way through the ranks, starting as a driver. He had gleaned lots of information from passengers that he used for rewards and promotions.

For the time being, they left the issue of The Butcher unsettled. They agreed to revisit it because eventually it would have to be dealt with, perhaps at a Commission meeting. They would not put the subject of The Butcher on the agenda, but they wait to see if anyone else raised it. If so, they might find someone else with whom to strategize. That was assuming The Butcher did not plant the implied criticism to trap his real critics. Whom to believe? What a conundrum.

As Marcese and Galente debated and analyzed possible scenarios, they raised the issue of Valenti's disappearance.

"You a-know where he went?" Marcese asked.

Marcese posed the question to Galente because Valenti would trust his long-time friend.   Galente answered that he did not, but added that he expected Valenti, being a pro, to have gone underground, deep underground.

"He's been around," said Galente. "He knows what to do."

They both expected that Valenti would reappear someday, somehow, because they knew he would not abandon Gisele and his children.   Yes, believing in *famiglia* was a virtue, and they respected Valenti for his loyalty, but it could also be a weakness in these kinds of situations. They worried about him.

Ignoring Galente's claim of ignorance, Marcese said, "Tell him, not-a to stick his head up too high if he no wanna lose it."

Galente did not react to the implication that he had information about Valenti's whereabouts. Both hoped that one day they would again have the services of the best hit man that the Big Apple had seen in many a year. They missed him -- in their own way.

Marcese turned the conversation to the publicity the car bombing had generated. Unlike Galente, he did not like the media attention. Galente was Page One news in New York, but the incident also spawned other stories on the mob. The papers, particularly the tabloids and gossip columns, were filled with stories about "alleged *Mafia* dons," and mobsters in general.

The headlines were huge because nothing sold more newspapers than the *Mafia,* the Yankees or some public official playing hanky-panky in the bedroom with someone other than their spouse, in that order.   The Galente bombing took up most of the news space in the papers. The only one more upset than Marcese and the *Mafia* lawyers was New York Mayor Ed Koch because the media was ignoring him.   Publicity is the lifeblood of politicians. It was unfair that he had to fight for news coverage, and was pissed that he was losing the battle. He should have realized it was an easy decision for those who daily decide the news agenda for the public. What would excite the news consuming public more: the mayor bragging how he was making New York a better city or mobsters blowing themselves to bits? It was no contest.

Galente's face was everywhere, in the papers and on TV. "Reliable sources" "Unimpeachable sources" and "sources beyond reproach" were quoted endlessly about the hit. The information on the murder and reasons cited by the sources were as different as the sources. The media circus over the story, inevitably, brought the *Mafia* and its families into the spotlight.

"I no like reading about us," Marcese said. "It no good. Hurts us all. What-a they mean by 'alleged'?"

Galente had an entirely different philosophy. He liked the publicity, he loved it. He would buy several newspapers and magazines and devour all the stories about himself and organized crime. He liked walking down the street and being recognized.

He relished his special relationships with a couple of columnists whose beat was the mob, frequently feeding them "exclusive" information. Those in the media handled informants with care, and Galente had the sophistication to understand that anonymous sources had much to gain, and nothing to lose, in partnering with reporters. If reporters screwed their sources, the information well dried up. Thus, with reporters wanting Galente to continue to hand them exclusives, Galente always seemed to fare a little bit better in stories than other mobsters. He was painted as a mobster with a white hat, a likable guy with a sense of humour who, since he talked to the press, obviously had nothing to hide. The fact that such logic would not hold up to the slightest scrutiny did not bother the media. Exclusives were sometimes based on a little philosophical inconsistency.

In a sense, he was a "reliable but anonymous rat." He ratted in a carefully defined but limited context. He did not point fingers at others nor did he squeal to the cops. All he did was exercise his constitutional rights, protected by the First Amendment, to say his piece anonymously, and he expected his news contacts to refuse to reveal their sources, even at the risk of going to jail. Yes, it was true he constantly fought to stay out of the slammer. He did not see any contradiction in his view. Perfectly understandable. Reporters had to be prepared to pay a price for those much sought after exclusives.

"Eduardo, they treat us like heroes," explained Galente. "Everyone loves us. They fantasize about us. They live their dull lives through us. They want to do what we do. They hate the cops."

"Tommy Boy, I no like being in the paper," Marcese said. "I no like my *famiglia* reading about me. It's all bullshit. I no understand how they print lies. We no do half the things they say. Who they talk to? They never asked me."

Besides feeding his ego, Galente had another strategy for his complicity with the press that he tried to explain to Marcese.

"My mouthpiece says shut up," said Galente. "He says don't say a word to the press. But I wanna get some information out. I ignore my mouthpiece. I call reporters, give them information. It don't even have to be the truth. The jury reads it, I win and I don't have to pay my attorney, who's nothin' but a fuckin' leech. He asks how that get in the papers. I shrug my shoulders. I don't know nothin'."

While Marcese still did not like the publicity, Galente's argument seemed to make some sense. Appearing before juries was a regular part of their lives. It seemed to happen every four or five years, particularly when a new major public official was elected.

Marcese shared Galente's distaste for attorneys who sold their souls for a buck, mega-bucks. At least mobsters were men of honour who had a set of beliefs. Damn attorneys would represent anyone, say anything, swear on The Bible while telling the most outrageous lies, all in pursuit of billable hours.

Marcese had to admit that Galente had a point. He just believed his method of handling jurors was a little more "sophisticated," less prone to chance. Giving jurors ten grand or so was more effective than hoping they had read some fact in the newspaper. And all he had to do was find one in twelve. Pretty good odds. Since some juror always needed the extra cash, he was usually quite successful. An implied threat, also, was a good incentive to vote "not guilty." Wanting to live persuaded many a juror to vote for acquittals.

So Marcese did not waver on his opposition to publicity. "It gonna bite us in the ass," Marcese said. "I no want people to stare at me on the street. Tommy Boy this ain't no good."

Galente, trying to ease the tension, asked, "You wanna my autograph?"

Marcese was not amused. He was about to reply when he and Galente heard a car door slam. The first was followed by a second, then a third, and several more. Voices were giving instructions. They did not panic because it was all too familiar. Before long the front door crashed open, and more than a dozen federal and local cops, revolvers drawn, ran into the house.

Marcese and Galente hardly flinched. Their faces seemed to say, "Not again." The man in charge of the unscheduled and uninvited intruders addressed them both:

"Eduardo "The Brains" Marcese and Tomaso "Tommy

Boy" Galente you are under arrest for murder, conspiracy to commit murder, and sixty seven counts of racketeering, violations of interstate commerce laws in transporting prostitutes, money laundering, and illegal gambling.

"You have a right to remain silent. Anything you say can and will be used against you in a court of law. You have a right to have an attorney present during questioning. If you cannot afford an attorney, one will be appointed for you. Do you understand these rights?"

Marcese and Galente wanted to laugh. Understand? They gotta be kidding. They had done this so many times they could have recited the Miranda warning. Both, cooperatively and to speed things up, were already standing with their arms behind their backs.

Cops handcuffed Marcese and Galente, grabbed the two by the elbows and escorted them outside where, to no surprise to either Marcese or Galente, they faced a gaggle of reporters from, it seemed, the entire state of New York. Obviously, some politician wanted to show the public how he was fighting crime to make the world a better place in which to live.

The questions came from every direction. "Are you guilty?" "Did you guys kill Michelotti?" "Are you members of the *Mafia*?" "Are you dons?" "You got anything to say?"

Marcese did not have anything to say. He walked with the officer holding him to the appointed scout car with his head down. He tried not to have his photo taken. When he saw a photographer kneeling in front of him, pointing his camera up, Marcese brought up his right foot to kick the persistent and inventive news pest, but the photographer leaped out of the way.

"*Bastardo*," Marcese whispered to himself. The cop,

with his hand on Marcese's head, pushed his prisoner into the back seat from where Marcese saw his colleague holding an impromptu press conference.

"We ain't done nothin'," Galente told the city's press corps. "We's innocent of everything."

"You members of the *Mafia*?" one reporter asked.

"Never heard of it. You make my mother sad writing that stuff."

The news reporters laughed.

"You blow up Michelotti?"

"Hey, that was my car. That could have been me, and I couldn't answer your questions."

Again, the news reporters roared.

When he added, after a pause, "I liked that car," the media could not control their laughter. Galente's timing was as perfect as that of professional comedians.

"Fellows, I wish I could stay, but these officers are in a hurry," Galente said. "I don't wanna get them in trouble. Come down to the station. We'll talk some more."

He ended his impromptu press conference and headed for his own scout car. As he walked through the mob of reporters, several patted him on his back.

One young reporter, an attractive woman about twenty five with long blonde hair and a healthy bust, stepped in front of Galente with one hand on her microphone and the other on a button at the top of her blouse. Slowly, she unbuttoned it as she bluntly asked Galente, "Are you guilty?"

"Baby, I'm guilty of a lot of things. Set up an appointment with me, and I'll give you a real exclusive."

The reporter, picking up on the sexual overture, followed up, "Will it be on or off the record?"

"Your choice." Galente, pushed by the officers, brushed past her and, as he got into the scout car, he turned and gave her a wink. She started to wink back but caught herself. Wouldn't be very professional.

For Marcese and Galente, the arrests were more of a nuisance than a threat to their freedom. As in previous arrests, many arrests, they would be released within hours with their attorneys posting bail, no matter the amount.

The entire process would cost them hundreds of thousands of dollars, and it would consume years, but they would be able to continue their operations. And overall, given the work of lawyers and a few bribes, the odds of being found innocent were in their favour. Indeed, their strategy had worked fairly well. Thus far, their records were perfect. Lots of arrests -- they had lost count – but no convictions. They believed in the justice system and, overall, had no complaints.

They were much more concerned about The Butcher. Court dates and hearings along with depositions and trials all would pre-empt and delay what had been their primary goal: to get rid of The Butcher. They could concentrate on only so many crises at one time.

They would have been in better spirits as they sped away in scout cars with sirens blaring, if they had any inkling that Valenti, in the not too distant future, would undertake the objective to assassinate The Butcher.

CHAPTER 24

VALENTI'S LIFE IN RENO was as uneventful as it was in Vegas before he screwed up and got involved with the hooker-spy. His biggest problem? He constantly wanted to get laid. Controlling his sexual appetite was not easy. Like in Vegas, all he saw in Vegas' sister sin city were long legs and tits. Only so much a man could take.

And he was becoming homesick. It had been months since he disappeared after ruining a pizza deliveryman's life. He needed and wanted to see his family. He thought about them constantly.

So he took a risk. He considered it a small risk, and called Giancamilli, asking him to meet him at a motel on the highway in Kansas. Valenti did not pick up on the tension in his friend's voice on the telephone. There was no joy in Giancamilli's voice in hearing from his friend to whom he had not talked in months. Instead, the voice was filled with sadness and despair.

They met in Valenti's room, and after the usual greetings which were shorter than under normal circumstances, Valenti asked, "Luigi, where are they? How are they?"

Giancamilli did not answer. He looked nervously around the room, avoiding eye contact with his friend. He nervously coughed into his hand curled into a fist. He did not say anything.

"Luigi, I asked you. Where are they? Come on. Don't just sit there on your fat ass. I want an answer."

Giancamilli got up from his chair. He paced back and forth within a few feet. He again coughed into his fist. He went into the bathroom and drank some water. He returned quickly and tried to answer his friend.

"Johnny ...," he started, but stopped.

"What is it? You're my friend, talk to me."

Slowly understanding Giancamilli's reluctance to answer his questions, Valenti plaintively asked, "No?"

It was not so much a question as a statement. The "no?" turned into a very painful, "No ... no ... no." He repeated the "no" many times, more loudly each time he said it. Valenti shot up from his chair, he stalked the room, and punched a hole in the dry wall with his fist.

"They're gone? Gisele, Little Johnny, and my Lucia?" Valenti asked. It was a rhetorical question.

Giancamilli said nothing. He saw what he thought he would never see. Tears welling in Valenti's eyes. Tears. Tears from a man who could look another in the eye and kill him without even blinking. Tears from a man who, after a hit, could have dinner, go to a movie or read a newspaper. Tears from a man who would feel worse stubbing his toe than seeing a man slumped over before him with a bullet between the eyes.

"How? When?"

"Two weeks ago."

"How? Luigi, I also asked you 'how?'"

"Johnny, what's the difference. I don't want to do this. Just make you feel worse. I ain't gonna go into it."

The story that Giancamilli pieced together from talk on the street and which he did not want to share with his lifelong friend began a month after The Butcher met with teams he had assigned to his get-Valenti project.

Giancamilli learned that The Butcher was coming to New York, and he assumed something big was up. The Butcher would not leave the secure surroundings of his villa in Cinisi unless it was urgent, a matter of life and death, mostly death. His decision to leave his safe haven was evidence of how much Valenti bothered him. Valenti did not have a high rank. Yet, The Butcher personally wanted to manage the Valenti project. Valenti was an unbearable thorn in his side.

The pipeline told Giancamilli that The Butcher had met with Joe "Banana Fingers" Palucci to discuss Valenti's fate. When The Butcher discovered that Valenti's family lived in Brooklyn, he decided to go after Valenti's wife and two children. He believed killing Valenti's family would be a greater punishment for his adversary than even whacking Valenti himself.

While Giancamilli had often raised the issue of safety with Gisele, she regrettably rejected his warnings, not able to fathom that The Butcher might consider her family a tempting target. She could not believe that the man would kill innocent women and children. That was beyond comprehension. Unfortunately, she could also not grasp that The Butcher was devoid of a conscience.

When Palucci and a two-man backup team got the assignment, they objected. Even by the mob's standards, this was unacceptable brutality. Palucci, particularly, wanted no part of this. *Famiglia* – family – was considered off-limits. Even the families of rats were to be immune from retribution. What's more and worse, Valenti had not ratted. Palucci protested as much as he could, as much as was safe. Ultimately, he acquiesced.

Giancamilli's sources told him that Palucci picked up The Butcher at his hotel room at two a.m. one night, and drove to Valenti's home. Palucci's two-man backup team followed in a separate car.

They arrived at about 2:45 a.m. Palucci got out of the car, and went to the side of the sprawling ranch home while the backup team stood guard. He pried open a window, raised it and climbed in. Palucci completed the assignment and was out of the house within a few minutes. The backup team stayed to pick up the bodies and dispose of them. They worked on the premise that the family would be reported missing a few days later.

Facing his friend, Giancamilli refused to tell Valenti what he knew about the slaughter of his family, how his wife and children were killed while sleeping in their beds late at night. He was unable to talk about such barbarity, especially since his best friend was involved. He also blamed himself for not insisting that Gisele and her children go into hiding. He should not have given in so easily.

"Johnny, please don't push me on this. I ain't gonna say no more."

Valenti started to protest. He wanted to know, but he did not want to know. He relented and did not press the issue. He felt sweat on his forehead and a little running down his back. He was weak, and unsteady on his feet. Would he faint? These were new sensations to him. They confused him. Underneath them all was anger, a raging anger. An inferno. Even while reeling from the news of the murder, the slaughter of his family, he was already thinking of how he would get justice. Ultimately, The Butcher would be held accountable. Would he ever. This act would not go unpunished. That much he had decided. Gisele, Little Johnny and Lucia would be avenged.

"Luigi, he may believe the stuff on the street, but I ain't no rat," said Valenti. "I never ratted. I did eighteen for nothin' and never ratted against that prick DeSante."

"Johnny, who you talking too, huh? You think I don't know. You're talking to Luigi."

Valenti sat on the bed with his hands on his head. He stood up. He paced. He cried. Giancamilli did his best to console his friend. He recognized that given such a loss his friend was inconsolable.

The two sipped drinks from a bottle of whiskey until Giancamilli, totally drained emotionally, passed out in a chair. When he awoke, he found his friend sitting at a table with papers strewn all over it. It was obvious, Valenti had been busy.

"You been up all night?" Giancamilli asked.

"Yeah, couldn't sleep. Been working."

"On what?"

"On what, Luigi? Whatta you think? On that fuckin' Butcher. How I'm gonna get that son-of-a-bitch. I had lots of ideas. And I think I got it."

"Yeah? So tell me."

"Luigi, you gonna see soon enough."

Valenti looked at his watch. It was 10:30 a.m. The U.S. government's offices would be open.

He stood up and picked up the telephone. "Give me the number of the federal organized crime division."

Giancamilli was aghast. His friend could not be calling the feds. He rushed forward and grabbed the phone out of Valenti's hands.

"Johnny, what the ... you can't."

"Luigi, I got to do this. He killed my family. You think I'm just gonna sit by and do nothin'. That what you think? Give me the damn phone."

"Johnny, I understand, but this, you can't. It's against ...."

Giancamilli could not bring himself to say "*omertá*," not under the circumstances. He had difficulty accepting that his friend would violate the principle by which he lived his life. Giancamilli did not want to confront his friend, who was grieving, with the apparent contradiction. It did not seem right. Without another word, he handed Valenti the phone.

Valenti got the number, made his call and reached Bruce Johnson. "Johnson, this is Johnny Valenti. I'll come straight to the point. I wanna deal, and I think you and your fed friends will like what I gotta say."

Valenti listened closely, and then told Johnson, "I need three days to get back. After that, as far as I'm concerned, the sooner the better." With Johnson apparently agreeing, Valenti ended the conversation with, "I'll be there," and hung up.

With some hesitation, Giancamilli gave it one more try.

"You sure about this?"

"Yeah. No question what I got to do." He did not tell his best friend that in meeting with Johnson, he would be working with a chameleon, a mole in the feds with whom he had dealt for years. Johnson, who had saved Valenti's life in Vegas, played both sides of the street. He was a federal agent as well as an informer for the mob. He made a good living at it, but he probably would be considered a high risk, very high risk, by life insurance companies.

Overnight, Valenti had developed a complex and diabolical plot to avenge the murder of his family. He would get justice. And justice was all he wanted. Regrettably, he would need the help of the mole. He had no choice. Sometimes one just has to swallow hard to accept undesirable realities. Can't be helped.

Valenti kissed Giancamilli on both cheeks and gave him a bear hug.

"Don't worry, Luigi, I never heard of you."

CHAPTER 25

VALENTI COULD NEVER EVEN have imagined that one day he would be in the offices of the government's special organized crime task force with the very people who, for most of his life, had hunted and haunted him and his friends. They had worked to destroy him. They had made life miserable. Johnson and his cohorts were pricks, never giving them a moment of peace.

They tapped their phones, followed them, and took photos at their funerals. Why did they need photographs at funerals? They had thousands in their files along with tapes from wiretaps. Hell, they could name most of those who would be attending these funerals. Did they really believe no one knew they were watching the mourners at graveside? Sometimes Valenti wanted to shout, "As long as you're here, you want to say something about the dead?"

What really pissed Valenti off was that given all the countless photos the feds had in their files, they always released the worst to the media, the ones with the five o'clock shadows. Why not release the more flattering ones?

At the moment these thoughts were far from Valenti's mind. Under the circumstances, he was prepared to help the guys who chased the mob. They lived for only one objective which was to destroy the undestroyable, and they never gave up. Talk about being stubborn. It was true that every once in a while, they caught a big-time mobster that earned them big headlines. None of their work ever achieved the destruction of organized crime. It never would. The entire program, Valenti always thought, was a waste of taxpayers' money. If only the *schmuck* on the street knew.

All these thoughts were running through Valenti's

head when he realized it would be with these bastards that, for the first time in his life, he would violate *omertá*. Actually, pretend to violate *omertá* to get the information he would need to achieve his objective, one the feds had tried to accomplish for a long time. He had a trick or two up his sleeve.

Admittedly, it pained him that he had to work with Johnson. Valenti had absolutely no respect for him, given his duplicity. At least, the "regular feds" abided by some principles. This guy Johnson would sell out his mother.

Valenti was sitting in a small conference room at a table with a tape recorder on it. In the room were Johnson and two of his colleagues. The three wore white shirts and ties. With their coats off, they revealed their shoulder holsters which were empty.

"Tell your two friends to get the hell out of here and take that with them," said Valenti, pointing to the recorder.

Johnson did not argue. He handed the recorder to the agents and waved at them to leave the room. After they were gone, Valenti asked, "Before we start, you got bugs in here anyway?" Receiving no reply, he offered, "I guess I'll trust you. I really can't debug the place, can I?"

They both laughed as Johnson gave Valenti a knowing wink. They played it straight just in case the office was, indeed, bugged. Johnson scribbled a short note – a *pizzini* – that said, "How about a thank you for Vegas." In return, Valenti scribbled, "F you." Both gave each other knowing looks as they tore up their notes with Valenti putting all the scraps in his pocket. Couldn't be too careful.

"So, Mr. Valenti, what brings you to the house of the enemy, to Team U.S.A?"

He didn't have to answer the question. He still had time to turn back. It wasn't too late. But he didn't want to. He was warming up to the proposal he was about to make. He was exhilarated, excited. He was taking the first step to whacking The Butcher.

"I want to take out The Butcher."

"What's new? So do we. You think we've been sitting on our asses since he hit Hawk?"

"Yeah, but the difference is you guys are incompetent. I can make it happen. It takes a mobster to get a mobster."

While Johnson did not like Valenti's assessment of the government's work, he thought Valenti's point made sense. He would know, from the inside, how The Butcher operated, his habits, weaknesses. All that would help immeasurably.

"Let's hear what's on your mind and try to do it without all the nastiness. We are very sensitive in this office."

"I'll go to Sicily to take out The Butcher, but I need your help. I need a new identity, passport and the book you have on him. Everything."

"What's in it for us?"

"You get a dead Butcher, and the names I give you when I come make will make your career. Just don't give me any credit."

Valenti outlined an elaborate plan. The feds would hire a plastic surgeon who would change his face, so that even his mother would not recognize him. The plastic surgeon would also alter his fingerprints.

Valenti would fly to Cinisi to execute his plan – execute The Butcher. When he returned from killing The Butcher, with his new face, he could have a regular life in

New York. No witness protection plan for him. Witness protection was an oxymoron. In fact, the mob had a whole corporate division assigned to do nothing but take out members of that program. And its record was pretty good. He didn't want to look over his shoulder for the rest of his life.

For his recuperation period, he demanded they provide him with a secure place in New York along with the medical attention he would require.

The feds would make the travel arrangements to and from Sicily. They would provide the appropriate housing (He would give them the instructions when his research was completed). They would install a secure telephone line and arrange for all his needs, such as food, emergency medical teams just in case, a maid to clean his place, anything he would need.

The most important part of the deal required the feds to turn over the "book" on The Butcher. He needed everything – daily routines, his habits, quirks, medical records, transcripts of wiretaps – everything the feds had collected over the years. That was the key for him to develop his plan, a plan that would be immune – immune as possible – from failure. When the job was completed, he would return and sing, not happily, but he would sing. He would perform an aria.

Johnson exhaled audibly when Valenti finished.

"Anything else you want us to do, like having the Pope invite you to dinner?"

"Nah, he's boring. He won't want to talk about broads."

"How do I know you'll come back?"

"Trust. Are you saying, Johnson, you don't trust me?

Can't believe it. Even if I didn't, but I will, you'll get The Butcher and you gotta admit that's big. You can even take credit for it, how you took him out. Come up with some bullshit story for the press. You do it all the time, and, I promise, I won't say a thing."

Johnson did not let on, but he liked the deal. The Butcher was worth it, and he also believed Valenti would keep his word, and rat.

Trying to bluff, he said, "We could take out The Butcher."

"Who you kidding? You guys need pros. If you had asked us to help with Castro, he wouldn't be in power. We could've done that for you, and for less than it cost you to screw up. We could have saved lots of taxpayers' dollars. You guys ain't nothin' but amateurs."

Johnson had to admit Valenti had a point. Efforts by the U.S. to assassinate Cuba's dictator, Fidel Castro, had failed repeatedly as had attempts to get rid of other "unwanted" leaders in the world. Valenti's record and those of his colleagues were pretty impressive. They always seemed to succeed. Maybe the CIA ought to establish a mob division.

"If it weren't for us guys in the mob, we'd still be fighting World War II."

"What the hell are you talking about?"

Valenti warmed with pride to tell Johnson the story he had heard many times over the years how underworld crime leaders "Lucky" Luciano, Meyer Lansky, a Jewish mobster, along with Calogero Vizzini, known by some as the "*Mafia* boss of bosses" in Sicily in 1943, helped organize support for the Allies during their invasion of the island.

"Valenti, you're full of shit."

"The *yids* and *dagos* got together for a good cause. And just because they don't teach this in the schools don't mean it didn't happen. Before they write all that bullshit, they should ask us about how we helped win the war. Our feelings are a little hurt."

Ignoring Valenti's history lesson and sarcasm, Johnson, more out of pretence than uncertainty, paced the floor. He rubbed his chin as if he were pondering Valenti's unique proposal. He had already made up his mind.

"Give me a minute. Gotta check this with the higher ups. Be back in a jiff."

After about forty five minutes, Johnson returned. "It wasn't an easy sell."

The two shook hands with Johnson giving Valenti another wink. Valenti reluctantly winked back.

So far so good. He had taken the first steps to whack The Butcher and to free himself from the feds and from his life in the underworld forever. It was a good start. Everything was working perfectly. Johnson had not suspected anything.

CHAPTER 26

DR. WALTER BECKWITH DREW on Valenti's face
with black markers. He drew lines on his cheeks, his nose,
eyelids, chin, forehead and on several other places.

Periodically, he looked at several photographs of
Valenti pinned to a board on the wall. He checked X-rays,
and grunted in apparent approval. He looked at Valenti
who was leaning back in a specially equipped chair.

"I'm just about ready, Mr. Jones," said Beckwith.
"Basically, you will feel nothing. As I told you, you will
have some pain and swelling for about a month. From
what I see, I think we will have a successful project."

"Think? What's with 'I think'?"

"Just a figure of speech. I have done this on a number
of Mr. Joneses and never had a problem."

So, Valenti thought, *I'm not the first.* Johnson had
been bluffing in pretending that he was asking for
something unusual, new.

"I also want to let you know, Mr. Jones, there will be
no records. All these X-rays and photos along with my
medical notations will be burned. I just don't like keeping
so many records around. I am not a pack rat."

"Good to hear."

He underwent several hours of surgery that included
breaking the jawbone, and other facial bones, and grafting
skin to Valenti's fingertips. Had Valenti known about the
surgical procedures he would undergo, he might never
have agreed to have his face altered as part of his plan.

He did not remember much as he was driven to a
secret safe house to recuperate. The woman driving was
dressed in a nurse's uniform. She had a medical bag by

her side on the seat. His face was covered with bandages as were his fingers. He had some pain – pills helped – and he was woozy.

"How you doing?" his nurse asked.

He grumbled an almost undecipherable, "'Kay."

"Glad to hear it. A couple of other nurses and I will be with you around the clock. We'll help you eat, bathe, everything for awhile. It won't be long before you should be able to manage yourself."

"'Kay." Valenti realized they would have to help him piss and wipe his ass. He was revolted, but he had no choice. He saw a bulge by her shoulder under the nurse's uniform. *She's packing heat,* he thought. Good, very good.

The nurses took care of all his needs, almost all of his needs. He was not disappointed by the omission because getting laid was the last thought – well, not quite the last thought – that crossed his mind. All his energy was devoted to recuperating as quickly as he could.

After about a month, Beckwith visited him and removed the bandages from Valenti's face. He examined his work closely, telling his patient, "Things look pretty good. You won't need these any longer."

He gave Valenti the assurance he was hoping for. "You won't look anything like the photos we have in our files."

Valenti was amused by the doctor using "we" and "our," meaning that he must be on the regular payroll of the feds.

After examining Valenti's fingertips, the surgeon had another good prognosis for Valenti, telling him, "A little more time and you'll be able to use your hands. You're doing fine. See you in a week."

When the surgeon left, Valenti looked in the mirror only to discover he was so bruised – black, blue, swollen – he looked like a deadbeat whom he had tried to convince to meet payment deadlines.

"Holy shit, I'm a goddamn mess." He felt a little sorry for himself but not for long. All this was worth it if he succeeded in his goal.

As time passed, Valenti was getting restless. Just so much daytime TV a man could take. Worse, he couldn't even try to screw the nurses. True, they weren't beauty queens but under the circumstances, they would do. Despite the sexual pressures, he was not going to fool around with federal agents. When, throughout his career, he said "screw the feds," he did not mean it literally.

A week later, the doctor removed Valenti's bandages from his hands, permitting him to do things for himself. That helped. It was an upbeat day for Valenti. Ready to begin his research on The Butcher, he picked up the telephone that had a secure line, called his contact, telling him, "Send the stuff over."

The "stuff" involved the records on The Butcher. He wanted everything, and that's exactly what was delivered, everything. More than twenty boxes, filled with transcripts of telephone taps, photos, federal agents' notes, and other information, were stashed in Valenti's room.

It would be a gigantic research assignment, but he was ready. As he looked at the boxes, he thought the job foreboding, but he was anxious to start. If he wanted to succeed, he would have to do his homework, as laborious as it might be. No pain, no gain.

With a notepad at one side, a Coke on the other, he began. He read through the transcripts of wiretaps, he reviewed notes, looked at photographs taken surreptitiously by cops on surveillance. He looked for a clue, any clue that would help him with his self-appointed assignment. It was time-consuming, boring work.

He was amazed at the amount of information the feds had collected. They even seemed to know how many times The Butcher got up at night to take a piss. He wondered if they had such an extensive file on him. He was tempted to ask Johnson.

As the days and weeks slipped by, he started to lose hope. Maybe he would never find what he was looking for. Maybe he would have to search elsewhere. Although he was having doubts, he remained persistent, and his persistence paid off.

He came across the notes of an agent stationed in Sicily. His assignment was to follow The Butcher and record his every move. The agent was very thorough. Valenti was grateful as he read:

"TB (The Butcher) creature of habit. Likes sidewalk café called *DaNino* in the centre of the city. Never misses; visits at least once a week, always in p.m. Usually on Tuesdays but may vary. TB always sits at the same table and chair; three tables with four chairs each are outside. If his chair is occupied, owner moves customers. Orders lunch, always the same. Never pays. Owner treats him like royalty. Two TB's security guards stand by about twenty yards away. Stays forty minutes; like clockwork. Locals stay away from table. Seem to know who he is. No one joins him. Likes sitting alone. Tries to engage good-looking women walking by. Makes obscene comments. They ignore him. He gets pissed. Laughs like hell."

The agent's report continued for several more several pages. The package with the notes also included photos taken of The Butcher at the café with a long-range lens. Valenti studied everything carefully. He had the lead worth pursuing. He had sufficient information to implement his plans that would take him to Cinisi once more.

He prepared for his visit but, like the last time, he would not be able to tour the sites or have any reunions with distant family members. Too bad. Maybe on another occasion.

CHAPTER 27

CAPTAIN BRUCE JOHNSON KNOCKED on the door of Valenti's room. Five short taps, followed by two seconds of silence and five more. That combination would change each time he visited.

Valenti unlocked the door and, while he did not want to admit it, he was anxious for some company even if it was with a duplicitous fed agent.

"You don't look so bad anymore," said Johnson.

"Thanks for the compliment."

Valenti handed notes he had prepared to Johnson. They included these instructions:

> *I want/need*
> 1. *1 Car/driver to airport.*
> 2. *2.Rifle with scope and a .45 calibre (backup in case of trouble. Don't expect.)*
> 3. *3.$5,000 in cash in Sicilian money.*
> 4. *4.Safe apartment or room across from café. Must have window facing café.*
> 5. *5.Secure telephone line.*
> 6. *6.Car/driver on 24-hour call. He needs to be no more than five minutes away.*
> 7. *7.Driver from Sicily airport to place.*
> 8. *8.Food, supplies for three weeks. May not need all. Depends.*
> 9. *9.Medical personnel available on call (if I get sick.)*
> 10. *10.Car/driver to airport after mission completed. Car/driver to pick me up when I return. I'll come straight to your office to keep my part of bargain.*
> 11. *A hooker for each night. (Kidding. I'll play*

priest.)

Valenti is sure thorough, Johnson thought.   Didn't leave much to chance.

"Whew!" said Johnson, feigning surprise.   "Is that all?"

"Yeah, that'll do it.   If I think of somethin', I'll let you know."

"I'm sure you will," Johnson said, heading for the door.   "I'll be in touch."

The next job was to test his face.   Valenti waited another couple of weeks when he called Giancamilli whom he had not seen since his meeting in Kansas.

"Johnny, where the fuck you been?"

"It's a long story."

"I been looking all over hell for you.   Meet me at Arturo's.   I got good news.   Real good.   Move your ass."

"What's the rush?"

"Just get over here."

Valenti could not understand Giancamilli's urgency. He seemed desperate.   Good news?   What good news?   He sure could use some.   He was anxious to hear the "good news" and also share his plans to whack The Butcher with his friend.   He made his way to Arturo's.   The meeting would give him the opportunity to test his new identity. He wondered if Giancamilli would recognize him.

Valenti saw Giancamilli on a bar stool, his back to the bartender.   He was scanning the crowd for Valenti and, at the same time, eyeing broads.   He did not see Valenti approach.   When Valenti was about three feet away, he addressed his friend.

"So, where's the fire?"

Giancamilli was perplexed. He glanced at the man in front of him who resembled Johnny Valenti. Confused, he concluded maybe he was just a look-alike. He was puzzled.

"I know you?"

"Luigi, yeah, you know me. You owe me a hundred smackers."

The voice did it. "Johnny, what the ...?"

Valenti grabbed his friend by the elbow and led him to the back of the bar. They sat in a booth where Valenti explained his plastic surgery, and all aspects of his plot to whack The Butcher. Giancamilli listened impatiently. He had important news. When would Valenti finish?

His patience ran out, and before Valenti said another word, Giancamilli interrupted, "Shut your trap already. Johnny, your family is alive. Gisele, Little Johnny and Lucia."

Valenti was not sure he had heard correctly. "What are you talking about? You told me ..."

With a big grin, Giancamilli nodded. "They're alive. Safe."

Valenti, totally confused, just sat and stared at his friend. He shrugged his shoulders, signalling Giancamilli to tell him what had happened.

"The Butcher assigned the job to Palucci, but he couldn't do it. Neither could the two backup guys. Wife and kids, no way. It ain't our way. Never been done before. And they got kids too. Palucci and the others faked the killings, told Gisele to take the kids and get out of town. He took a big risk. He and the others have disappeared. Gisele called me, asking for help. She's in a safe place."

Valenti was shocked, speechless. Again, his eyes welled up with tears but this time out of joy. He left the booth, went to the john and washed his face. He looked in the mirror and did not move for several minutes. When his emotions were under control, he went back to join Giancamilli.

He had lots of questions. For the next half hour, he interrogated Giancamilli for information. While Giancamilli did not have many details, he tried his best to give Valenti a full picture of what occurred.

"Johnny, I don't know much. Told you what I picked up on the street. All that matters, they are safe and you know I will take care of them."

Valenti relented in his pursuit of the full story. Maybe he would learn the full story at some later date. He decided to bask in the most unexpected but welcome news that his family was alive.

"Yeah, you do that, Luigi. I wish I could tell Palucci I owe him. I owe him big. Any ideas where he went?"

"We ain't never gonna find him because if we can, he can."

Valenti agreed. Understandably, he had a difficult time digesting the news. He was working to comprehend what appeared to be incomprehensible. He wanted to talk about his family but he did not have much time so he returned to outline, in some detail, his elaborate scheme.

"Why the fingerprints?"

"Those are for Cinisi. No telltale signs left in my room. The face is for here. I want to live a normal life, if

I come back."

The "if" bothered Giancamilli. Would he see his friend again when this was over? He would have to wait and see. It was obvious that Valenti had it all thought out. Was it a sure thing? In life, particularly in the underworld, nothing ever was. Something always seemed to happen. Whenever you thought you had it made, shit hit the fan. True, there were lots or risks, lots of unknowns, lots that could go wrong. After all, Valenti was going after a big fish, a very big fish. Giancamilli's conclusion? Valenti had a reasonable chance of success. That was all a man could ask for.

"You were my test on the face, Luigi. If you hesitated, I don't have to worry. See you in about a month or so. I'll call."

"Wish I could go with you," said Giancamilli. "We could work together." Giancamilli made this suggestion half-heartedly. He knew his friend would not accept his offer, that Valenti had to go it alone. Valenti had to solo.

"You watch the home front, Luigi. I'm gonna get that son-of-a-bitch. He ain't never gonna have the chance to go after me or the family, ever."

The men embraced and kissed each other on both cheeks. As they let go, Giancamilli took one last look at the face. All he could do was shake his head.

Giancamilli asked about Johnson. "Can you trust him?"

"Like my own brother. He's a worm, a mole. Used him even before doing my time."

"No shit!"

"Gave me the tip in Vegas. Don't need to worry about him. Luigi, you take care of them. I'll be in touch."

"Don't worry. As if they're mine." He added, "I'm sure glad I ain't The Butcher."

When Valenti returned to his room, he found a large package on a table. He opened it carefully and emptied the contents. Important phone numbers/contacts, check; five grand in liras, check; and a key to an apartment, check. There was also a note:

1. *"1.The passport still needs a photo of your new mug. Will send a photographer tomorrow. When ready, I'll get passport to you.*
2. *"2.The equipment you need will be in apt. along with food, and other things you asked for.*
3. *"3.The driver to take you to apt. on arrival is waiting for call.*
4. *"4.A secure telephone line installed.*
5. *"5.A driver to take you to the airport is standing by and his telephone number is in apt. along with emergency medical phone number. A doctor has been briefed. A driver to bring you to my office on your return is ready on call.*
6. *"You can drink the water. Everything is go. Oh, no hookers since you passed on them. Not that we would have provided them. Government doesn't pimp. Happy hunting."*

Happy hunting! Sick bastard, Valenti thought. He considered the good wishes appropriate. He was going hunting and, indeed, he hoped the ending would be a happy one.

CHAPTER 28

VALENTI LANDED AT PALERMO International Airport for the second time. The first time was when he flew with Marcese to Cinisi to meet The Butcher. This time, the second meeting, would not be so cordial.

One of his main objectives was to avoid rattling the various crime organizations that had their corporate headquarters in this part of Sicily. He wanted no entanglement with them not knowing their politics or their opinions about the boss of bosses. If he got in trouble, he did not have Luigi Giancamilli – The Fixer – to step in.

He did not want to become an item on the agenda of Sicily's Commission that settled disputes between various *Mafia* organizations. He did not think the commission would look kindly on a self-starter who, without any kind of official portfolio or sanction, came to its turf -- from the U.S. of all places—to do in one of their leaders. *The* leader. His former boss, no less. The Butcher may have had it coming, but there were rules to follow, jurisdictions to respect, clearances to be obtained, hits to be approved. One couldn't have crime flourishing in anarchy. There was a reason the *Mafia* and *Cosa Nostra* were said to be engaged in "organized" crime with the emphasis on "organized."

Recognizing the political crisis his self-appointed assignment could create, all he wanted was to do his job quietly, without fanfare and get the hell out of Cinisi as quickly as possible.

His driver took him to Cinisi, ending up on a small, narrow side street where a sign caught Valenti's eye. *DaNino*. The driver pointed to the other side of the street. "You're over there," the driver said as he dropped Valenti off.

Valenti reached into his pocket for a key Johnson had included in his package. He unlocked a door next to a candy store and made his way up the stairs. The key also fit the door of his room.

He dropped his bag, and on the bed he saw a .45 calibre revolver and a rifle – an AR-15, a lightweight, air-cooled, semi-automatic weapon, the civilian version of the military M-16. He picked up the rifle which looked new. Barrel spotless. Didn't have a scratch. Good feel. Without parting the curtains, he pointed the rifle through the window and, using the scope attached to this model, fixed the cross hair on the letter "D" on the sign, "*DaNino.*" He liked what he saw; he didn't anticipate a problem. It was easily within the rifle's maximum range of six hundred yards. Everything had been taken care of just as Johnson had described in his note. The guy was good at follow up.

The feds had some trouble getting the apartment facing *DaNino*. The occupants were tourists in Sicily for three months who did not want to move. After a tear-jerking story about a family from Argentina wanting to use it while holding a vigil for its dying grandmother, the renters agreed to move out. It won't be long, they were assured. "We'll call you when it's over." What really did it? The feds paid them three times the rent along with a five hundred dollar bonus.

The room wasn't much. A double bed, chest of drawers, a couple of chairs, and some pictures of landscapes on the wall. A reading light was next to an overstuffed chair. It had a bathroom in the hall that was also used by other renters. Valenti did not like having neighbours nearby, people he might run into on his way to the bathroom or in the halls. Not much he could do about it, though. As to the apartment, whatever the feds paid in rent, it was too much.

As he unpacked, he placed a photo of his family on the chest of drawers. He walked to the window. The chairs and tables on the sidewalk of the café were only about sixty yards away. The street was narrow. Things could not be any better.

He counted. As the agent noted, there were three tables with four chairs each. Valenti looked at his notes which reminded him that The Butcher always sat at the same table. He hadn't noticed that the fed agent didn't identify which one. Damn!

He picked up his rifle, and peering through the scope, aimed it through the closed window. For the next few minutes, he focused on each one of the twelve chairs to see if there were obstructions. A couple would give him problems, unwanted problems, but not major ones. He was a little upset but accepted that which could not be changed. He couldn't go to the café and move the chairs to spots that would give him the best shot. The good news? It was the weekend so he had a couple of days to adjust and practise.

That's exactly what he did, hour after hour. He pointed the rifle at each chair, squeezing the trigger to work out any kinks that he might encounter. His plan was as follows: He wanted The Butcher to know he was being assassinated. If he had his choice, he would like to stand in front of him and see the fear as he did with others. Under the circumstances a confrontation was not possible. Thus, he developed a fifteen-second plan. He would wound The Butcher first, surprising him, but he would not immediately conclude he was about to be whacked. Valenti would wound him again, and this shot would bring the reality of the hit into The Butcher's consciousness. And finally, *the* shot – the deadly one.

Valenti figured that he only had fifteen seconds, about

the time The Butcher's protective henchmen would jump into action. It wouldn't take them long to figure out where the shots came from. He would have to move and move fast.

He spent the weekend, hour after hour, looking through the scope. While somewhat tedious, for Valenti, the chore was not onerous because he had immersed all his energies and focus into achieving his objective. Whenever he was fatigued, depressed or annoyed by the boredom, he looked at the photo of his family.

At night, he walked the streets, stopping in bars for a beer or two. He kept a low profile, talking to no one. He was extra careful. If someone tried to engage him in a conversation in bars or on the streets, he pretended he did not understand. Which was partly true. While not fluent, the Italian he had learned from his parents was still very good. But the Sicilian dialect in this part of the country was not easy to understand even for someone with some knowledge of Italian. He could make out a few words, but simply waved off anyone who tried to talk with him. He wanted to avoid taking any chances, adopting a very strict no-risk policy. Better safe than sorry.

The wait gave Valenti lots of time to think. Think not just about The Butcher but about his future. After his mission, which he assumed would be successful, what would he do? How long could he continue in this job? He was getting older. His instincts and reflexes were not as good as they used to be. This was a job for a younger man. Even "The Greatest," the heavyweight champ, Muhammad Ali, who at thirty six was younger than Valenti, could no longer float like a butterfly and sting like a bee.

He thought about his family. Eventually, Gisele might figure out how he supported his family, if she did not know already. If she discovered, specifically, that he killed people for a living, could she accept him? It would take some woman to accept the argument that, "You married me for who I am not for what I do to put bread on the table." Then he had to consider the kids. What would he tell them if they asked, as they would, when they grew older? What if they found out on their own? What would he do if he were invited to school for show-and-tell or a career day?

He was hoping for a marriage like the one his parents had. They had a simple life entirely devoted to each other and their son. Could he achieve that while maintaining his present profession? That was unlikely.

This line of thinking led him to review his recent unprofessional behaviour. How could he explain his effort to save the cop in the subway? What about failing to whack the dry cleaning store owner in the woods, at the risk to his own life? In Vegas, he had set free the spy-whore who would have had him killed. As he reviewed his performance in the last few months, it shocked even him. He would never hire a hit man with that kind of record. What in the world was happening to him?

These questions and many others dominated his thinking. Worse, underneath it all, he sensed he was beginning to feel some guilt. True, it was just a tinge of guilt. A hit man, a professional hit man of Valenti's calibre, could not afford any second thoughts. Compassion, vacillation, uncertainly, sympathy, depression were qualities, at whatever degree, murderers could not afford to indulge in. He sensed how these feelings were getting stronger by the day. Perhaps Gisele had unlocked them. The root cause for his ambivalence about his job did not matter. He was becoming damaged goods.

Who would want to hire a hit man who needed counselling or sympathetic reinforcement after a job? A hit man with guilt was like a major league batter stepping into the bucket when facing an approaching inside slider. The batter usually struck out. For a hit man, any hesitation before blasting a bullet into someone's gut or skull could mean failure, and failure could translate into death or imprisonment.

He was worried that, ultimately, his bosses, like the baseball manager watching the batter whiff when swinging at the curve ball, might notice. When assigned a contract, he might not be able to hide reluctance, no matter how slight it might be. He was not good at faking it, putting on a false front, and his bosses would have little patience with an employee who had second-thoughts when ordered to whack a rat or some other double-dealing bastard. If his bosses found out, he would be fired, and a firing by his bosses would not be accompanied by severance pay. If a hit man like Valenti were canned, there would be greater finality.

He was facing a dilemma that he would have to solve himself. Obviously, he could not talk to anyone. He could not see a psychiatrist and ask him to restore him into the cold-blooded guilt-free murderer he had been all his life. He could not ask a career counsellor to explain to him what had gone wrong, and to set him on the right path. He could not seek the counsel of other hit men or ask them how they overcame second-guessing or equivocation. Talk about embarrassment. He would not be able to live with the inevitable gossip that would spread about him in the underworld. In short, he had no confidant.

All these ruminations didn't matter. He knew he would never work again in his specialty. His career, which had been an excellent one, was over. No one would hire him after the assassination of The Butcher. He would become an untouchable. That was very clear to him. Indeed, in effect, he had made the decision to retire when he drew up his plans in the motel room in Kansas.

Moreover, should he surface after killing The Butcher, he would become a target. Someone would try to take him out. Little question about that. He probably would have the highest price on his head in the history of organized crime. Someone would want that money. And some of The Butcher's supporters would have a dual motive: revenge and the money.

So why was he thinking about the deterioration of his skills and future career opportunities? He did not want to return to work. Enough was enough. He felt it in his gut. He was needlessly wasting psychic energies trying to analyze what was wrong with him as it relates to his professional talents. It really didn't matter. He could never go back.

All these thoughts led him to consider seeing a priest. He remembered that whenever his parents, the only people he ever loved besides Gisele and his children, had problems, they would counsel with Father Rosetti. Admittedly, their sins hardly equated with those of their son. Their moral violations were more in the category of gossip, inadvertently short-changing a customer in their bakery, sometimes using a swear word, or occasionally not going to church. Compared to their son's wrongdoings, this was kid's stuff for a priest.

When his parents left for church with dour faces to confess their sins, they always returned happy, apparently free of whatever guilt lay heavily on their shoulders. The world was again a beautiful place, and they would advise their son, "When you gotta problems, you do bad things, Johnny, you go and talk-a to Father Rosetti."

At the time, the young Valenti had no interest in

talking to Father Rosetti or anyone else in authority. He did not think that even Father Rosetti would understand, condone or forgive him. Indeed, Father Rosetti, no matter how patient and understanding, probably shared his teachers' desire to punish him. He would not have been happy with Valenti and his friends stealing the money from collection plates, breaking windows, or their generally antagonistic behaviour in the neighbourhood.

That was long ago. He was a middle-aged adult. He had obligations, family obligations that he had to assume after he carried out his next, and final, hit. This time, unlike the promise he broke after whacking DeSante, he meant it. He was hanging up his revolver(s).

He decided to give it a try. He'd go to church. What's to lose? He wouldn't feel worse and he might just feel better. No one would ever know, which was the best part. He was not in New York where, by chance, he might meet someone he knew. He faced absolutely no risks.

All these thoughts led him to visit the Santuario della Madonna del Furi Church.

CHAPTER 29

HAD VALENTI BEEN A tourist, the visit to Santuario della Madonna del Furi Church would have been a once-in-a-lifetime highlight. He might have used an entire roll of film to take photos, maybe even shoot two or three rolls of film. He might have been a little awed, read the brochures, toured the building, admired its architecture and/or reflected on its holy setting.

The Santuario della Madonna del Furi Church was no ordinary church. It was built in the 1700s next to an adjacent creek with the same name where churchgoers had, through the years, reported seeing miraculous apparitions of the Virgin. Thus, this church had special holy standing in the community. The local populace was extremely proud of this very holy structure.

Valenti, strutting with determination and decisiveness, was not aware of the church's unique history nor would he have cared if he had known. He approached his mission as if he were on the way to a business meeting. And, as a matter of fact, he was. He had some business to take care of, the quicker the better.

His confidence waned as he stood in front of the church. Suddenly, the idea of unburdening himself to a priest did not seem so smart, so inviting. Valenti had never talked to anyone in his life about his problems, let alone about the problems he created for other people. What good would it do? If he told all, the priest would have to be appalled. The priest would not be able to understand. In that, Valenti was probably correct.

He started to walk away. This was all crazy, too crazy. What could that guy with the strange collar do for him? If he spilled the beans to the priest, then what? He was perplexed, to say the least.

After a few minutes of vacillation, he suppressed his misgivings. He would feel his way through the process, and if he experienced any doubt or had second thoughts at any point, he would just leave. The priest could not force him to talk. Even the feds couldn't do that.

He opened the front door, stepped inside and found the church almost empty. A few parishioners were kneeling, reciting prayers quietly, and a priest was lighting candles at the altar.

He stood in the doorway somewhat confused. This was new territory for him. For a few minutes, he did not know what to do. He did not want to ask for help from any of the parishioners, or interrupt their prayers. He decided to approach the priest, and headed down the centre aisle. Nervously, he looked from side to side at those praying. Mostly, he kept his head down.

When he reached the front, he stopped and waited. He did not know whether to interrupt the priest who had his back to Valenti. After a few minutes, Valenti coughed to get the priest's attention. The priest turned around, and was somewhat surprised to see Valenti standing there.

"I'm sorry, did you want to see me?" the priest asked gently.

Valenti's first instinct was to say that he had made a mistake. Instead, he admitted, "Yeah, I want to talk to you or someone else."

The priest, sensing the uneasiness of the hit man, motioned for him to sit down on the bench. "How can I help you?"

Good question. Valenti wished he knew the answer.

"I don't know if you can," Valenti said. "I done ..."

Valenti stopped. He did not know how to tell the

priest that he committed murders, lots of them.

"...bad stuff. Thought I would talk to you or another guy – priest – about that."

"You want to confess?"

The word "confess" sent shivers up Valenti's spine. No, he did not want to confess, to rat. The cops always wanted him to, but "confess" was a foreign and hated concept. Didn't this priest know anything? Didn't he ever hear of *omertá*? He's gotta be kidding. Confess, indeed!

"No, I don't wanna confess. I never confessed to anyone about what I did. Cops questioned me many times but I never confessed. I came cause my parents said they always were happier after talking to Father Rosetti. I wanna feel better."

The priest suppressed an urge to laugh. He recognized the connotation the word "confess" had to Valenti.

"May I ask when was the last time you were in church?"

Valenti thought back. The last time he was in church to pray was when he was a young child and attended Sunday services with his parents. He was confident the priest would not be impressed with other visits in which he and his pals stole money from several churches and the wine used in communions from the sacristies. He was certainly not going to tell him about his presence in Harlem's First Baptist Church with the Rev. Willie "Diamond Fingers" Johnson. The Cinisi priest would hardly consider that a religious experience. To his credit, Valenti didn't either.

He answered, "Never."

For the next few minutes, the priest patiently explained the Sacrament of Penance and Reconciliation –

confession – to Valenti. He assured him it was not like being questioned by the cops. It was a much gentler, more healing process.

"You mean, I tell you what I did, and you forgive me for everything?"

"Basically, yes. Priests have been given the authority by God and Jesus to forgive sins here on Earth."

The priest stood up, took Valenti by the elbow and led him to a more private area of the church. When they were seated again, the priest asked, "Have you sinned?"

"You kidding? Yeah, a lot."

"Do you want to tell me about your sins?"

"Do I want to tell you? No, I don't. I ain't feeling so good, and my parents told me long ago, if I feel bad to see Father Rosetti. Well, he ain't around so I come here.

"Look, Father, I sinned many times. I was in prison for a long time. I come out and started sinning again."

Trying to put Valenti at ease, the priest offered, "Jesus understands and forgives. I will explain what you can do for absolution after your confession."

"Abso ... what?"

"After you tell me of your sins, I will explain what you need to do for forgiveness."

Valenti sat still, confused, nervous, not sure he had made the right decision. All this was becoming a little too complex for him. He scratched his head and was tempted to leave. If he did, how would he come to peace with himself? There was no one else he could turn to so he continued.

Valenti tried to explain that what he did involved "big

stuff" not little sins like his parents committed. He was in the big leagues, the majors.

"Some of the things I did, well…" Valenti could not finish the sentence. No way could he reveal his secrets.

The priest waited, hoping Valenti would open up. It was not to be. Valenti, it was obvious to the priest, would have to be coached.

"Do you want to tell me about what you call 'big stuff'?"

"I ain't sure. If I tell you, you can tell the cops."

"I cannot tell anyone. I am required to keep your confession, all confessions, secret. I cannot and will not tell anyone. If I ever did, I would be excommunicated."

I heard this before from other guys promising not to rat, thought Valenti. At the same time, if this guy won't rat, if he was telling the truth, Valenti thought, this priest was really a disciple of *omertá*. If the priest had that kind of a commitment to keeping his mouth shut, maybe he could be recruited. Valenti was not convinced. He was hesitant. He had never trusted anyone in his life with his darkest secrets, and this priest, a total stranger, was asking him to unburden his soul, to tell him of crimes that could make him subject to several life sentences.

"I don't know," said Valenti. "I done some bad things."

The priest continued to explain that God forgives those who repent.

"He forgives past sins for those who pledge themselves to a new beginning," the priest assured Valenti. "Everything in the past is forgotten and forgiven."

"Everything?" Valenti asked.

"Yes, my son, as long as you are sincere and turn your heart to Jesus. You begin with a new slate."

Valenti was impressed but still sceptical. A life like the one Valenti had lived would make one cynical. Everything, huh? That's some forgiveness. He would never have forgiven or forgotten what DeSante did to him even if DeSante had turned to God or even became a priest. No way. DeSante had to be whacked. The son-of-a-bitch had set him up. Cost him eighteen years. How can anyone forgive that? For Valenti, there were limits to forgiveness. Could he trust the priest to know that God has different and more liberal standards?

The priest watched Valenti process what he had told him. He changed the subject. He asked Valenti why he was in Cinisi. Was he on vacation, on business, visiting relatives?

Valenti did not know how to answer. He sure would not tell him about his plans even if the priest swore on a stack of Bibles that he wouldn't blab. Maybe he could buy into the promise that the priest would not betray him about past sins. What about future sins, and such a big one? No way could he trust the priest with such a secret.

"Well, I gotta do one more big stuff."

The priest was shaken. He could not hear confession and absolve Valenti if he planned to sin again, and so soon, and apparently commit the same sin. At least that was the implication.

"Are you saying you plan to sin again?"

"Yeah, I guess."

"Then, I am afraid, I cannot help you. At least, at this time. In your confession, you must be firm in your purpose of amendment. I can't extend forgiveness if, while you're confessing, you are planning to sin again."

"People sin after confessing, don't they?"

"True, but they don't plan to sin while confessing as you're apparently going to do. Their future sins aren't premeditated."

Valenti was confused. He did not understand all the nuances of the confession process. The priest's references to "purpose of amendment" and "premeditation" sounded much like the jargon and gibberish used by his lawyers when trying to convince him to accept certain deals from prosecutors.

Though confused, he understood enough. It was déjà vu. This situation was something like the one he had faced when he appeared before the parole board. When board members asked him if he would "do this" again – they meant kill – if he had answered that his first job on the outside would be to whack DeSante, he probably would still be behind bars.

The priest was under the same constraints. It was clear to Valenti that he would not receive forgiveness if he still planned to go ahead with more one job – The Butcher. God had certain rules and the priest had to abide by them.

The confession process called for him to abandon his mission to whack The Butcher in exchange for forgiveness, and feeling better. No way. Sorry, God, that was not in the cards. Too much at stake. Giving up on "Mission: The Butcher" in exchange for absolution was not an option. His reward, were he to agree with the priest, was all too intangible. He would not compromise on The Butcher. Some things were simply not negotiable. God would have to understand. Equally important, there was this thing called "risk" to Valenti if he let The Butcher live. He had to consider that as well.

Couldn't God bend the rules of confession a little given that Valenti's life was at stake? He could not pose that question to the priest. He would have had to divulge his plans and the reason behind them. That was out of the question. It was either seek forgiveness by letting The Butcher live, or sacrifice, for the moment, being absolved and pursue his mission.

For Valenti, the decision was easy. He had his answer. There was no indecision. He knew what he had to do. No ands-or-buts or "Hail Marys" about it. He stood up, shook hands with the priest, telling him, "Thanks, Father. I will see you or another priest after my next sin."

CHAPTER 30

ABOUT THE TIME VALENTI decided he could not confess because he still had more sinning to do, the target of his next sin was expressing his frustration at not being able to find the sinner who was, literally, in his backyard.

"Whatta you mean, you cannot find him?" The Butcher shouted into the telephone.

"We're working on it."

"I giv-a you one more week," The Butcher said. "I wanna him and I wanna him fast. You no do this, and I no be very happy."

He slammed the telephone down, and ranted while stomping around his house. He would not endure another defeat. He had his limits.

He sat down in an overstuffed chair and did some deep thinking. He had lots of questions but few answers. Where would Valenti go? Where would Valenti believe he was safe? Who were Valenti's closest confidants whom he might ask for assistance? Surely, Valenti needed help and had to trust someone. He couldn't execute a Houdini disappearing act on his own.

What about Tomaso "Tommy Boy" Galente? He was a good friend of Valenti's. He was probably miffed at The Butcher for trying to spy on him with Michelotti. Of course, The Butcher did not know if Galente ever found out. Regardless, he decided to pass on Galente.

How about Luigi "The Fixer" Giancamilli, Valenti's best friend? He would be The Butcher's best bet. If anyone knew Valenti's whereabouts, it would be Giancamilli. He would most likely have the information, but would he divulge it? Probably not but he decided to call anyway. He had nothing to lose. He would use a carrot approach not the big stick.

He called Giancamilli on the pretence of offering him a promotion in an organizational restructuring. He described a "management shakeup," and implied that Giancamilli would receive a key spot in the new organization.

"I'm a-making some changes," The Butcher started. "I have-a big plans for you."

Giancamilli was suspicious. "I like working for Eduardo. He treats me good."

"Luigi, I need-a you up at the top," The Butcher replied. "I need-a good men. Lots more money for you."

Giancamilli did not take the bait. The Butcher would never appoint someone to the top like him, someone who was opposed to the kind of violence The Butcher thrived on. Someone who was Valenti's friend, a very close friend of The Butcher's number one enemy.

"Well, when you're ready, let me know," Giancamilli said.

"I'll think about it, and talk to Eduardo."

The Butcher asked him, "You hear-a anything about

Johnny?"

Giancamilli's suspicions were confirmed. The jump from a discussion of greater job opportunities for Giancamilli to the whereabouts of Valenti was too quick. There was no transition, no logical bridge. Giancamilli had no doubts about the reason for The Butcher's call.

"Haven't heard from him. I know nothin'. Wish I did. He's a good friend."

"You know-a nothin' huh?"

"That's right."

After they hung up, The Butcher was convinced Giancamilli was lying. Now what? If he had Giancamilli beaten to make him talk, word would leak out, and employee morale would suffer. Giancamilli was well liked, and The Butcher, at this sensitive time, could not afford more alienation among his troops. He was trapped. He made several other strategic telephone calls but to no avail. Valenti had kept his secret well and covered his tracks.

Then he made a call to the mole, the same one used by Marcese, Galente and Valenti. The mole was not fussy; he took payoffs from anyone, conflicts of interest be damned. He rationalized that the payments from The Butcher did not create a conflict since he was the boss of bosses. His other benefactors might conclude he would sell them out to The Butcher if the payments from The Butcher were lucrative, more lucrative than theirs. And he probably would.

Despite his duplicitous standards, the mole, Bruce Johnson, felt some anxiety while talking to the man whose assassination he had helped plan.

"I wanna something for my money," said The Butcher.

"I need-a information on Valenti."

"Wish I could help," said Johnson. "Haven't heard from him"

"I no believe you."

"Sorry, but ain't seen him or heard from him. Not since he returned from Reno. Wondered about him myself."

"I better not find-a out you lyin'.'"

Again, The Butcher hung up in frustration. It appeared he would just have to let it go, as much as it hurt. It was totally against all he stood for. Grudges were to be sated, not endured.

Wait a minute. Didn't Johnson say he had not seen Valenti "since he returned from Reno?" Reno? What's this about Reno? Valenti had disappeared again after Vegas. No one knew where Valenti went, yet the mole said "Reno." It was unlikely that Johnson misspoke. It must have been a slip. The Butcher was confident Johnson had some information. How he got it, The Butcher was not sure. Had Valenti contacted Johnson? If so, for what?

The Butcher was optimistic that he would get the information. His next move would be to launch an anti-Johnson plan, similar to the one that took care of Hawk, but the first step would be to make Johnson talk. His methods of persuasion were fairly reliable. They worked almost a hundred percent of the time.

With the Reno lead, The Butcher was confident that the search for Valenti, thousands of miles away, would prove successful. With this breakthrough to find his nemesis, he decided to make his usual visit to his favourite restaurant.

Meanwhile, Valenti waited for his encounter with The

Butcher across from *DaNino*, a mere fifteen miles from The Butcher's villa.

CHAPTER 31

MONDAY, THE WORKWEEK BEGAN not just for residents but for Valenti. The Butcher came every week, usually Tuesdays, the report said, but it contained a qualifier – "usually." That was a little disconcerting, but there was nothing he could do about the implied uncertainty.

Valenti moved a chair to the window and watched from behind the curtains. He had checked from the street to see if he could be seen. He was safe. Someone staring very closely might make out a figure behind the curtain. They certainly could not identify the individual or even say whether it was a man or woman.

So he sat. Sometimes he would read a newspaper or magazine looking up almost every minute. At times, he watched a television that he had moved into his line of vision. When he had to piss or take a crap, he did all he could to hurry the process. He ate at the window. Hour after hour he looked out, not taking his eyes off the three tables and twelve chairs. He was totally focused, almost to a fault.

Nothing Monday. He was a little disappointed. These things take time. His inner voice warned him not to get too anxious, too nervous. That might impact his performance. He needed to be calm, collected, patient. He had to remember, he told himself, the report said Tuesdays.

Tuesday. Nothing. A little doubt began creeping into Valenti's consciousness. What if the fed had screwed up? What if it was a bogus report? Maybe he had never stalked The Butcher and wrote the report to collect his paycheck. Maybe he was out getting drunk and he made up all those facts.

Valenti fought his doubts. Come on, Johnny, get a hold of yourself, it's only been two days. Let's worry if he doesn't show by the end of Friday. The report said every week, usually Tuesday. That still leaves Wednesday, Thursday and Friday.

Wednesday. It was 2:25 p.m. There he was. The Butcher. He looked even heavier than when Valenti had met him. Seemed like he put on another twenty to thirty pounds. He probably tipped the scales at three hundred pounds, maybe more. He was walking slowly with two bodyguards about ten yards behind him. He approached a table, his table, that from Valenti's view was on the far left. Not the best location but not the worst either. He could work with it. The Butcher sat down facing the street. Valenti could not keep his heart from beating faster. He wanted to remain as cool as he always was on his assignments. This was different. This was more important than getting even with a stoolie/rat like DeSante. This was seeking justice for his family. This was personal, very personal.

He went to the phone. "It's time," is all he said. He waited a few minutes, left the apartment and went to a window in the hall. He saw the driver arrive and park with the motor running. Back in his apartment, he opened the window about an inch. He picked up the rifle, knelt in front of the window, and poked the end of the rifle through the opening. The barrel rested on the sill. He parted the curtains just enough to have a clear view.

Slowly and carefully he got The Butcher in the cross hair of his scope. He took a deep breath and held it. When he was ready, he squeezed off one round. The Butcher felt a sting before the pain in his thigh. Instinctively, he grabbed his thigh and immediately his hand was covered with blood. Three seconds later, Valenti squeezed the trigger again. The Butcher grabbed his other thigh. Valenti had used six seconds. He counted: one, two, three, four, five, six and followed with the final fatal round. The Butcher got one through the neck. It took twelve seconds, three seconds fewer than he had allotted for the job. The Butcher was dead.

The Butcher's security guards did not respond to the first shot other than to look around when they heard the "pop" in the street. They moved quickly on the second. When they reached their boss, he was already wounded in both thighs. They did not have time to protect him against the third shot.

As The Butcher's security team scrambled, Valenti took the rifle, his small suitcase, ran out of the building and jumped into the waiting car. Valenti did not have to say a word. Without any instructions, the driver raced toward the airport. When they arrived, Valenti got out, leaving the rifle in the car. He assumed Johnson had given instructions how to handle its disposal. After all, Sicily was surrounded by water.

He went into the terminal, and sat down. He held his head in his hands, and reflected on his successful mission. He tried to collect himself while reflecting on what he had done and all its possible consequences. He had killed The Butcher, one of the most powerful men on two continents. He had killed a man who had politicians and power brokers at his beck and call, a man hunted by police agencies for years. He, Johnny Valenti, had accomplished what others, much more powerful, were unable to achieve. Valenti felt some pride. He would not have to fear being stalked. He felt as free as he did the day he walked out of Ray Brook. He had feelings he could not explain. Overall, it was nothing but joy.

What did it all mean? The media would have a field day with the story. Presidents and premiers would make statements while the underworld would be agog with rumours and gossip. Organized crime leaders would meet to discuss the hit, what to do about it, if anything. And, many in the top echelon would immediately implement a variety of strategies to replace him.

Valenti really did not care about the aftermath. The Butcher would be replaced and someone else would take the reins. The Butcher was dead but organized crime would live. All Valenti cared about was that his family was safe. He had protected Gisele and the twins.

As he sat mulling over the circumstances, he tried to focus and concentrate on his future, his family. He scanned the flight schedules not just for departure times but for destinations. He made his decision which confirmed thoughts he had while planning his post-Butcher future. He wasn't going back to New York, at least for some time. He was confident that was the right move. For the time being, any place in the world, except New York, seemed attractive. That would have to wait, maybe even forever. Who knew?

No question, he would have to leave Sicily. Where to? Somewhere back in the U.S.? The Middle East? Russia? France? Yes, France it would be. He had made the decision on France even before leaving the U.S. Now, he confirmed it while waiting in his room across from *DaNino*. Not just France – Paris. The city for lovers. He probably would not visit the Louvre or other cultural institutions. Not his thing. He did not even know the Louvre existed. At this moment in the airport, he concluded that he and Gisele could make a life in this historic and cosmopolitan city. Yes, Paris. It seemed the right choice.

"Luigi," he said in his telephone call to his friend. "Send them to Paris tomorrow." He was reluctant to answer Giancamilli's questions.

"Yeah, it's done," he said. "Don't want to talk about it on the telephone. Some other time.   You've been a good friend, the best. I'll see you again."

As he prepared for his flight, he only had one regret. He could not thank Palucci and his friends. They had put their lives on the line for him. Someday he would thank them.

CHAPTER 32

NEWS OF THE BUTCHER'S demise spread like wildfire. The world was abuzz from the President of the United States to the man on the street.

Within minutes of the shooting, news organizations throughout the world issued bulletin after bulletin. Sources, always anonymous, quoted in the media described the killing as a *coup d'état* conducted by dissident organized crime factions. Others claimed that The Butcher had met his fate in a shootout with his bodyguards who were part of a revolt against him. All sources were identified as "reliable" or "unimpeachable" or both.

"The American mobsters got tired of being bullied by The Butcher," said one source in a major paper. "They wanted more independence, and more profits."

Added another in a radio interview, "It was not just the Americans, but the Sicilians hated him too. He treated them like they were his slaves."

A third, with his face blacked out and voice distorted, offered on television, "The Sicilians and the Italians worked together to get rid of him. They both shared the same goal."

Reporters descended on Cinisi like flies to an unguarded plate of food. The travel and airline businesses experienced a much-welcomed increase in revenues as did hotels and restaurants in Cinisi. Municipal officials were grateful for the unexpected financial windfall. They might not have liked the damage to the city's image, but they appreciated that the publicity put Cinisi on the map. It may have been bad publicity – the story was about the murder of the world's most powerful mobster – but in life, the Cinisensi rationalized, one always had to adjust to trade-offs.

The media conducted interview after interview, asking Cinisensi their opinions on the killing. No one ever said they had absolutely no idea what happened or why. Everyone had an answer. No one, using good sense, said "good riddance." Interestingly, those at *DaNino* at the time of the shooting or others in the neighbourhood said they saw and knew "nothin'." First-hand accounts from witnesses were not available. The only people who talked openly were government and police officials.

On both sides of the Atlantic Ocean, government spokesmen, in almost identical detail, said the shooting of Giuliano "The Butcher" Monteleone, resulted from attempts to apprehend him. Monteleone, they said, was to be arrested for the murder of Henry T. Hawk, the late FBI director, and on numerous other charges. As Sicilian agents approached him, Monteleone drew a weapon, forcing agents to respond with gunfire, killing the internationally renowned and feared gangster.

Sicilian officials, pleased to receive credit, said they took the lead but had the support of the U.S. in the investigation and the subsequent attempt to apprehend The Butcher. In line with being a good neighbour, the Sicilians gave some credit to the Italians, stating they also played a role in The Butcher's demise.

With the official version of the shooting established in the media, the President of the United States, never one to miss a PR opportunity, called a press conference. The White House press corps was more excited than usual. Most of the time the president, whoever he was, talked about world peace, budget problems, and his political troubles with Congress. Hardly exciting Page One news. This issue was another matter. The murder of The Butcher was newsworthy, and   its coverage was guaranteed to increase TV ratings and to sell papers.

Before he took questions, the President read a prepared statement in which he said:

"I promised when Henry T. Hawk was brutally murdered that those responsible would be brought to justice. That has happened with the death of Mr. Giuliano Monteleone. We believe he orchestrated the murder of Mr. Hawk from his headquarters in Cinisi, Sicily. The U.S. government worked cooperatively with the Sicilian government and Italian officials on this matter.

"This combined and cooperative investigation led to an attempt to arrest Mr. Monteleone. Unfortunately, he resisted and was killed in the process. Let me add that we will continue to pursue, relentlessly, all others who participated in the murder of Mr. Hawk.

"I want to commend all the brave and courageous U.S. agents who took part in this effort. I also want to extend my sincerest appreciation and gratitude especially to our Italian and Sicilian friends. They proved invaluable, and without them, we might never have been able to proceed effectively."

The President made no reference to his previous remarks about the Italian and Sicilian history with organized crime. He thought it better not to raise that sensitive subject. It didn't cost anything to commend the Sicilians and Italians, and maybe his words might help him mend whatever political fissure he caused at his previous press conference.

A reporter asked, "Mr. President, can you give us some particulars such as how many agents were involved, where did you get the leads, and why do you believe The Butcher was responsible for the Hawk killing?"

"This is still early in the case. We are still putting

together all the details. So I don't want to be premature. I will appoint a special liaison to brief the media when we have collected all the information."

Another reporter also asked for more specifics, saying, "Mr. President, this is all very vague. Can you help with a little more information?"

The President hung tough. He did not want to make the slightest error that might unravel the internationally conceived plan to give credit for Valenti's work to the Sicilians and Italians.

"That's a good question. As I said, you will get more facts as they become available. Most important, I want to thank all involved for their outstanding work, and express our admiration for all the law-abiding people of Sicily and Italy." Then he added:

"The world is free of a despicable, brutal man who contaminated society. I want to conclude by observing that all the civilized nations of the world should be grateful. This is a time for celebration."

The word "conclude" was a signal and, as the President hoped, the reporter assigned to end press conferences, yelled out "Thank you, Mr. President." The President shrugged his shoulders, suggesting he wanted to continue but what choice did he have? He left the lectern and was gone.

In the eye of the rumour hurricane and "official" explanation by none other than the President of the United States, Galente called Marcese, asking simply, "Whatta you think?"

"Whatta I think?" Marcese repeated. "I no think. I know. Johnny."

Galente agreed. "That's what I think. I sure would

like to know how he done that. Wish I could kiss him."

"Tommy Boy, you call-a Luigi. He'll know. Johnny always talk-a to him."

A few hours later, Galente was sitting in a dark bar in lower Manhattan and when he heard the "unofficial" version, all he could say was, "You shitting me? He done it all?"

"Down to crossing all the t's," said Giancamilli as he outlined the entire plan. "Got the mole to help him."

"That fuckin' Johnson?"

"Yeah, he gave Johnny all the files, made all the arrangements."

Galente was impressed, more than impressed, by what he heard. Valenti was good, very good. This "project," however, exceeded all of Galente's expectations, anyone's expectations.

Giancamilli and Galente decided that no one in the mobster world, except Marcese, would be told of how The Butcher met his demise. That's how Valenti would want it. That's how they wanted it. The fewer people who knew the better. Let the President have his publicity. Why make him out to be a liar?

"I'm sending Gisele and the kids to Paris," Giancamilli said. "When they get there, they'll all disappear, probably forever."

"Before they go, I wanna give them a few grand. You pick it up and give it to Gisele for me. They're gonna need it. He deserves it for what he done. Got rid of that bastard for all of us. Tell him to call anytime he needs somethin', anytime."

Giancamilli and Galente clicked their glasses and

downed their drinks with a hearty, "S*alute*."

CHAPTER 33

WHILE THE PRESIDENT AND Giancamilli/Galente did not agree on the facts of The Butcher's murder, they did see eye-to-eye that it was a time to celebrate but for different reasons.

Giancamilli and Galente along with their colleagues were elated because their world was free of The Butcher whom they considered a real *bastardo*. The Sicilians did not think much of The Butcher either nor, for that matter, did the neighbouring Italians. He had given a lot of people a bad name in that part of the European continent. The Butcher did not have any fans as the boss of bosses.

The President hoped that The Butcher's death would lead to a weakening, if not eradication, of the mob. He told the American people he expected that before long organized crime would be disorganized, in disarray, and, ultimately, destroyed. Whatever the facts, the President was free to hope and express his somewhat unrealistic expectations. Makes a person, especially a president, feel good.

The fact was, the jockeying to replace The Butcher as the boss of bosses would begin immediately. The top job would not be decided by popular vote, the Electoral College, or white smoke from a chimney. Nor could anyone predict how long it would take for someone to assume the crown designating him the boss of bosses.

The process was an evolving one with the winner one day, recognizing his power, proclaiming, "I am the boss of bosses." No one would disagree given their position of weakness. Not enough fire power.

While there have been many bosses in the mob's history, there have been relatively few *capo crimini* – boss of bosses. Despite the understandably high risks of the job, those that held super boss status had surprising longevity. What's more, there were no constitutional term limits to hold the highest office in the underworld.

One thing was clear. All the bosses in the U.S., Sicily and Italy, at least those aspiring to the job, would begin strategizing, manoeuvring, intimidating, conniving, deceiving, and implementing a variety of devious tactics required for a winning campaign.

Whoever won would be completely ruthless, greedy, extremely jealous, totally fearless, and hopelessly paranoid, believing that someone was always after them. Paranoia was almost a required characteristic for the job. Most of all, the winning candidate would, at the same time, have to be a man of honour who had an uncompromising commitment to the principles of the underworld.

In Paris, Valenti paid no attention to what the U.S. President or anyone else said about The Butcher's death. He concentrated on his own future.

After spending the night in a Parisian hotel, he took a cab to the Paris Charles de Gaulle International Airport some twenty miles northeast of Paris, to be reunited with his wife and two children, and pick up the pieces of his life.

As he passed a newsstand, he saw photos of The Butcher in several newspapers. He looked for a paper in English and bought a copy of *The New York Times*. There, on Page One, he read:

"Powerful International Mobster Slain in Alleged Shootout

With Sicilian Agents; U.S. and Italy Reportedly Involved

"CINISI, Sicily – Giuliano "The Butcher" Monteleone, arguably the most powerful organized crime figure in the world, was shot and killed when he resisted arrest, Sicilian and U.S. authorities said today.

"Sicilian police said that they approached Monteleone in a restaurant to arrest him when the suspect, known as The Butcher because of his penchant for extreme cruelty, random and unnecessary violence, refused to surrender. He allegedly pulled a revolver and aimed it at agents, but was killed in a hail of gunfire, police said.

"Monteleone not only headed organized crime in Sicily but, for years, had been identified by U.S. authorities as having control over six Mafia families operating in New York City.

"Sicilian authorities said the plan to arrest Monteleone was developed in cooperation with and assistance of Italian and U.S. police agencies."

At the end of a long story that began on Page One and continued for another half page on A-24, *The Times* reported, *"The accounts by Sicilian and U.S. authorities could not be independently verified."*

The last sentence caused Valenti to laugh out loud. Not bad giving the Sicilians and Italians credit for the hit. Made them look good by showing that they are fighting against organized crime. Couldn't have been Johnson's idea, Valenti thought. Ain't that bright.

Valenti was pleased that someone in the fed's shop accepted his suggestion that they take ownership of the murder. The feds went a step further by playing second fiddle to the Sicilians and Italians. They could count on him not to say a word.

When he looked up from his newspaper, he saw her coming through a narrow aisle at Gate 9. There was

Gisele, in all her beauty. Before getting up, he looked at her beautiful face, her curvaceous figure, her full breasts and her long legs. He was overcome with desire.

He saw Little Johnny and Lucia, two years old, just ahead of their mother. His family was back together. His heart quickened, and it took all his power to control his emotions.

When Gisele Valenti stopped to ask a question at the ticket counter, the two children began to cry. Valenti walked over to them, knelt down, and engaged them in small talk. Almost immediately, he had them giggling.

"You should teach me how to make them stop crying so quickly," said Gisele Valenti from behind her husband.

Without turning around, he told her, "Children always recognize their father's voice."

He stood up and faced his wife. She was momentarily confused, recognizing while not recognizing, the face in front of her. The hair and eyes were the same. The rest of the face was not. The cheeks, nose and forehead were different.

When he tried to embrace and kiss her, she stepped back. She was tempted to walk away, call security, but didn't.

"Johnny?" she said.

He touched her elbow lightly. He did not want to frighten her.

"It's a long story. I'll explain it all to you later."

Hearing the familiar voice gave her some reassurance. Her eyes continued to examine the man in front of her who insisted he was her husband.

"Your face ..."

"I thought Luigi might have told you."

She relaxed more when she heard Luigi's name. No one else could have known that.

He moved closer and gave her a light embrace. He could feel the tension. She relaxed a little because his body seemed familiar. Holding her hand, he sat down and she beside him. Neither spoke.

She held her head down as he fumbled for words. Her eyes caught a headline in *The New York Times* that Valenti had on his lap. All she could read was, *"Powerful International Mobster Slain ..."* The rest of the headline was obscured by Valenti's hand. She could see a little of The Butcher's face in the front-page photo. She tried to read the first three paragraphs that were visible but was unable to do so no matter how hard she strained.

The headline was enough to raise her suspicions, concerns. Was her husband involved in this murder? What was he doing with this newspaper? He was not a man who read *The New York Times*. *Sports Illustrated* maybe. *Playboy, Penthouse*, yes. Not *The New York Times*.

Valenti suddenly noticed her interest in the story and slowly moved his hand to cover the headline and photo. Both of them went through their motions, hoping the other would not notice. Just as he was aware of her effort to read the story, she was cognisant of his efforts to hide it.

He started to talk, give her some kind of explanation, when he had an idea. He would call Giannola.

"Wait here," he said. On the way to the telephone, he threw *The Times* in a trash can. After about ten minutes on the telephone, he called to her.

"It's your uncle," Valenti said. Giving his wife the

privacy she needed, Valenti left the phone, and went to watch his children as she talked to her uncle.

Valenti did not want Giannola to reveal the details, any details, to his wife. He just wanted Giannola to reassure her that he was her husband, that she had nothing to fear.

Valenti looked at her from a distance. He watched her face for the positive sign he was looking for. After a few minutes, he was rewarded. He saw small a smile form on her face. She hung up the telephone, returned to Valenti, embraced her husband, although still with some hesitancy.

"Give me some time," she pleaded. "This will take a little time. He said you would explain."

"Yes, I will. I understand your confusion, but don't worry, Gisele, it's all over." He did not explain the "it." Maybe later. The fact was that he would never discuss all of "it" no matter how much she might insist. Much of "it" would remain his secret forever.

And, it was over as the Valenti family left the airport. What about his promise to the feds to return to the U.S. and rat? Who gave a shit? They got The Butcher for what Valenti thought was a minimal investment, a few grand. The Butcher, Numero Uno on two continents, was history, as they say. He had taken all the risk, and they got credit in the media for assisting in the assassination of the mobster who was responsible for many murders, including that of the director of the Federal Bureau of Investigation of the United States of America.

The Butcher might be gone, but Valenti was confident his death would not end the Hawk investigation. The FBI would continue to try to hunt down every single mobster who had any part in ending the life of a real American hero. The President's order would be carried out to the letter. He was confident that the feds would not come after him for not keeping his pledge to return, or for his many hits. His confidence rested on a tape from a little recorder he had hidden in his shirt pocket in Johnson's office. That would protect him for a long time, indeed, forever.

The ruse about the feds tape recording him in their office had worked. He had turned their attention away, and they did not think to search him. *I told Johnson we were smarter than the U.S. government,* Valenti said to himself, very self-satisfied. *I ain't gonna have to look over my shoulder – ever. Alleluia*!

Undoubtedly, Johnson would be pissed. Valenti could care less. Johnson would find another mobster benefactor, someone to pay him off. He had others lining his pockets anyway.

"Wait a minute, Gisele," he said. "It ain't over ... not quite." He opened his suitcase and removed four little packages. Each was about five-by-three inches and was marked "confidential." These were copies of the tape he had made in Johnson's office. One copy was addressed to Johnson and the other three to his superiors.

He dropped them into a nearby mailbox. "Now it's over. All over," he told his wife. At last, he was a free man, really free.

He had his family. The Butcher was dead. The feds would be off his back. And he did not break. Life didn't get any better than that.

Valenti was proud of himself. He considered himself *uomo d'onore*, a man of honour. He went to prison because he would not violate *omertá*. His principles had almost cost him his life because The Butcher did not believe Valenti was totally committed to *omertá*. He could hold his head up high. What about all the murders he had committed? Valenti was not prepared to quibble as he walked out of the airport, a family man.

He had made his point. It was the destiny of only a few, like him, to believe completely, uncompromisingly in *omertá*. Those that didn't were frauds that gave the *Mafia* a bad name.

Yes, now, he was ready to go to confession.

ABOUT THE AUTHORS

GIOVANNI GAMBINO

Giovanni Gambino is the author of Prince of Omerta, Undercover Secrets and Mulberry Street to Rome B.C. He was born in the province of Palermo in Sicily and grew up in Torretta, located in a mountainous area overlooking Palermo. Thirty-seven years old, he is the youngest in a family that includes four sisters and a brother. His family moved to Bensonhurst, a neighbourhood in southwestern Brooklyn in 1985. He grew up in the underworld as the son of Don Francesco "Ciccio" Gambino. Don Ciccio was senteneced to 30 years in federal prison in 1988 and passed January 4th 2012 honorably in prison. Giovanni was raised and cared for by real men of honor, out of respect for Don Ciccio these men of respect taught Giovanni about the real underworld and how to avoid precarious situations. Visit him online at giovannigambino.com

12946200R00173

Printed in Poland
by Amazon Fulfillment
Poland Sp. z o.o., Wrocław